# Praise for Alexa Martin

"Martin is an incredible storyteller and has a unique ability to blend fiction with real-life situations in the sports world."

—*New York Times* bestselling author La La Anthony

"The kind of book that's destined to be passed from friend to friend."

—PopSugar

"An emotional journey with an intoxicating romance."      —NPR

"A fun and sexy romance novel set in the sports world."      —Bustle

"If you like steamy romance with a side of sports, this fun, fast-paced novel is for you."      —HelloGiggles

"The writing is snappy, the pacing is quick, the romance is sublime, and the humor is off the charts. Alexa Martin delivers a stellar love story, and I can't wait to see what she writes next."      —*USA Today*

"Martin scores a touchdown of a debut with *Intercepted*, a witty rom-com set in the world of professional football players and their wives."      —*Entertainment Weekly*

"Fast, fun, and absolutely engaging. A smashing debut!"

—*New York Times* bestselling author Kristan Higgins

"Alexa Martin's books are the ultimate reading escape, filled with fabulous characters; witty, dazzling prose; and swoon-worthy romances."      —*New York Times* bestselling author Chanel Cleeton

# Better than Fiction

# ALEXA MARTIN

Berkley Romance

New York

BERKLEY ROMANCE
Published by Berkley
An imprint of Penguin Random House LLC
penguinrandomhouse.com

Library of Congress Cataloging-in-Publication Data

Names: Martin, Alexa, author.
Title: Better than fiction / Alexa Martin.
Description: First Edition. | New York: Berkley Romance, 2022.
Identifiers: LCCN 2022009307 (print) | LCCN 2022009308 (ebook) |
ISBN 9780593337226 (trade paperback) | ISBN 9780593337233 (ebook)
Classification: LCC PS3613.A77776 B48 2022 (print) |
LCC PS3613.A77776 (ebook) | DDC 813/.6—dc23
LC record available at https://lccn.loc.gov/2022009307
LC ebook record available at https://lccn.loc.gov/2022009308

First Edition: November 2022

Printed in the United States of America
3rd Printing

Book design by Elke Sigal

*For my grandma. I miss you every day.*

# Better than Fiction

# CHAPTER 1

I KNOW IT'S NOT THE POLITICALLY CORRECT THING TO SAY, BUT school is most definitely for fools.

Listen, I get it. I won't tell the kids, but I already fell victim to the great con. I was a good student—not full-scholarship good, but solid—went to a decent college, majored in something other than art. And where did it get me?

A high-paying job on Wall Street where I laugh at the peons around me complaining about school debt?

Not even close.

It landed me as the owner of a bookstore I most definitely didn't want to own, pretending to care while this woman drones on and on about the difference between women's fiction and romance. But, you know, good thing I aced that AP Chemistry exam.

"I'm so glad you're able to find something you love here." I pull out one of my many well-rehearsed responses. I hope it will send her on her way so I can do inventory—or pull out my hair—but then she cuts me off and hits me with something no amount of rehearsal could prepare me for.

"And I want you to know . . ." She reaches over and grabs my hand. I fight the urge to yank it back. Physical touch is def not my love language. "I'm just so sorry about Alice, she was always so kind to me."

My fingers curl into hers, my aversion to touch temporarily forgotten as I seek the comfort I have yet to find since my grandma passed away a year ago.

"Thank you." I can't get the two small words out without my voice breaking. Sympathy swims in the woman's eyes the same way I'm sure unshed tears are swimming in mine.

The woman, whose name I don't remember, gives my hand one more gentle squeeze before walking away, off to bury her problems in a book with a happily ever after that's so elusive to actual humans.

Alice Young was the best person I've ever known. The best person anyone has known. Every stranger who walked into her little bookstore walked out with more books than they probably wanted— and a new friend. The Book Nook sells books, obviously, but the real draw was getting to come and chat with Gran. She was wise beyond her seventy-two years and had a way of listening that made you feel like your biggest problem was actually just a pebble in your shoe. She made you feel as if you could accomplish anything. In the age of the e-book conglomerates and chain bookstores dominating the market, the Book Nook never struggled.

Until she left it to me.

It's not that I have self-esteem issues as much as I know my strengths and weaknesses. And my strength is definitely not sitting with a sympathetic ear and listening to other people's problems. I've never been good at it, but I'm especially terrible at it when my own problems seem so big.

Huge.

Gigantic.

Insurmountable.

Because yeah, this isn't my dream job or anything, but Gran left the bookstore to me. And sure, sales were through the roof the first couple of months after she passed away, with well-wishers coming to show their support. But now that the months have crawled by, people are going back to their lives. Unfortunately for me, that doesn't include spending money at a store where Alice no longer greets them with her cheerful smile and welcoming ear.

If I don't figure it out soon, I will lose the only tangible link I have left to my grandma.

On that thought, the bell above the front door rings and I look just in time to see Collette, Vivian, Mona, Ethel, and Beth file through the front door.

Oh shit.

I really need to check my calendar more often.

"Drew!" Mona's voice bounces off the overstuffed bookshelves. Even at seventy, she strides through the store in her trademark three-inch stilettos, which make my feet wince. Her gray hair has not a strand out of place and her pink-painted lips stand out on her pale, gently wrinkled face, which has aged gracefully over the years. "What are you doing standing over here looking all sad? Is it because you're wearing those sandals again?"

"The way you come for me every time you see me is still completely unnecessary, Mona." We live in Colorado: Birkenstocks are not only a completely reasonable footwear choice; it's practically mandatory for all Denverites to own a pair.

Also, it's still strange for me to call her Mona instead of Mrs. Fuller, but as I transitioned into adulthood, she insisted that I call her by her first name only. It's weird, but I acquiesced. Respect your elders and all that jazz.

It is kind of nice to feel like I'm on an even field with them now. Even though they're a lot older than me, they're still the coolest people I know.

"Coming for you? I just want you to join us and sit with some old ladies for a little while."

"Well, if you insist." I play it cool, but there's actually not a chance in hell I'd ever pass on the opportunity to listen to them very self-righteously talk shit about every person they know.

I aspire to be just like them when I grow up.

Minus the book club, obvi. Maybe I'll start a podcast club or something.

She links her arm through mine. Her nearly translucent skin is a stark contrast against my golden-brown skin.

"How's Mr. Fuller?" I always ask about her husband of almost fifty years when I see her.

"Old and cranky. Happy golfing weather has returned, though not as happy as I am to get him out of the house." The snide words don't match the dreamy look that crosses her face whenever his name is mentioned.

I love seeing how happy she still is. My best friend, Elsie, married her high school sweetheart before she could even legally drink—I still tease her relentlessly for her sparkling grape juice toasts—and is blissfully happy with four kids. As for me, however, I'm very much *not* into the idea of marriage.

I don't even like myself half the time and you're telling me it's a good idea to latch myself on to one other person until death do we freaking part? Or more likely, until they cheat, get bored, or whatever other reason fifty percent of marriages end in divorce.

Yeah. No thank you.

It's probably a good thing I have no interest in marriage. I'm not fighting off a swarm of potential suitors. Apparently my winning personality isn't doing it for them.

Their loss.

When we reach the back corner of the bookstore where the Dirty Birds—the name they chose for their book club—meet on the second Wednesday of every month, they're cackling just like their name would suggest. Copies of whatever romance novel they decided to read this month are sitting on the coffee table and each woman is in her unofficial-official chair. None of the chairs are the same. Gran and I would take weekly trips to the flea market, and she'd treat me to a fancy coffee and pastry before we'd spend hours wandering around, hoping to find the next treasure to grace her store. It took us months before we found all seven chairs that now occupy the nook portion of the Book Nook. I sanded and painted them all a creamy shade of mint while Gran sewed cushions to top them.

Now when I look at the chairs filled with all her friends, laughing and chatting like she imagined, I struggle to remember the joy we had creating them. All I see is the empty seventh seat.

Her seat.

"Did you finally read this month's book?" Collette, the most crass of the Dirty Birds, narrows her eyes when I sit. Her hair is dyed a bright red that turns a little orange and always clashes with her red lipstick.

"You know I didn't." I've never participated in a book club and I never will. Once I watched the movie instead but was shamed so intensely for it, I avoided them for a week. The Dirty Birds are vicious.

"You do know you own a bookstore now," she reminds me, as if I've thought of anything else since the lawyers read Gran's will all those months ago. "You have to read books. You can't keep this place running if you don't know the products."

"Geez, Collette, give the girl a break. She just inherited the place!" Sweet Beth sticks up for me. "Not even you could read all the time when you were working. Just because you're retired now doesn't mean she can do whatever you think she should be doing."

I want to high-five Beth, but I resist when Collette's knowing glare cuts my way.

"Fine," she mumbles, leaning back into her seat. "But you're going to need to start reading something. You can't own a bookstore and hate books!"

She's not wrong. This is why I thought Gran was only leaving me her necklace I loved so much.

My fingers drift to the pendant always resting on my chest. She still left me the necklace; it's just that now it feels more like an apology than a gift. Especially since she left me to fight off her son too.

"I'll figure it out." I wave off her concern, sounding much less worried than I actually am. "What book are you reading this time?"

Vivian leans forward, the creak of her chair cutting through the quiet chatter. "*Last Hope*, by Jasper Williams." Color fills her cheeks as she summarizes the book for me, and I can't help but wonder exactly how dirty these Dirty Birds are getting. Maybe I should start reading along, given how single I am. "Oh, and it was just so lovely. The way he writes. I'll never get over it."

"You've read him before, haven't you?" I recognize the name right away. It's a popular one in the store; soccer moms and pierced pixies alike request his work weekly. Jasper Williams stands out among the shelves of female romance authors despite the understated covers that grace all his books.

"You'd know that if you'd read the damn books with us." Collette's raspy smoker's voice rises and I bite back my smirk. I didn't mean to, but getting her worked up is one of my favorite pastimes.

"Maybe next month," I lie. And by the exaggerated roll of her eyes, she knows I'm full of it.

It's not that I don't like stories. Of course I do. I'm human, after all. I just like my stories told to me in a different way. I like visuals. The countless stories photographs can tell. The real-life images where the curve of a mouth can tell more than any book can. The perfectly framed shot of a mountain that allows your imagination to drift to the countless lives that have graced the landscape. Those are the stories I'm drawn to. I love conjuring hope myself, not being force-fed broken promises or lies telling me love is for everyone and I'm right around the corner from a happy ending of my very own.

"Oooorrrr . . ." Ethel drags out the word. My spine snaps straight. I recognize that tone and the meddling that always follows it. "You could read it before this weekend because Jasper Williams has agreed to come to the store. He's going to join our book club and do a reading."

I shake my head, trying to understand. "What do you mean? Shouldn't I know about in-store events?"

"Well, now you know, dear." Mona reaches for her copy on the table . . . the one with about eight hundred sticky notes popping out from the pages. "It's Saturday evening. The reading begins at five, followed by a discussion lasting until six or so, but he said he's flexible. I put it on your calendar. I thought you would've seen it by now."

I grab my phone out of my back pocket and open up my calendar, but nothing is there. I swipe around a little more, trying to see if she entered it somewhere else by mistake.

"It's not on my calendar."

"Oh no, not on your phone." Mona laughs and shakes her head like I'm being silly. "I said your calendar. The one on your desk."

I barely manage to fight back my groan.

This is just one of the problems that come with inheriting a business from your grandma. Mona and Ethel helped me get organized when I officially took over about nine months ago. And by that, I mean they nagged me about how I did everything and tried to force a day planner on me. For some ridiculous reason, I assumed that once the adjustment phase was over, they would step away completely. I should've known better.

"Mona, you know that was Gran's planner, not mine." And I avoid it like the freaking plague. I made the mistake of opening it once, and seeing her heavily slanted penmanship covering the pages with plans she would no longer be here for broke me.

"Well, she left you the store and that includes everything in it. Besides"—Mona lifts her chin in the air, looking down her nose at me—"if I don't put it in there, how am I supposed to schedule things for the Book Nook?"

"Ummm . . . I'm not sure?" Sarcasm is heavy in my voice. "Maybe don't? Or ask me?"

"Nonsense. It's going to be amazing. You'll thank us." She waves me off like I'm the little girl I was when she met me and not a grown woman trying—and fine, whatever, maybe failing—to run a business. "Now, where should we start? I think that little bit by the lake in chapter two was interesting."

On that note . . .

I stand up, ignoring the way my chair groans beneath my weight, and make my way to my office in the back to cancel the booty call—I mean the date—I had scheduled for Saturday and add Jasper Williams to my calendar.

A Saturday night spent listening to some old guy mansplain what women want?

Can't freaking wait.

# CHAPTER 2

In movies, when a person gets home after work, we watch them visibly deflate right in front of us. All the stress from the outside world melts away. They rip off their bra and crack open a bottle of wine. The luckiest of them all lounge on a gigantic couch with too many throw pillows as they snuggle up with an extra-fluffy puppy thrilled to finally be back with their human.

That's not me.

I toss my purse onto my entryway table in my too-quiet apartment. The distressed turquoise piece needs to be refinished, but all the equipment I needed was at Gran's house, and Dad sold the house . . . and everything inside it . . . months ago. I look around for a moment and consider putting my purse back on and getting the heck out of Dodge.

It's not that I haven't tried to make my home my sanctuary.

Quite the opposite, actually.

My credit card bills can vouch for the number of candles and pillows I've purchased since moving into this place. I've taken up new hobbies, cluttering my space with an overabundance of yarn or calligraphy pens, hoping they would fix everything.

It hasn't worked yet.

The framed prints of photos I've taken over the years used to bring me joy. The photo of beautiful red rocks set against the stormy gray sky still hangs on my wall beside the shot of Lake San Cristobal surrounded by green-covered mountains and the bright blue sky reflecting off the water—that one won me an award. The black-and-white print of miles and miles of snow-covered trees in the frame Gran gave me for my birthday was the first time I was paid for my work. The large canvas off to the side, of the ice-covered lake with the fire-hued sunset peeking through the mountains, was featured in a national travel magazine.

But now when I see these pictures, these visual representations of my true, authentic self, I don't envision more adventures to be had or goals to reach. I fight back the memories of looking through my camera and feeling the world fall from beneath my feet as I framed the perfect shot. Now all I feel is a familiar twinge in my chest, a constant reminder of all the things I lost when Gran left.

Another dream forgotten.

And that's okay.

Not everyone can live their biggest dreams. Not everyone can feel at ease.

Maybe it's the constant edge of wondering *what next?* that keeps me going, and I just need to get used to it.

Or maybe I should get a cat like my mom has been pushing me

to do since she moved back to her tiny hometown in the Smoky Mountains after I graduated college. I've been fighting her on it, but maybe she's onto something.

Maybe a skittish, mildly detached creature is the perfect remedy to all my problems.

Unfortunately, before I can sit down to plan a day to go to the animal shelter and find the answer to my loneliness, there's a knock on my door. Part of me wants to hide and pretend not to be home, but considering the only person who ever shows up on my doorstep unannounced is George from across the hall, who watches me through the peephole—which is only slightly creepy once you get to know him—there's no point.

I guess it's a good thing I'm not one of those people who rips her bra off straightaway after all.

I swing the door open, plastering a smile on my face to greet my neighbor and whatever puzzle he's brought by this time. But it falls off instantly, because of fucking course I'm met not with a jigsaw treat, but instead, the last face I ever expected to see.

Ever.

My mouth falls open and I struggle to come up with words other than *fuck no* or *why me, God?* or something else that properly expresses my feelings. When in reality, I should've slammed the door in her face and broken out the tequila hiding in the back of my pantry. Because while I wait for the right words to come, my sister shoulders her way past me, right into my apartment.

Again I ask, why me???

"Oh my goodness!" Daisy looks around my eclectic apartment (by lack of direction, not an actual design) with wide eyes and a wider smile. "Your place is so cute!"

"Um, thanks." I lock the door behind me and try to unscramble my brain. "Come in, I guess."

"Oh!" Daisy spins around and shows me a bag I didn't notice her holding. "I brought food. You like Thai, right?"

I want to lie and say no.

I want to say anything to get her out of my apartment as fast as possible, but I am actually very hungry. Plus, Thai is my favorite, and even if it wasn't, it sure as hell beats the Velveeta shells and cheese I was going to eat for dinner.

I guess spending an evening with her will be fine. It's not her fault that her presence causes my anxiety to spike and the insecurity constantly lingering beneath the surface to claw at my skin.

Also, if I kick out my dad's favorite child, I will no doubt hear from him ASAP. A quiet evening with her should keep him off my case for a while. Anything is worth that.

"I love Thai." I point to the dining table I've only eaten at once before. "You can take it out while I grab plates."

"I hope your plates are big, I got a ton of food," Daisy's perpetually sunny voice says.

Five years my junior, Daisy couldn't be more different than me. And not only because of the blue eyes, blond hair, verging on six feet tall, physical stuff either. She's rainbows, sunshine, glitter, and green juice. She was a cheerleader in high school and I'm pretty sure her superlative was "Most Likely to Achieve World Peace" or some bullshit like that. Whereas I love thunderstorms, I hate glitter with a fiery passion, and my senior year, I was quite literally voted "Most Likely to Leave and Never Come Back."

I push my stack of paper plates to the side and grab the plain white porcelain set Gran gave me when I moved in. I send her a quiet thank-you as I set them on the counter. Even though Daisy is fresh out of college and should be riding the struggle bus, she's always lived that Uber Black life. Her mom is old money, and whenever I'd visit them, I'd return home with insecurities about my secondhand denim and our tiny two-bedroom rental house. I don't even know if Daisy would notice, but the tiny bit of pride I have won't let me serve dinner on paper plates.

"I didn't know you were in town," I call from the kitchen as I rattle around my silverware drawer. "When did you get here?"

"Dad didn't tell you? I got in last weekend." Sweet Daisy, after all these years living with Andrew Young, still manages to have the faith in him that I lost in kindergarten. But he's never been the same person to her that he is to me, and when I'm not bitter about it, I'm glad at least one of us might avoid spending countless hours with a therapist.

Because Andrew Young, our father—and tragically, my namesake—is trash.

How he's the absolute freaking worst is still a mystery. Obviously Gran was the best, and from what she told me, so was my grandpa. But genetics are weird and maybe the awesome gene skips generations. Add that to the long list of reasons I should never reproduce.

"No, I haven't heard from him in a while, actually." I haven't had to ignore any of his calls recently, and it's been blissfully quiet from him as of late. "How long are you staying?"

"I'm here to stay!" Daisy, who always sounds like she's talking in all caps, says. "I nailed down an internship with Nella Moon, a designer here."

If I hadn't amassed hours of practice faking peppiness with

people at work all day, I'm not sure I could've prevented my jaw from hitting the table. I don't know if I'm angry or frustrated hearing this news, but I do know I'm ashamed for not being happy.

She isn't responsible for a grown-ass man abandoning me for his new, shiny family. It's not Daisy's fault she was born into a life where her existence minimized mine.

But logic doesn't supersede emotion; it hasn't prevented resentment from coloring every interaction we've had together.

"Wow! That's . . . wow!" I force the words out, hoping they sound light and friendly. "Congratulations."

I feel like I should ask some questions, or better yet, already have an inkling of the goings-on in my sister's life, but the sad truth is, I'm sure her Instagram followers know more about her life than I ever will.

"I'm really excited about it. Dad wasn't thrilled I chose fashion merchandising as my major, and you know him, so I really wanted to find a job to shut him up as quickly as possible." She shovels noodles out of one of the six take-out boxes she brought onto her plate. "Lucky for me, my mom's sorority sister is a bigwig at Nella Moon so she was able to pull some strings. It's an unpaid internship, but we're not telling Dad about that part."

I grab a spring roll and shove it into my mouth. I chew as slowly as possible to give myself some time to think of something to say other than my thoughts on nepotism or the inherent systemic racism in industries still using unpaid interns.

*She means well. She means well. She means well.*

"Well, at least you found something you're interested in," I manage to say after I swallow. "Where are you staying?"

"The Highlands area. Close to downtown, but not in the heart of it." She explains this to me like I wasn't born and raised in this city. "My apartment is really cute. My mom forced me to get a two-bedroom so she can visit. I know Aspen isn't far away, but I didn't realize how close it was. She's totally going to kill my single-in-the-city vibe."

I stay quiet, nodding with what I hope is a polite smile and not a grimace as I relive some of my deepest childhood trauma. Aspen is 198 miles away from Denver, but with the distance it put between me and my dad, it might as well have been millions.

"There are a ton of bars and restaurants within walking distance, though, so maybe you could come over one night. I mean, if you want to, no pressure. I know you're busy. I'll understand if you can't."

Daisy is always composed. She has perfect posture, and when she enters a room, it's like she assumes everyone is glad she came—even when she shows up unannounced at your door with Thai food. It's the kind of thing that must come from living a life of privilege where mistakes aren't the end of the world and second chances seem endless.

This rambling, nervous Daisy is foreign to me, and I can't help but end her misery.

"I'd love to," I cut in, squeezing her hand across the table. Her cheeks warm to a pink cosmetic companies must spend years trying to formulate. "It doesn't take much convincing to get me to explore new restaurants and eat food."

"Same!" Her face brightens and part of me wonders if I imagined the insecurity to be able to relate to her on some level. "Great, I'll find a few places that look good and then you can tell me when you're free."

"That sounds fun! I'll check my schedule and let you know." I'm trying so hard to sound excited, but my fake smile is making my cheeks hurt. I doubt I'm putting on an award-winning performance.

I leave my hand in hers for a second longer before I pull it away. I tuck it in my lap and ignore the flash of hurt in Daisy's eyes at the movement.

I don't want to be like this.

I want to be able to call her sis and invite her to my home. I want to go on vacations with her and know all the little details about her life. I want the easy relationship that sisters have where, sure, they'll fight on occasion, but it never lasts. I wish we had years of togetherness, whispering secrets in the darkness of the room we shared, giggling while we braided each other's hair or walked to school together.

But Daisy and I don't have that foundation.

What I have is hours of sitting in the passenger seat of my mom's sad little Toyota sedan, which struggled to get up the mountain roads. My mom tried to her best to keep her thoughts to herself, but those trips always ended with her mumbling beneath her breath about my no-good dad, who only cares about his new family. I remember the way her eyes would well with tears that never managed to fall as I waved goodbye and turned to walk up the long cobblestone driveway leading to Dad's new house. All I have is the disappointed look on my dad's face when he'd open the front door for me. And the way his entire face would light up with joy when he saw Daisy.

"So when do you start work?" I ask, pulling myself out of those dark thoughts. "Do you have any fun plans before you start?"

"Not for another month. I wanted to spend a few weeks getting to know my new city. Oh my god!" Daisy practically leaps out of her seat and startles the ever-loving crap out of me. "Dad got me tickets to see one of my favorite bands at Red Rocks on Saturday! You should come with."

Have you ever had a piece of candy, and when you put in it your mouth, at first it's the best thing your tastebuds have ever encountered—sweet and delicious—but then, after a few seconds, you start to register a different flavor and it's so god-awful you have to use every single ounce of self-control not to spit it all over the floor? That's this offer.

I love live music and I really, really love Red Rocks. I'm not a religious person, but if I was, Red Rocks Amphitheatre would be my church. It's one of my favorite places on the planet, and most of the time, I would jump at this offer with zero hesitation. But hearing that Dad is the person providing the tickets causes a pause. A major one. If there's one location I can't have tainted by Andrew Young, it's Red Rocks. The last thing I need is to pull up to Yoga on the Rocks—Red Rocks' alter ego during the day—seething as I remember whatever douchebag move he inevitably pulled in my presence.

But I guess it doesn't matter since I already have plans.

"I really wish I could, but I have an event at work that I have to be there for." Only a few hours ago, I never thought I would've said this, but thank the freaking lord for the Dirty Birds.

"Bummer." Daisy sticks her bottom lip out much like Elsie's toddler when he's forced to take a bath.

"I know, I wish I could make it. You're going to have so much fun." I think about leaving it there, letting myself live in blissful ignorance, but I need to know. "Is Dad going to go with you?"

"God no!" She throws her head back and laughs while I let out a breath I didn't realize I was holding. "He came down with Mom to help me move into my apartment but didn't even spend the night. I was surprised he came at all, you know he hates leaving his mountain retreat."

"Yeah, you're right about that." Unfortunately, thanks to years of him missing every milestone in my life, I do know that.

However, ever since Gran died and he was more upset about losing the Book Nook than losing his mother, he's made more exceptions in order to make his way to my part of the state. Between stressing about my new title of bookstore owner and his unpredictable appearances, I'm a ball of anxiety. At least I can relax a little knowing he's not here right this moment.

"But speaking of work . . ." Daisy lets her sentence trail off and my anxiety picks back up. "You mean the Book Nook, right? Gran always told stories about the store when she came to visit."

"Yup, the Book Nook." I nod, afraid to say anything more because I have no idea where she's going with this.

"How's it going there? Gran told me the two of you had been giving the place a little face-lift. I'd love to come by one day and see what she was always going on about." She pulls her lips between her teeth and glances away from me, but I don't miss the familiar way her eyes glisten with unshed tears before she does.

It's weird.

I was always on the receiving end of their pity. I was the poor girl growing up without her dad. I'm pretty sure Dad convinced everyone my heartbroken mom was batshit crazy. The birthday cards sent in the mail were from my dad, but signed with my stepmom's writing . . . even the checks that funded my back-to-school wardrobes had her name in the corner.

Honestly, until this very moment, I thought Daisy had everything. But now I realize that she missed out on one of the absolute best things life had to offer. A relationship with Alice Young.

Since my dad—for lack of better words—abandoned me, Gran stepped up to the plate and put his responsibilities on her shoulders. She was at every school play, every soccer game . . . she even took me to the two Girl Scout meetings I went to before I quit. If Mom was working, it was Gran's old Buick that met me outside school to take me to the Book Nook. She had a special cabinet in the back filled with snacks, and I'd spend hours there, doing homework, helping organize, and, at the end of the day, just reveling in time spent with my favorite person, who never made me doubt that I was her favorite person too.

For the first time all night, I let my eyes wander to Daisy's hand to see Gran's modest diamond, which, even years after my grandpa died, never left her finger. It was what she left Daisy in the will. I knew Daisy was getting it. Gran asked me what I wanted, her ring or the pendant necklace passed down to her from her mom. Even though Dad was/is trash, I loved the idea of having a family heirloom from my Young family. I didn't think twice about choosing the pendant.

I just wish that while we were having that conversation, she had told me she was leaving me the Book Nook too. It would've been nice to have a heads-up before I sat in a room with Dad for the first time in years while the lawyer read out her will. Until the day I die, I will never forget the shade of red that colored my dad's fair skin or the way his deep voice turned into that of a schoolgirl's as he shrieked. But mostly, I'll never forget the look of pure hatred and disgust in his green eyes as he gave me one last look before he walked out of the room.

I still don't really understand his problem. Gran left him her house, his childhood home—my dream bungalow in Washington Park, which he sold for a small fortune—it wasn't enough for him. I didn't think things could get worse with him, but I was wrong. Because ever since that day, he's made my life a living hell trying to get control of the bookstore so he can sell it to the highest bidder.

I can deal with it. I can take pretty much anything he throws at me by now.

I just hate how disappointed Gran would be.

Even though she stopped urging me to call him when I was in college, I know she still harbored hope that one day we would mend our relationship. I think she thought she was being fair, splitting her belongings between the two of us. Not that she had to—it was her stuff, for goodness' sake! She could've given it all away and left us with nothing at all.

That's what's so hard for me to comprehend through all this.

Even though the Book Nook was never my dream, I'm so grateful she trusted me with this piece of her heart. Whenever I walk into that store, I can feel her around me. Memories of her linger in every nook and cranny of the store; every customer who tells me a story about their time with her is another link to the person I will never stop missing. My dad just wants to sell that.

Money can turn even the best person into a monster, and Andrew Young already sucked, so this has brought out an entirely new level of vile.

But in this moment, my sympathy for Daisy, my sister, exceeds all that.

"Come by whenever you want. Gran would love for us to be in there together." I don't have to fake a smile, for the first time since she walked into my apartment—hell . . . into my life. Sincerity drips from my every word. "And if you're up for it after your concert and want some more Red Rocks in your life, I do yoga there on Sunday mornings. You're more than welcome to join."

"I'd love that! I'm not big on exercise but this could be the exception." Her eyes light up and the guilt I feel from pulling my hand away from her earlier starts to fade. Sure, we didn't grow up together, but now that we're adults we have the opportunity to forge a relationship without our dad.

"Anything at Red Rocks is the exception. You'll love it." And shocking the hell out of me, I think I might actually love it too.

"Okay, so now that we have bookstores and yoga sorted, I think it's time to move on to the important things." Daisy drops her elbows onto the table and leans over, the unmistakable whisper of gossip perking her right up. "I could really use a Denver boyfriend—where can I find one?"

"Even though I'm intrigued by the idea of you having boyfriends in multiple cities and really wish I could help, my dating history is troubled at best." *Much to Gran and the Dirty Birds' dismay.* "I wouldn't even know where to begin to look for you."

"Oh, sister dearest . . . we have so much to catch up on." Mischief twinkles in her eyes as she looks at me and winks . . . *winks!* "I have a feeling I might be able to teach you a thing or two."

Well, fuck.

As if the Dirty Birds meddling in my life wasn't enough, let's just pile it on.

# CHAPTER 3

Saturday mornings are my favorite time in the Book Nook.

Besides hosting a few book clubs and being an overall wonderful human being, Gran didn't have any ploys to drive business to the store. Shortly before she passed, though, she mentioned she wanted to do something for our in-need-of-much-love children's section.

And you know what helps you ignore the death of your beloved grandmother? Painting walls, assembling shelves, and constantly bothering your best friend about the latest and greatest in children's entertainment. I spent every waking hour I had making sure the children's nook was everything Gran would've wanted. I even reached out to a local company that hires out princesses and superheroes for birthday parties. We worked out a steal of a deal to have someone come every Saturday to read to the kids. Where other sales have dwindled over the past few months, our children's book sales are through the roof.

And today is the most packed yet.

"You should see how much it costs to put a coffee bar inside," Elsie says while simultaneously bouncing the baby strapped onto her chest, wrangling my favorite one-year-old right before he goes limp noodle, and also keeping her eyes focused on her twins, sitting like the angels they are as they listen to Elsa. "I'd kill for a freaking latte right now."

"I don't understand how you don't have a caffeine IV constantly pumping into your veins. You're like superwoman." I can't function without a strong cup of coffee or two—fine! three!—and I get full nights of uninterrupted sleep. Or at least I used to. Sleep has been a little harder to come by lately.

"I think I've been in survival mode since Willow and Wren." She readjusts her grip on Milo's wrist while poor baby Finn just bounces around on her chest. "Add in these two, and it's a miracle I manage to leave the house at all."

I take pity on Milo—or Elsie, not sure which one, to be honest—and swoop him up into my arms. His tiny gap-toothed smile widens and his squeal of laughter cuts through the whispers of the moms around us when I squeeze his side.

"Well, I appreciate your commitment to child-rearing so I don't have to." Milo settles on my hip, content to watch Elsa now that he's being held. "And you know I can babysit for a little if you need a break or a power nap. Five hours is my max though. I don't think I could last longer than that."

"Don't tease me with a good time. Brandon has been working like crazy and it would be nice to spend time with him again without having to separate toddlers, whip out my boob, or clean butts." Even though she's talking about dirty diapers, her face goes soft and does that annoying thing it does whenever she talks about her husband.

"First, fix your face. You and Brandon have been together for like a million years. There's no reason you should still look like a heart-eye emoji whenever you talk about him." I mean, yeah, Brandon is six foot six inches of a perfect male specimen who worships the ground she walks on, but it just feels unnecessary at this point. "Second, I'm pretty sure whipping out your boobs is how you got here in the first place."

The moms standing around us giggle, but instead of looking the tiniest bit embarrassed, Elsie looks thoroughly and utterly pleased with herself.

"Well, you know, part of the reason I'm not sleeping is self-imposed." She winks at me and high-fives Angie, one of the other moms who come to story time every week.

Show-off.

Not that I can exactly blame her though. Elsie and Brandon have been the epitome of Black love since they were high school sweethearts. Now Brandon is an investment banker (and not a douchey one either), and Elsie graduated with a degree in freaking aerospace engineering. She was looking at master's programs when she found out she was pregnant. She was still looking to apply, but when she found out babies made four instead of three, she decided to put a hold on school until the twins were in preschool.

I just don't think she realized her uterus was the baby-making equivalent of Pringles, because once that thing popped, it did not stop.

So again, college loans: two, Elsie and me: zero.

Cool.

"Whatever." I try to roll my eyes, but my heart's not in it. "But back to the coffee bar, I have been considering it. I was actually thinking dual purpose. Coffee in the morning for circle time, wine in the evening for book clubs."

I have the exact spot in mind and everything. If I was only going off the profits from the store, I wouldn't be able to afford it. However, Gran did leave me some money, not a fortune, but enough. I've avoided touching it until I figure out the best way to use it. This might be the perfect cause.

"Oh my goodness! Yes!" Elsie turns her wide chestnut eyes to me. "I love that idea so much! I have a few mom friends who have been wanting to start a book club. If we could host them here, away from all of our children, and drink wine? I'd join in a heartbeat."

I can see the wheels turning in her head and I don't know if it's good for me. When Elsie gets an idea in her head, she doesn't let it go. So, I use this moment of distraction to drop a casual bomb on her.

"Anyways . . ." I tuck Milo a little higher on my hip, playing with his curls to avoid looking at his mom. "Did I tell you that Daisy dropped by the other day?"

The air goes static around me.

"Angie, would you mind keeping your eyes on the girls for me?" Elsie asks before wrapping her fingers around my wrist. "I have to talk to Drew really fast."

"Of course." Angie aims her bright smile at us, ignoring the way I'm shaking my head no. "Take your time."

And to think I was going to give her free coffee one day.

Traitor.

"You're the best!" Elsie's voice is about five octaves too high before she tightens her grip on me and pulls me through the crowd filled with leggings and buns.

I share a look of sympathy with Milo as we follow helplessly behind my best friend.

When we're securely tucked out of earshot of the majority of the mom squad, she drops my arm and narrows her eyes. "What do you mean Daisy dropped by? And why would you drop that freaking bomb in the middle of story time?"

"It was after I got home from the store on Wednesday." I half shrug, Milo seriously cramping my ability to pretend to be casual. "She showed up with Thai food. We had dinner and chatted. It was . . . nice."

"Nice? You call me no less than once a week about some new scheme your dad's concocting to take the store." She leans in and I want to roll my eyes and tell her she's exaggerating, but she's actually being quite generous. I call her at least twice a week about Andrew Young shenanigans. "And it was nice?!"

She finishes on a shout, and Milo, instead of being startled, starts to laugh. Laugh! Wow. That's it. Never having kids. Nobody on this planet is more intimidating than Elsie Cooper when she's angry, and this tiny human is amused by her wrath. Children are monsters.

I look from the giggling kid on my hip to my well-intentioned but super-pissed best friend. "Your kid thinks you're a joke."

"Welcome to my life." She brushes me off. "Now, spill. What happened? Did your dad show? Did you tell Donna about this?"

"Oh god no. You know I try to avoid telling my mom anything that will freak her out. She's finally not asking if I want her to move back from Tennessee every time we talk. Father Dearest hasn't shown up yet. If he did, it would've been anything but pleasant." My dad's special like that. He has the distinct ability to ruin my entire day without even trying. "We just ate dinner and talked. You know Daisy has always been nice—"

Elsie cuts me off. "I swear to god, if you say *nice* again, I'm going to freaking scream."

I look at Milo. He's bored with me and his mom. His chubby little toddler fingers are busy trying to grab the pendant resting on my chest. "Milo, dude. Your mom's a little cray-cray, yeah?"

His big brown eyes, which are an exact replica of his dad's, meet mine as he nods and repeats after me. "Cway-cway."

I pull my lips between my teeth and try to swallow my laughter.

"Great." Elsie rolls her eyes. "Thanks for that."

The snort of laughter lodged in my throat breaks free. I should feel guilty, but I don't. "Please, Willow and Wren said the f-word when they were this age; this isn't that bad."

She puts her hands on her hips, but some of the intended effect is lost with the sleeping baby still strapped to her. "First of all, ma'am, no need to remind me of that. If you had twins and were pregnant again, you'd swear a lot too. Second, I fixed my mouth and we haven't had that problem since, thank you very much."

"Well, what is Aunt Drew for if not providing your kids with absurd amounts of noise-making presents, sugar, and slightly inappropriate words that sound very cute coming out of their little mouths?"

It's not like I'm out here teaching them four-letter words; I'm not a total troll. But Milo can't say his *r* sound. Him saying *cray-cray* is adorable and I'm not apologizing.

"Whatever." She shakes her head and lets out a sigh so deep I fear she might pass out. "I know you're deflecting. Tell me what happened."

"Fine." I purse my lips and scrunch my nose, probably looking much more like her children than is socially acceptable for a woman of nearly—but not yet—thirty. "It was kind of weird. I left the night almost feeling bad for Daisy."

She starts to laugh and only stops when she looks at my face. "Wait." Finn begins to stir on her chest, and without skipping a beat, she starts rubbing his back through the carrier and doing this mom-bounce thing she's always doing. "You're being serious?"

"Yeah, it was weird—"

"*Weird* feels like a massive understatement." She cuts me off again.

"Are you going to keep cutting me off or do you want me to tell the story?" I sound more irritated than I am. This is a huge change of tune for me and she's right to be confused.

"Proceed." She waves me on and now I'm the one rolling my eyes.

"As I was saying, I felt bad for her. She was asking about Gran and trying to make all these plans with me. I've been so wrapped up in my loss and dealing with the store and my dad that I never really thought about what she was going through." I remember the sad smile that crossed Daisy's face when I told her stories about going to the flea market with Gran to fill my apartment and the Book Nook. "My loss was huge, but at least I have a lifetime of memories to think back on. Daisy missed that. Gran would go visit them occasionally, but Daisy has never even been to the store. I don't know, it just made me realize how lucky I was to get Gran when Daisy was stuck with our jackass of a father."

"Wow." Elsie is still bouncing baby Finn; her knees must be made of steel. "I never thought about that. You know you're family to me, but forging a relationship with Daisy might be good for you."

"I hope so." Milo starts to fidget on my hip and I set him on the ground, holding his hand instead. "She invited me to a concert at Red Rocks tonight, but I have that stupid author event." Damn Dirty Birds. "I talked her into doing Yoga on the Rocks tomorrow if you want to come."

Elsie has only ever heard stories—mainly of me complaining—about Daisy, and it might be nice to introduce them.

"Aw, that's nice of you to invite me to your sister time." The bell over the front door, which I'm pretty much immune to, goes off and pulls Elsie's attention over my shoulder for a second before she looks back at me. "You're nervous to be alone with her, aren't you?"

"It's very rude that you know me so well that you won't even let me lie to myself."

"I know." She smirks her annoying, smug smile and closes the space between us. "You know I only like yoga pants, not the actual craft. I'll go, but only under a few promises."

"Anything. I'll do anything." It's not that I'm nervous to do yoga with Daisy as much as I'm terrified about the drive to Morrison with just the two of us so early in the morning. I can take a lot of things, but long stretches of awkward silence isn't one of them. "Name your price."

"One." She holds her hand in the air, ticking off her fingers. "You pick me up with a latte, no way am I waking up before my children on a Sunday without being properly caffeinated. Two"—she adds another finger—"we do brunch after. I miss brunch. If I have to embarrass myself with my lack of flexibility in public, on a rock, I deserve a mimosa and French toast after."

"That's fair. I feel like I will also deserve a drink or two for spending time with Daisy. You know this is a big step in the direction of being less petty for me."

Considering who my parents are, I'm pretty sure pettiness is hereditary, and I have it in spades. This is a big deal for me.

"Big facts." She squats down to the floor—no wonder her ass looks even better after four kids than ever before—and swoops up Milo without disturbing Finn. "But my final requirement is the most vital."

"More important than brunch?" I was so distracted seeing her pick up Milo and stand holding these two babies, I forgot she wasn't finished yet.

"Oh yeah, way more important. If you want me to go, you need to go over there and talk to the hottie who just walked into your store." She uses her chin to point in the direction of said hottie since both of her hands are full of baby.

I turn, prepared to follow her line of sight, but I don't need to. This hottie is not just hot. He's fucking *Fine* . . . with a capital *F.* And my eyes, like the eyes of damn near everyone in the store, are drawn straight to him.

I mean, I never thought I'd pick someone up in Gran's bookstore while Elsa read in the corner and my best friend's toddler watched.

Never say never, I guess.

Discretion has never been my strong point. I blame it on my photographer's heart. I can't help but envision the perfect shot when I'm met with beauty. I can't look away until I have it set up in my head and it's as if the image has already been printed and framed on the wall. I just really hope my tongue isn't hanging out of my mouth as I take mental picture after mental picture of the DILF in front of me.

"He's probably here to find his wife and kid at story time," I say to Elsie without looking away from Mr. McHotterson. "He's clearly looking for somebody."

And he definitely is. Even from across the room, I can see his eyes scanning the store.

Which sucks for me because even though I don't really have a type—or, honestly, standards—per se, if I was forced to pick, my type would be this guy. He stands next to our bookshelves, and his head hovers above them, putting him at a solid six feet tall. His tan skin jutting out of his short-sleeve button-up—which could look a little goofy on most people, but on him just looks hot—points to a Mediterranean heritage. Black hair right on the verge of being too long falls in thick waves over his forehead. And even though it's covered in scruff, nothing can hide the hard, cutting lines of a jawline that up until this point I've only seen on movie screens. I half expect to see paparazzi (which I've never seen in Denver) chasing after him, the flashes from their cameras pulling me from whatever lust-induced fantasy he's thrown me into.

"No way he's married. If he had a wife, she would've already snatched his behind up and been wearing him like a freaking trophy." Elsie nudges me forward, but my feet are stuck. "Trust me. When Brandon walks into a room, I make sure everyone knows he's mine."

It's not that I have confidence issues. I'm not a supermodel or anything. Unlike Daisy, I got Gran's height and topped out at an impressive five foot, two inches tall. I also have an undying love for baked goods and French fries that keeps my abs of steel nice and protected, but YOLO or whatever the kids are saying these days. No matter, I'm still nothing to sneeze at. It's just that this guy is H-O-T hot and I can't be rejected in my own damn store.

Talk about embarrassing.

Elsie and I, along with ninety percent of the adult clientele, watch him and his very tight, very nice jeans as he wanders through the Book Nook. We're all waiting with bated breath for him to walk back to story time, where he'll inevitably find his spouse, wrap his thick, strong arms around her dainty waist, and kiss her forehead.

Yeah.

He's definitely a forehead kisser.

But instead, he walks to the front of the store, where sweet Dani is staring at him with hearts in her eyes and her jaw on the desk. We're very professional at the Book Nook. I'm too far away to hear their conversation, and when Dani leans around him to point at me, I all but panic.

"Did Dani just point at me?" I ask Elsie. I'm frozen in place, watching the scene in front of me, where the man of my dreams slowly looks over his shoulder and we lock eyes. "Is he looking at me?"

Listen, I live in Colorado. I've been grappling with the aftereffects of grief and a lifetime of daddy issues. Would it be accurate to assume that I have occasionally taken advantage of the healing powers of THC? Yes. Did I partake this morning? No. Or at least I don't think so? I've never been so high that I hallucinated, but it feels like the only explanation for the way his lips pull into a wide smile and he starts walking my way.

"Oh my god. He's coming over." Elsie breathes out and—unless we're having a shared trip—confirms that I'm not imagining things.

My brain finally kicks into gear again and I spin to face Elsie. I step in front of her, but she completely ignores me and the wiggling child on her hip.

"Elsie!" I whisper-shout to get her attention, but she looks right through me.

"Holy freaking cow," she whispers. "He's even hotter than I thought. Wow."

It takes every bit of restraint I have—and I don't have much—to not turn and gawk with my best friend. Something that gets even harder as her eyes go soft and dreamy and a goofy-ass smile pulls on the corners of her mouth.

"Hi," she says.

"Hi," a deep voice returns, very, very, very close to my ear.

Chill bumps race down my arms and something weird happens to my stomach. My brain and my body are not on the same page. I might talk a big game when it comes to flirting and men and whatnot, but I'm panicking here!

I don't want to turn around. I'm worried I'll be blinded by his beauty this close-up. I feel like he should come with those little glasses we had to wear to see the solar eclipse or something. But the manners hammered into me growing up kick in, forcing my feet into gear.

And sadly, when I come face-to-face with him, I find out that Elsie was correct.

He is, in fact, even fucking hotter.

*Rude.*

"Hi," I echo the elegant word—singular—as I try to gather my wits. It's a struggle to do anything other than just stand here and gaze into his truly hypnotizing eyes, which fade from a brilliant blue to a vibrant green. "How can I help you?"

I don't let my mind wander to all the different—and slightly inappropriate—ways I would like to service him.

"Are you Drew Young?" he asks, and for the first time, alarm bells start to ring in my head.

Maybe Daisy was wrong and Dad is back in town. This could be a freaking trap. Mr. Hotty-Hot is probably a lawyer, ready to serve me with papers. I bet he uses his overabundance of charm and good looks as a distraction to catch people off guard before dropping the gauntlet.

"I am." I narrow my eyes at him and take a step back. "And who, may I ask, are you?"

For some reason, this seems to amuse him even more. The lines by the corners of his eyes deepen, doing nothing to detract from his handsomeness. "I'm Jasper Williams." He reaches out an oversized hand as I search my mind trying to place the familiar name. "A woman named Mona reached out to me, she told me to find you."

Jasper Williams? He talked to Mona?

I shake his hand, trying not to be distracted by the way it engulfs mine, when recognition of the familiar name finally dawns on me.

"Oh my god. Jasper Williams." I pull my hand away. "You're the author guy?"

I don't mean for my tone to come out so incredulous, but I can't help it. This giant hunk of a man is Jasper Williams? Explainer of women, writer of unbelievable romances, Jasper Williams?

"That's me." He nods, no longer looking amused, and maybe a tiny bit offended. "The author guy."

Oops.

"Sorry! I mean . . . wow! Okay!" I'm a little too loud and probably sound a little too excited to meet a person I had exactly zero interest in meeting. "That's great to know."

I can feel Elsie's glare burning into the side of my face as relieved laughter falls out of my mouth, but I don't even care.

Mr. Perfect isn't perfect after all! He's a freaking author! This changes everything.

# CHAPTER 4

"Why do I get the feeling it's not actually great?" says Jasper Williams, Author, and his thick, Instagram-worthy eyebrows scrunch together, the lines on his forehead dancing above them.

I feel a little guilty. Just the smallest, tiniest amount of guilt for not being the kind, welcoming hostess Gran taught me to be. But the rest of me is so relieved that while Jasper might be literal physical perfection, who he is as an actual human is the last thing I'd want in a boyfriend. Because I'm busy, you know? I don't have time to pine after a guy who will undoubtedly leave me high and dry and sadder than I already am. Unlike Jasper's books, real life does not come with happy endings. My entire fucking life is proof of it.

"Yeah, Drew, why does he get the feeling that's not actually great?" Elsie echoes his sentiment. However, her look is less confusion and more a promise of her cussing me out later. Out of earshot of her small humans, of course.

"I don't know." I widen my eyes at her, giving her my best "shut the fuck up, I'll tell you later" look. I hope she gets the message, and then I plaster on my biggest, fakest smile maybe ever and look back to Jasper Williams, Author. "It is great. You're an author. This is a bookstore. This is great."

I know I don't sound very convincing, but lucky for me, before Elsie can call me out on it, yelps of goodbyes and tiny squeals of laughter drift to the front of the store.

"Sounds like story time is over," I say to Elsie, a real smile tugging at my mouth. "You should probably go get the girls."

Saved by Elsa! Look at story time paying off in spades.

She purses her lips together and shoots me a death glare that has only become more potent since she's given birth. "You're so lucky right now," she murmurs beneath her breath before turning her attention to Jasper. "Nice to meet you, Jasper. I read *The Beginning* when I was pregnant with this one"—she gestures to a still-sleeping baby Finn—"and adored it. Clara was so relatable and I loved watching her transform."

"Thank you so much," Jasper says. "I see you have your hands quite full, so it means more to me than you know that you would spend any of your time reading one of my novels."

I don't know where to look. At the man who casually used the word *novels* or my best friend, who is apparently a secret romance reader. All I know is that Elsie better have bought that book from here. If she ordered the e-book, we might have to fight.

"I can't wait to read more," she says to Jasper before turning back to me. "And you. Behave." She scolds me like I'm one of her kids and speaks again before I can defend myself. "Call me later so I know when to set my alarm for yoga tomorrow."

Yoga.

Dammit! Thwarted again! I can't even pretend to freeze her out for treating me like a child in front of a hot author.

"Will do." I give her a quick hug, wrapping my arms around her, Finn, and Milo. "Have a safe drive in the swagger wagon back to the burbs."

"Always do."

Then she's gone and I'm alone with Jasper Williams.

Awesome.

"So . . ." I drag out the short word, trying to ignore the way the other moms are going out of their way to get a better look at Jasper. "How can I help you?"

"I was in the neighborhood and thought I'd come sign some books ahead of tonight." I don't know if he's used to being the subject of everyone's attention or truly doesn't notice the women gawking at him, but he's not fazed at all as he speaks.

I, on the other hand, am not used to feeling like I'm inside a fishbowl, and I do not like it one bit. "Oh, okay. Yeah." I trip over my words. "That sounds good."

"If this doesn't work for you, I can do it tonight instead." He must see the discomfort written all across my face, but he reads it wrong.

"Oh no. I'm sorry." I wave off his concerns. "Now is fine. Your books are over here."

Thankfully he's one of our most requested authors, so I know exactly where they're located. After my not-so-graceful realization of who he was, it'd be nice to look at least semicapable.

I weave my way through the shelves, smiling and waving good-byes to the moms and their minis as they head to the checkout with arms loaded up with picture books. With each step, I feel a little more confident. The nerves of knowing one of America's most popular authors is trailing behind me fade as we approach the table always covered with multiples of his titles.

But when we get there, his books are missing. And I don't mean one or two—I mean all of them.

"Ummm . . ." My skin starts to tingle as my eyes dart around the space, searching for the familiar covers. "They're usually right here."

I move to the aisle, locating the *W* authors in a snap, but feeling heat rise in my face when his books are missing from there as well. Leave it to me to lose an author's books—books I see every day!— the day of said author's event.

"Mona told me she had them gathered in the back." Jasper's deep voice jolts me out of the panic spiral preparing to pull me under. His deep voice soothes my nerves as efficiently as the words he says. "I don't know if that helps."

Freaking Dirty Birds.

I love them, but I swear, their "help" is going to put me in an early grave.

"It does, thank you so much." I offer him a grateful smile. "Do you want to sit while I go grab them?"

"Sure." His full lips spread into a wide smile and I try to ignore the way it causes the butterflies I thought went extinct years ago to take off.

I don't say anything as I make my way to the corner filled with empty rocking chairs. I assume he's following close behind, not only because the gazes of customers nearby still drift over my shoulder, but also because of the way the hairs on my arms are standing up. It's as if he's full of electricity. Like lightning preparing to strike.

"Wow. This is great." His voice, which must sound so wonderful wrapped around the words he writes, startles me from my thoughts when we get to the nook. "I guess I see why this place is called the Book Nook."

"Yeah." My smile is more wistful this time, taking in the space alongside him. The constant ache in my chest lessens for a moment as I remember the way Gran beamed with pride each time she showed off our hard work. "It took us forever to find all of the pieces, but it was worth it."

"Us?" he asks. I think I might see him glance down at my hands before returning his eyes to mine.

"Oh, um, yeah. My grandma." I can't stop my hands from wringing. I'm a nervous fidgeter and the anxiety I feel whenever I have to talk about her in the past tense sends me into a semi-tailspin. "This was her store. She left it to me, hence the slight disorganization right now."

It's not hard to see the moment his beautiful eyes—I still can't decide if they are blue with green or green with blue—register what I'm saying to him. The way they soften at the edges and he moves, probably unconsciously, toward me and places his large hand on my shoulder.

It's enough to break me.

Since the day she passed, I feel like I've been in survival mode. From planning the funeral, because Dad sure didn't, to taking over the store, it's always been something. Add in the fact that my mom caught the first flight out of Tennessee and showed up on my doorstep with so many suitcases, I knew she was planning on staying longer than the week we had initially planned on. I had to pretend to be fine and unbothered for weeks before she booked her return flight.

I haven't been able to grieve. And I don't want to. The sheer magnitude of what I lost is too big to be felt. If I even begin to let it in, I know I won't ever recover.

"Let me go find those books." I infuse so much peppiness into my voice, it sounds like I've sucked helium. I step out of his reach and try to ignore the way his hand falls back to his side before I turn and damn near sprint to the stockroom.

I slam the door shut behind me and lean on it, grateful to be alone for a minute.

"Fuck," I hiss into the dark, quiet room, the thousands of pages stacked around me absorbing my words.

I might not love to read—okay, fine, I hate it—but I'd be lying if I said I didn't find an odd comfort in the smell of a book. Maybe some of it is because of the familiarity of it, but nothing calms my frazzled nerves more than taking inventory back here. The weight and feel of a book in my hand, the crisp pages beneath my fingertips, the bright and colorful covers that are all so similar, yet so different. It's almost hypnotizing.

And it's the exact place I need to be after Jasper Williams almost put me under whatever hot-guy spell he's wielding.

"Get your shit together, Young," I scold myself. Now is not the time for whatever the fuck that was out there. There will *never* be a moment for that.

I squeeze my eyes shut for a moment before pushing off the door to go in search of the abundance of Jasper's books that Mona moved, or—more accurately—hid.

I know the Dirty Birds say they're trying to help me, but part of me is convinced they're secret sadists. Nothing else could explain all the shit they put me through. Including inviting the world's hottest author to the Book Nook.

"Okay! I found them!" I don't know how long it's been since I left—fine, ran away from—him, but I do know I'm out of breath and the hair at the nape of my neck has started to curl up when I drop one box of his books on the floor next to him. "Mona put them all in boxes and in the back of the storage room for some reason I'll never understand. There are still two more, but you can start signing while I grab the other ones."

Instead of thanking me or complimenting my strength and pulling out the feather pen I've convinced myself he carries with him at all times, he unfolds his much-too-tall, much-too-muscular body out of the rocking chair and closes the small space between us.

"Why don't I help you grab the rest?" he asks, the stupid timbre of his voice doing stupid things to my stupid body. "Teamwork makes the dream work, am I right?"

Teamwork makes the dream work? This guy, who is an award-winning writer of words, just said that?

His cheeks redden beneath my gaze and a kinder person would move on, pretending that didn't happen.

"Did you really say that?"

I guess I'm not very kind.

"I honestly regretted it the second the words came out of my mouth. I was hoping you would let it slide." His smile widens, and I'm not one hundred percent sure, but I think it's the only thing that could distract me from the topic at hand. This must be why hot people get away with so much. They say something stupid, hit you with a smile, all is forgotten. Repeat.

What a vicious cycle.

"Sorry." I toss the word over my shoulder as we walk back to the storage room. It's easier to interact with him if I'm not looking directly at him. "One of my more toxic traits is pettiness; I can't let most things slide."

Okay.

Is the reason I'm going to be single forever because I loudly—and proudly—announce my toxic traits to virtual strangers within minutes of meeting them? Yeah. One of about a million reasons, actually.

"Good to know," he says without hesitation. "One of my more toxic traits is enjoying people telling me their toxic traits."

My feet and not my heart—absolutely *not* my heart—stutter. Who is this guy?

"Put that on a dating profile," I half joke before pushing open the door and pointing to the corner with stacked boxes before he can say something else I find amusing. "Your books are over here."

I let him step in front of me, and not because I want to look at his ass when he bends to pick up the box.

No.

Not at all.

But because I don't want him to look at mine. Duh.

"Be careful," I warn as he squats down to grab the biggest box. "Don't get hurt. I have enough things going on with the store, I can't deal with a lawsuit because you lift with your back and not your legs."

He stops moving and looks over his shoulder. His eyebrows knit together and questions linger behind his eyes. I think over what I said and realize I might've shared way, way, way too much information. All I need is for Jasper Williams, Author, to be convinced I'm running some sort of shady business out of here. The Dirty Birds would make my life a living hell.

Well, more of a living hell.

I open my mouth to defend my honor and probably share some more information he doesn't need, but he speaks first.

"Are you questioning my form?" The confusion on his face vanishes in an instant. He arches a single eyebrow, looking nowhere as cool as the Rock, but also not looking as ridiculous as he should. "I'll have you know, I do CrossFit. This is perfect form."

I feel like a cartoon character. I'm pretty sure my jaw hits the floor. Out of everything I thought he was going to say, CrossFit wasn't even in the top one thousand!

"Nope." I shake my head. "Absolutely not. I'm pretending you aren't here anymore."

His deep, throaty chuckles echo in the small room as he straightens—his form is actually very good, but I can never admit that now—and I squeeze by him to get the final box. My arm grazes his as I pass by, and for some reason my body ignores that he's an author who does CrossFit and lights up in previously dead places.

"What?" He walks to the door and pushes it open, keeping a close eye on me as I approach. I'm convinced he can read every filthy thought in my mind. "I was told CrossFit is very cool."

"I refuse to engage with you anymore. Won't do it." As a yoga stan, I cannot condone the phenomenon that is CrossFit. I took one class and promptly left when the others finished before me and didn't leave, but instead stood around me and clapped as I struggled through burpees and dead lifts. It was a nightmare. Give me my yoga mat and a semblance of peace and quiet over that nonsense any day. "But thanks for holding the door open."

My manners beat out my initial desire to ice him out. I'm not sure why, but for a reason I refuse to investigate, I think a part of me wants him to like me. Even if he is absolutely the exact opposite of everything that I enjoy in life.

Weird.

The ache in my back distracts me from the fact that I'm going to look like a sweaty mess trekking across the store and into the cozy nook where he can sign all bazillion of his books.

"There we go." I mean to set his books down with a gentle flourish, but unfortunately for me and the poor arm muscles I try my hardest to never use, I just drop it. "Shit." I hiss the elegant word in front of the world-acclaimed author. Super professional. "I mean shoot! I'm so sorry. I didn't mean to drop your books or swear."

Gran must be rolling in her grave.

"Not a problem." His lips twitch at the corners as he sets his box down on the ground all slow and controlled. Show-off. "There might not be tons of it in my books, but my language isn't always pristine."

I guess that's the author way of telling me he says *fuck* too.

I smile at him, not really knowing how to respond, and awkward silence settles around us.

"Why don't I help you unpack these books." It's not a question so I don't wait for an answer before moving to a box and cracking it open.

All his books have similar covers. Unlike the fun and colorful covers on most of the new romances we've been getting in, his are a little more muted. No fun illustrations on the cover, always scenic pictures, never a model. His name is in large bold print, in most cases larger than the title of the book. I always thought they seemed a little pretentious, but now, after only a short time around him, I see them with a different set of eyes. Like the soft colors and delicate font are a promise of gentleness inside. Just like the author.

My fingers trail across the covers as I place them on the large coffee table, careful not to bend the corners or disturb the crisp pages. It's a familiar dance. One I've been doing since I was a kid. One I've been practicing solo for the last few months. And maybe that's why any lingering awkwardness fades as Jasper works in tandem beside me. The silence provides a comfort I didn't think would be possible alongside Jasper.

"Wow." His voice pulls me out of the comfortable silence we've been working in as he takes the last book out of his box. "Sometimes I forget how many of these things I've written."

He drags his hand through his thick hair before tearing his gaze from the table and moving it to me. A faint shade of pink tinges his cheeks as he shrugs his shoulders, his lips curving up into a shy smile that changes his entire face and, if it were possible, makes him a million times more attractive.

"You have written quite a few," I agree with him, the understatement not missed by either of us. "Are you working on a new book now?"

I don't know how this writing thing works. At some point, he has to stop, right? Like one day, there will be no more stories to tell? Maybe he'll want to move on to something else. Get out from behind the computer and actually experience the world he writes about.

"I am." His long legs make quick work of the small space before he pulls one of the rocking chairs closer to the table. My heart stutters in my chest when I realize what chair it is. I watch as he folds into my grandma's chair. The old, unused wood creaks beneath his weight. "I just started it, actually."

"Oh really? That's exciting." I say the words, but there's no emotion behind them. I'm too busy trying to think of an excuse to get him to switch chairs.

"It is. I've been wanting to tell this story for a while now, and the time is finally right. It's kind of like *Need You Now* meets *Party of One*. Have you read either one of those?"

I'm too lost in my thoughts to think about what I'm saying before I open my mouth. Too focused on the past to be in the present.

"No, I don't read."

The way the pen falls out of his hand and his gaze snaps to meet mine would be comical if I saw it happen to anybody else. But instead, I shrink beneath his disbelieving gaze. I know the incompetence I always feel is on full display. At this moment, he knows I'm a fraud.

"You don't read?" Confusion mars his gorgeous face. "But . . . you own a bookstore?"

"I *inherited* a bookstore." I repeat my earlier words, not loving how exposed I feel. I look at my phone, which is definitely not ringing. "I have to make a call and take care of a few things before tonight. But you met Dani already and she can help you if you need anything or have a question."

He leans forward, his lips parting, but I cut him off before he speaks.

"Thank you again for doing this. Mona and the other ladies are so excited." I spin on the well-worn heel of my Birkenstock, forgetting all about manners and only focusing on the fastest route away from Jasper Williams, Author. "Okay. Bye!"

I don't wait to hear what he says and I sure as hell don't look back. Not even when his deep, throaty chuckle drifts after me.

# CHAPTER 5

I'M NOT AN ATHLETE. BACK IN HIGH SCHOOL I PLAYED FIELD HOCKEY for the simple reason that it was new, they needed enough people to make up a team, and I really loved the plaid skirts we played in. We were terrible, but I was able to get a letterman jacket and that was all I wanted.

Sports are not my thing.

Where my talent lies is in taking normal situations and making them as awkward as possible.

If awkwardness was a sport, I'd be a goddamn Olympian.

It truly is a gift.

To be fair, though, this is Jasper's fault too. I thought I had prepared myself to see him again. Yes, he's an attractive man, but I saw him once and I was prepared.

Joke's on me, folks.

Because what did he do? Oh, that's right. He walked into my bookstore to do a reading for an old-lady book club looking like a whole-ass glass of water—and there's been a drought in Colorado practically my entire damn life.

Damn thirst trap.

Even Collette, who's been in a perpetually bad mood for the last five years, pepped right up. She might've even blushed. I don't know for sure, though, because after I waved at him like a freaking three-year-old, I turned and ran.

Again.

I stayed behind the front desk, using the customers as human shields until Mona introduced Jasper and it was safe to venture out.

"How do you find your inspiration?" Vivian is leaning forward in her seat, her eyes glued to the man in front of her. In her former life, Vivian ran etiquette classes out of her home to make a little extra money. This is the first time I've ever seen her posture anything but perfect.

"It comes from different places." Jasper takes his glasses off and leans an elbow onto the podium I pulled from the back room when I was setting up for tonight. I swear I hear a collective sigh from the crowd. "The easiest answer is from other creatives. I love to go to museums, concerts, and even movies. For me, creativity sparks creativity. But it can come from anywhere really. For instance, the premise for my next book came to me while I was at the grocery store."

I lurk in the back, half spying, half hiding, listening as Jasper's deep voice enraptures the crowd, which—despite me only posting on our social media channels a few times—is standing room only. I'm going to have to buy Mona a gift for setting this up, which sucks because now she's never going to stop surprising me with events. But between story time this morning and copies of *Last Hope* and the rest of Jasper's catalog that people are buying, this has been the best sales day we've had since I took over.

"Oh! Another book?" someone shouts from nearby, and when Jasper looks to the crowd to find whoever yelled, his eyes meet mine instead. His lips, which I know seem much fuller up close, quirk at the corners. I don't know if it's a trick of the light, but I swear he winks before he looks away.

It took a few months longer than I thought it would, but it seems as if I'm finally losing it.

Cool, cool. No big deal.

"Yes, and it takes place right here in Denver. It's why I'm able to be with you lovely people tonight. I like to explore the places I write about and spend my time drafting in the city of my characters. I'll be here for a few months, until I finish writing this story. Getting a deep understanding of my characters and their setting is a crucial part of my process."

*A crucial part of my process.*

See, this is why I'm watching him speak instead of doing paperwork or any of the other hundreds of things on my to-do list. When he says stuff like that, I realize that while he may look better than anyone has a right to in a blazer and turtleneck in the middle of summer, we have nothing in common. We'd probably hate each other if we spent more than twenty consecutive minutes speaking to each other.

But what about time together not speaking?

I'm standing beneath the air-conditioning vent but my cheeks still burn. I'm sure that, though they're nowhere near me, the Dirty Birds can read my thoughts.

On that note . . .

As much as I enjoy the view and—begrudgingly—how passionate Jasper is when he speaks, it's time for me to move on.

"I'm going to do a little work in the back, but come grab me if you need help at the register. Are you good out here on your own for a bit?" I ask Dani before I head back into Gran's—I mean, my office.

"Oh, um, yeah! I got it, no problem!" Dani answers a little too brightly, even by peppy Dani standards. She looks away from Jasper and her face turns a deep shade of red. You don't need to be a mind reader to know what she's thinking. *Solidarity, sister.*

"You're the best." I leave her with her lusty thoughts and navigate the familiar path between overstuffed bookshelves, dragging my feet across the worn-down carpet, which should've been replaced years ago.

I pause outside the door. I'm still not used to the obliterating silence that meets me when I walk into the small room filled with furniture much too large for the space. It's been months, but sometimes I'll close my eyes and shout, "What's cookin', good-lookin'?" when I enter the office, hoping Gran's laughter will surround me and wake me up from this freaking nightmare.

I twist the cold doorknob, hating the way the brass burns. The weight of the store, anticipating my dad making another move, and the bills piling up on the oak desk are the only things that may be able to distract me from Jasper Williams, Author . . . whose voice I can still faintly hear.

Personally, I've embarrassed myself in front of Jasper two times now. Professionally, however, this day has been fantastic.

The Book Nook had in-store events when Gran was still around. Since she passed we haven't had anything other than story time. I've been telling myself I'm too busy getting used to day-to-day practices and setting up our children's section to really invest in it. But if I'm honest, I've been afraid. When Alice Young put on an event, she found the authors, reached out, and set up entire itineraries. She was able to do this because not only was she an avid reader, but she was an avid listener. She always had one finger on the pulse of her customers, intent on creating a community inside the Book Nook, where there was something for every reader.

I've avoided events like tonight because I'm not prepared for the inevitable comparisons that will follow. I know I'm inadequate to fill her shoes—they are impossibly large—but I don't need everyone else to know that as well. That was the beauty of the children's section; it was her idea to build it, but it was mine to create. Nothing to hold it up against, just the feeling of accomplishment and hoping I made her proud.

I squeeze around the side of the desk and take a seat in her chair. The space might be small, but Gran lingers in every nook and cranny. The glasses she always forgot are on top of the filing cabinet. The book she was reading is on the bookshelf, her bookmark peeking through the top of the pages she'll never finish reading. Her favorite mug is still sitting on the desk in front of me. For all anyone knows, it could be superglued to the spot, because I've never moved it.

The only thing I've considered taking down is the framed article from a local magazine naming me the top up-and-coming photographer: "With style and grit, Young explores trails most photographers wouldn't dare take. Her keen eye for beauty in untouched places has us holding our breath as we wait for what she shows us next."

Gran was so proud of it. *I* was so proud of it. I felt like I was getting my feet beneath me; my future felt so bright. I would help Gran when I was around, but I was a photographer. I had found my path.

Then it was gone and all I had left were unfinished dreams, a grieving soul, and a new business to direct all my energy.

I should take it all out of here. Bring her mug home, pack away her books. There's no logical reason for them to be here anymore. But a part of me—the part I'm afraid to let escape—is terrified to move any of it. I'm comfortable right now. I can make it through days without crying. I've figured out how to keep moving forward. I'm afraid the smallest disruption will set me back or, even worse, cause me to forget something. Without the opportunity to create new memories, I'm clinging desperately to the ones I have. Even the ones as silly as giving her a hard time for not using a coaster on her beloved desk.

I open my computer and check the emails I've ignored all day.

Even though I am what some could consider a hot-ass mess, I'm a pretty organized person. I thrive with structure. Saturdays are my day to go over the previous week and prepare for the next one. Usually, I work the floor until the end of story time and then spend the rest of the day in here.

Unfortunately for me, I was so busy avoiding Jasper that all my work sat on my desk while I ventured to four different grocery stores until I found the flavor of Jeni's ice cream I wanted. What can I say? Eating my feelings is one of my favorite coping mechanisms. Just under shoe shopping but right above barhopping.

I click through the emails, making quick work of deleting junk mail, flagging important emails that require well-thought-out responses, and answering the rest with my standard prewritten response. Before Gran passed, I always helped her on the computer. I didn't know all the logistics of her day-to-day work, but it was nice to have a grip on one part of the business when I was thrown in the deep end.

The paperwork, on the other hand?

Gran was a stay-at-home mom until Dad started going to school and she got bored at home. Her husband was at work and she was the only person in her group of friends who had only one child. She decided to take her newfound spare time and get a job at Dad's school. She worked in the library, and although she always loved books, she said this is where it really went to the next level. It's also where she started filing papers like a madwoman with no damn sense.

Organizing her files was a form of torture that could've broken the most hardened criminal. I collapsed in tears more than once. She filed so many scraps of paper with three or four words scribbled on them that I almost convinced myself they formed a secret message and she moonlighted as a treasure hunter. I was about two seconds away from going full-on *National Treasure* Nicolas Cage when Mona came in and helped me decipher the shorthand notes.

There was no treasure, but there was a mystery. Tucked in the back of her scraps, I found a business card from an executive at Prose and Fable, the online source to buy books and a perpetual pain in my ass. I don't want to say they're the only reason I shop local as often as possible, but they're the only reason I shop local as often as possible. Since their rise in popularity, staying in business as a small bookstore has become harder than ever.

Gran never mentioned anything to me about them contacting her, and as much as I poked and prodded all the Dirty Birds, none of them seemed to know what she was doing with their phone number either. I should've thrown it away as soon as I found it, but as I grab a pen out of the desk, the business card peeks at me from the corner of the drawer.

*Just in case*, I remind myself as I slam the drawer shut. Everyone needs an emergency exit plan in place. I can't help that mine feels more like a betrayal than a lifeboat.

I don't know how long I spend looking at order forms and filling in spreadsheets, but before I know it, a hesitant knock on my door pulls me from my work trance.

"It's open," I yell across the small, cluttered space, shocked when the door opens and Collette walks in.

I'm not surprised that she's back here, but this is maybe the first time she's ever knocked instead of barging in.

And my Spidey-senses go crazy.

"Everything okay?" I close my laptop and push away from the desk. The night was going well when I left, but now all sorts of worst-case scenarios are running through my head, including, but not limited to, the Dirty Birds running Jasper out of the store and causing him to quit writing, therefore unleashing millions of angry readers upon the Book Nook; a small fire; or an angry mob accosting poor Dani at the register because I lost track of time. "I didn't realize how late it was."

"Oh yeah, fine. Mona helped Dani at the register and things went nice and smooth. Your sticker system went off without a hitch." Collette waves off my anxiety, but for some reason, that only makes it grow even more. "We know you close soon, but come chat with some old ladies for a bit."

I'm glad my sticker system worked. Since this was my first big event, I really wanted to keep the chaos to a minimum. Before Jasper started talking, I went through the audience, giving out different sticker colors for people who already had books and people who needed to buy them. We had stacks of his signed books at the register so the crowds were where they needed to be instead of in bubbles all around the store. Everyone had sticky notes with their names so it was easy for Jasper to personalize what he wrote for them.

"Oh good. I'm glad it went well." I keep my tone even and my steps slow as I approach her, but now I'm positive something is up. If they really just wanted to talk, they would've sent in Beth or someone who could take no for an answer. They sent Collette because she'd have no problem issuing threats if I declined. "And you know I always love a little Dirty Bird action."

Out of the corner of my eye, I'm pretty sure I see Collette roll her eyes, but her usual smartass response never comes.

Strange . . .

The previously packed space is almost empty save for a few stragglers browsing the shelves in the romance section. The store is reminiscent of a frat house after a rager. Dani and Jess, my part-time employee, are collecting the folding chairs we grossly underestimated the need for and stacking them in the corner. Display tables are rummaged through and look more like an eyesore than a selling point. Quiet conversation lingers, excitement from a night with a famous author still buzzing in the air.

"Did Jasper answer all of the questions you had planned for him?" I ask as we get closer to the nook, where I know all the Dirty Birds have assembled.

"Oh, you have no idea," she says without glancing my way. "He's been more than accommodating."

Alarm bells start to go off in my head, warning me to run and hide until the end of time, but it's too late. By the time the full extent of the incoming disaster registers, Ethel's bright smile is aimed right at me while Mona and Vivian are fawning over a very handsome man in a turtleneck and blazer.

"Oh, there you are!" Ethel pushes out of her rocking chair, moving toward me faster than I've ever seen her move in her sensible kitten heels. "We've been looking for you."

Collette is over whatever act she was forced to put on to get me out here. She rolls her eyes and deflates into her chair with an exasperated sigh. She's like a caricature of an old lady, and it'd be amusing if I didn't sense a massive setup happening.

"You have? I've been working in the back."

If there's one thing you learn being around a group of older ladies, it's that meddling isn't something that just happens out of happenstance.

No, no, no.

A lot of effort, planning, and logistics go into it. And as Mona's voice rises above the rest, I realize I have been played and played hard.

"Wasn't tonight so wonderful?" Mona leans into Jasper. "Our Drew here has done such a wonderful job with this store, taking over for our dear Alice. Did she tell you? She's so humble, I doubt she's told you everything she's done here."

Jasper, the poor, sweet man, nods and gives Mona an indulgent smile before turning his gaze to me. I've been on the receiving end of a look of pity. I have a dad who all but abandoned me for the new model and am living in the aftereffects of a dead loved one. But the one he gives me? With that perfect face and beautiful eyes? Nothing has ever been worse. All I want to do is run and squeeze my adult ass into the reading cubby in the kids' section.

Or move to Mexico.

Mexico seems like a good option.

"Don't answer that," I say to Jasper while avoiding looking at him. "You'll only encourage them."

"Encourage them?" Vivian repeats my words and I know I'm about to be scolded for whatever etiquette rule I've broken now. "It's not polite to speak about us as if we're aren't here. Jasper can answer if he wants. We've read his works and heard him speak tonight. It's clear he's a very intelligent man with great taste. I'm sure he agrees with our assessment of you and your work here."

I bite my tongue. I've been around these women too many times to think objecting will change the trajectory of this conversation.

"Exactly that," Mona chimes in. "You agree with us, don't you, Jasper?"

Jasper pulls his lips between his teeth, and I don't know if it's to hide an expression of fear or amusement, but both are fitting. Either way, though, he doesn't say anything.

As much as I want to appreciate his sudden vow of silence, part of me—a very hypocritical part of me—is offended he's not agreeing with them.

"Oh, don't be shy, now, boy." Collette's hoarse smoker's voice speaks up for the first time, and it's clear she's as happy with this conversation as I am. "You just spoke to a room full of people for an hour, we know you aren't a damn shrinking violet. And the sooner you answer, the sooner Ethel can drive me home."

There are many times when I take Collette's curtness super personally. I convinced myself years ago that she hates me. It's only in moments like these when I'm reminded it's not just me—it's everyone. Including the author she was fawning over only hours ago.

"I won't be driving you home at all if you treat Jasper that way!" Sweet Ethel is incredulous. "I know you're a grumpy old lady, but that doesn't give you the right to speak to him like that."

Collette leans forward in her rocking chair, her eyes narrowed. I'm horrified as I watch the scene playing out in front of me. I look at Jasper, and he also looks concerned that there may be a brawl in the Book Nook.

Thankfully—or not—this spurs him into action, his smooth, deep voice acting like a sedative to the worked-up women around us.

"I agree with you! Tonight was wonderful and I've had such a great time working with Drew," he half shouts.

I'm no lawyer, but I'm pretty sure this is what they would consider a coerced admission.

All the tension dissipates in an instant. Ethel, Mona, Beth, and Vivian all turn extremely pleased eyes to Jasper a moment before swarming the poor man. Collette, on the other hand, keeps her behind firmly planted in her chair and rolls her eyes so hard, I swear I can hear it.

"See!" Beth rests her hand on Jasper's arm and looks up at him with an expression so pure, it almost thaws my frozen heart. "We knew you were a smart one!"

"With exquisite taste too." Vivian grabs onto his other arm. "Now, didn't you mention that you're staying in Denver to write your next book?"

Jasper looks almost fearful for his life as he nods. "Yes, I'll be here for a few months."

"Oh my. That must be so lonely, all alone in a new city," Mona pipes in, and at the tone of her voice, all amusement I was feeling watching Jasper draped with Dirty Birds is replaced by dread. Because that tone? I know it well. It's the prequel to terrible blind dates and awkward phone conversations with their ideal male suitors.

"It's not too bad. I actually don't—" he starts, but is promptly cut off by Mona.

"Oh no, none of that." Mona clucks her tongue at him. "Did you know our Drew here is a Colorado expert?"

If I thought I could avoid this, I would do something to stop her. But not only do I know what Mona's going to say next; I also know there's no way to stop this disaster from coming to fruition.

"She's a very good photographer. She's always snapping her camera and driving all around to take pictures of these little towns and places I've never heard of." Mona is still talking, but Jasper's eyes flicker to me with curiosity working behind the ocean-blue center. Like this new bit of information about me has changed the way he sees me. It takes everything in me not to fidget beneath his intense gaze and put my focus back on a still-rambling Mona. ". . . she's been everywhere. You know! I'm sure she could tell you all the great places for your book. Maybe you could take her to dinner and discuss it?"

Annnnnndddd . . .

There it is.

I knew this was the destination, but it still doesn't lessen the recoil of my stomach when she finally lands the plane.

I love the Dirty Birds and their devotion to stepping in for Gran since she's been gone, but they are truly horrendous matchmakers. I've been dodging their attempts since the last one ended with me listening to their mutual friend's grandson drone on and on and on about Bitcoin and the trading market. He didn't stop until his room-mate showed up and he basically kicked me out of the restaurant so they could do Jägerbombs at the bar or some shit.

"Oh, that's not—" I start, waving off this terrible idea.

"That'd be great, actually." Jasper speaks over me—all the en-couragement I could need to want to spend an evening out with him. "I've been trying to network, but it seems like most people I find are transplants. It'd be great to see the city from someone who really knows it."

I try to keep the expression on my face neutral, but between the amused smirk on Jasper's face and the heart eyes the Dirty Birds—excluding Collette, obvi—are now sporting, I feel like my head might explode.

I want to say no.

It's one of my favorite words. I say it all day long. No. No. No.

Two letters.

So simple.

No.

But for some reason, it won't come out. It's lodged in the back of my throat and I'm choking on it. Maybe it's because the Dirty Birds have been there for me so much since Gran passed away that I can't bear to crush the hopeful looks on their faces. Maybe it's because even though I know Jasper's only going along with this to placate Mona and the rest of the ladies, part of me wouldn't mind spending a little more time with him. I know we have nothing in common and nothing will come from it, but taking a night away from the messy, depressing status of my current life to look at his gorgeous face doesn't sound like the worst thing in the world.

"Ummm . . ." I draw the word out, my eyes flickering between Jasper and the Dirty Birds, not knowing where to look. "Yeah, I guess that'd be fine."

I want to regret it, but the way Vivian and Ethel both begin to clap and Beth's and Mona's faces light up with joy makes it impossible.

"Great!" Jasper seems genuinely happy I agreed to this ridiculous plan. He pulls his phone out of his back pocket and extends it toward me. "How about we exchange numbers and we can touch base tomorrow on a date and time that works best for both of us?"

"Yeah, sure. That sounds good, I guess." I bite my lip to stop my nervous rambling. I take his phone and enter my information, only making a few typos with my shaky hands before I hand it back to him.

"Texting you now," he announces to the group, and I swear Mona nearly falls over with glee.

Even though I always question their motives, and I can't prove anything, I have a sneaking suspicion that the endgame of Jasper Williams coming to the Book Nook wasn't really to answer their burning questions, but an excuse to meddle further in my love life, if you can even call it that.

Cunning mother—

"All right. The boy got her number. They're going to dinner." Collette unfolds her tired body from the chair. "Can we leave now? Mr. Bennet is probably wondering where I am by now."

Jasper furrows his brows together and aims confused eyes at me.

"Her cat." I mouth my answer to his unasked question.

"Fine." Ethel rolls her eyes before grabbing her purse off the table and pulling the long strap over her shoulder. "Such a party pooper. You know Mr. Bennet only cares about you in the morning when he wants to be fed. Now, a dog, there's real loyalty and love."

"I'm not having this conversation with you again, Ethel Morris. You like needy, you get a dog. I don't like that crap, I got a cat." She starts to the front of the store, their familiar argument following them out. "We're old, for Christ's sake. What would I look like getting yanked around the neighborhood walking that big mutt of yours?"

Thankfully, before we can hear any more, the door slams shut behind them and they're out of the store.

"Are you good closing on your own?" Vivian asks. "I can stay and help clean up if you need."

I look behind me, pretending to put thought into her question to avoid getting scolded again for brushing her off.

"Thank you for offering, but it looks like Dani got most of it taken care of." It's not a lie. Dani is my number one for a reason: she's a lifesaver. "I'm just going to finish up a few things in my office."

"Okay then." She turns her smile to Jasper. "Then will you be the gentleman we know you are and walk some old ladies to their cars?"

"There's nothing I'd enjoy more," Jasper says. And with a move I'll probably dream about later, he lifts his elbows, making room for two Dirty Birds to latch on, which they do without any further encouragement.

Mona leads the way as I follow them to the door, trying not to laugh at the lovestruck expressions Vivian and Beth are both wearing, and quickly lock the door behind them.

"Soooo . . ." Dani crosses the room to stand next to me. "Wanna tell me what happened back there?"

"Absolutely not." Even if I did want to, I'm not sure I could articulate what happened. "But I'm pretty sure I got swindled by the Dirty Birds."

"Oh, so nothing new?"

And that about sums it up.

I knew tonight was not going to go according to plan, but I don't think even Jasper Williams, Author, could have seen that plot twist coming.

# CHAPTER 6

---

YOGA WAS PERFECT.

I feel like most Denver natives overlook the wonders in our own backyard. Before I tucked my camera away and shifted my focus to keeping the Book Nook up and running, I spent every spare second I had hopping into my old Jeep and exploring this beautiful state of mine. I was in talks with a local news station to create a segment finding the best places for staycations. I had dreams of making a coffee table book filled with photos from my hiking adventures in Colorado and then creating a show for the Travel Channel centered around the book. I try not to think about it much anymore. I keep the old map where I would mark off all my travels hidden in my bedside table. I only look at it when I really want to torture myself with thoughts of what-if or when I need to make a list of destinations for a famous author.

So much of this state goes unnoticed, but nobody can ignore the slice of heaven in Morrison. There's nothing better than closing your eyes, breathing in deep the fresh Colorado air, and being cocooned in the beauty that is Red Rocks Amphitheatre. It's the only place I let myself wander to anymore. Close and popular enough to give me the feeling of freedom without getting lost in it. When you're here, a part of your soul settles and you find a peace I'd be hard-pressed to believe you can find anywhere else.

Or at least you can find peace if you don't bring your best friend and sister with you and for some insane reason—I'll never be able to pinpoint it—tell them about dinner plans with Jasper.

"You're what?" Elsie's thunderous shout breaks the calm, Zen mood of everyone around us. The thin, shirtless man wearing tie-dye leggings and a headband standing beside us shoots daggers at us.

Yikes.

"Sorry, sorry," I say to the angry yogi before turning wide eyes to my lovely, wonderful, and loud best friend. "Shh! You can't yell after yoga."

"Girl, we are all the way the fuck outside." Elsie doesn't curse around her children, so when she's only around adults, she does it in excess to get it out of her system. "I got up before my sleeping baby to drive all the way to fucking Morrison for yoga—something my child-bearing hips are going to be very upset with me for tomorrow, by the way—and you just casually let it slip that you have a date with Jasper? I will damn well yell if I please and I don't care who hears."

She aims the last part at the man still glaring next to us, who—to his immense credit—only cowers a little bit before scurrying away.

"Wait . . ." Daisy tucks the yoga mat I lent her beneath her arm. "Who's Jasper? And why is a date such a big deal? Drew's gorgeous, I'm sure all these Denver men are falling all over her."

"You're not wrong about that, but Drew here has yet to say yes to a date in—" She sticks her finger in my face when I open my mouth to defend myself. "Don't even say it. Those booty calls you've manufactured are not dates."

"Manufactured booty calls?" Daisy repeats, and her blue eyes, which look even brighter in the morning sunlight, crinkle at the corners. "I think I need to hear more about those and also a detailed set of instructions on how you set them up."

Well, look at that. Looks like my dear sister and I have some things in common after all.

"Oh, it's really easy. Let's just say that dick is truly the only infinite resource known to humankind."

It's just too bad that only a small portion of it is quality.

"Vulgar," Elsie scolds me, like she wasn't just yelling obscenities only seconds ago.

"Ma'am." I purse my lips and give her my best side-eye. "You have four, count them, four children. You know all about this and you can't pretend not to."

"Whatever." Elsie rolls her eyes but doesn't fight me on this because she knows I'm right. "But Jasper is no booty call. Jasper Williams literally makes a living creating some of the most beautiful love stories ever written. And to top it off, that man is fine."

"Wait." Daisy sounds like she's on the verge of panic. She grabs Elsie by the shoulders and stares deep into her eyes. "Are you talking about Jasper Williams, author of *Rescue Me*? Creator of Jaxon Montgomery, my favorite book boyfriend of all time, who has ruined me for all actual, living men?"

Fuck. Does everyone read romance?

"Yes, that Jasper Williams," Elsie confirms for Daisy. "And let me tell you, that little square picture in the back of his books has nothing on him in real life. He should model every hero in his books as himself. Because yum."

"Really?" Daisy breathes out the word. Her cheeks are brighter pink now than they were during the entire hour of yoga. "Because even the little picture is good."

Besides the struggles of owning a bookstore, this might be the hardest part of refusing to indulge in the world of fiction.

I used to read. Gran was obviously an avid reader and she wanted to pass that love on to me. Every time I would see her, she'd have a new book for me. I had a bookshelf overflowing with every fairy tale I could get my hands on. I can still remember the way my little body would sink deeper into her lap when her smooth, warm voice would recite my six favorite words, "And they lived happily ever after."

But I also remember Dad starting to stay out longer and the way his smile never reached his eyes anymore. I can hear Mom's soft whimpers through the bathroom door when she didn't know I was listening. Those were the days I read my fairy tales the most, wishing and praying my family would get our happily ever after too. But we didn't.

I learned the hard way. I know books are unrealistic make-believe, whereas other people, like my best friend and apparently my sister, think they're goals. So they transfer these expectations and lovey-dovey emotions to people who might not deserve them. People like Jasper.

Just because he writes this stuff does not mean he subscribes to it.

I mean, sure. He did indulge the Dirty Birds by answering all their questions, offering to take me to dinner, escorting them to their cars, and calling—not texting, which felt like an attack—the same night to give me his schedule. But that doesn't mean he's an actual romance hero or anything.

Herein lies the problem with dating in the time of the internet and apps and texting. Basically existing in the twenty-first century. Our standards are so low that when someone is average, they jut above the crowd. Common courtesy should be the bare minimum, yet here we are, offering endless praise for being a decent human being.

"I hate to break up this lust-fest you both have going on, but you're making a way bigger deal out of this than it really is. The Dirty Birds coerced him into asking me to dinner." While I'm positive this is a sentence most people never utter in their entire lives, it's all too familiar for me. And thankfully, since Daisy and I share a father, she's heard about the Dirty Birds and I don't have to explain at least that much. "He's in town to write a book and Mona volunteered my native Denverite services. I doubt it'll go beyond this dinner without him being flanked by two old ladies forcing him to ask me out. I'm going to make a list of some good places and that will be it."

"What places are you putting on the list?" Daisy—bless her easily distracted heart—asks.

"I don't know. Casa Bonita and a Broncos game?" I'm only half joking. Casa Bonita did get a new chef and the food might finally be good, plus it is a staple of Colorado. Sports though? I can't. Especially in Denver. I feel like we should have an indoor arena. If someone tried to make me sit in the snow for three hours to watch grown men pummel each other, I'd never speak to them again.

"You're a horrible human and if my next Jasper Williams book has a couple falling in love over football and cliff divers you'll be dead to me." Elsie takes off her glasses and levels me with a glare that causes my bones to chill even under the hot Colorado sun. "Anyways, don't you have your map of the best places in Colorado or whatnot? This should be really easy for you."

I try to ignore the way my stomach twists into a knot.

As much as I'm pretending to be put out by this entire mess of a situation, part of me is thrilled to have an excuse to do what I love again. I want to tell Jasper about all the little mountain towns I spent countless weekends in, hiking empty trails until I found the perfect shot. I want to show him pictures of the little towns down south surrounded by open plains and blue skies. I want to tell him stories my way, by showing him the beauty that exists all around us and letting it speak louder than words ever could. But the other part is scared to remember how much I love it. Most days, I feel like I'm hanging on by a thread. I'm terrified getting lost in wanderlust with Jasper will be the thing that snaps the tiny semblance of sanity I have left.

Did I love the photography career I was beginning to build for myself? Of course. But I love Gran more. Running a bookstore may not be my dream, but walking in her legacy is. Standing in her store, surrounded by memories of her, feels like it's the only thing getting me through some days. I can't jeopardize that because Mona decided to play matchmaker and set me up with a hot guy who has a talent for spinning pretty tales.

"You can put your glasses back on and relax." I lean toward her to avoid getting caught in the selfie the couple in front of us is huddling together to take. "I'll make it a good list. I already have an idea for a few places I think would be a great setting in any story. But you need to calm down. Your hopes are way too high for something he's only doing to be nice to a group of sweet but very intrusive old ladies. You know they're impossible to say no to."

"I hear what you're saying," she says, but I know it's only to placate me. "But I need you to remember that Jasper is a famous author. He's busy, and even if he wasn't, he makes up things for a living. If he didn't want to go, he wouldn't have had a problem coming up with an excuse to avoid it. As usual, you're underselling yourself. He seemed into you when I was there."

Nobody makes me feel better about myself than Elsie does. She thinks I'm the shit and never fails to let me know. She's always there to give me a good pep talk when I need one . . . and I've needed quite a few over the years.

This makes her a good friend.

The *best* friend.

What it does not make her is a casual and impartial observer.

"I don't think he was into me as much as he's a nice guy to everyone he comes across." When I was watching him at the event, he was so attentive to every single person he interacted with. I'm almost positive each person he talked to that evening went home feeling like they had a new best friend or, if they were lucky, a potential love match.

"Well, you didn't see him approaching us. Trust me, the way he was looking at your ass was anything but nice." She leans back on her elbows, delighting in the shock that must be written across my face.

"You do have a fabulous ass," Daisy says. "It's the only reason I woke up this early on a Sunday morning. I figure we share some DNA, there's a chance I can get an ass like that if I can replicate your workout routine."

"Wow!" I'm a sucker for a good compliment. So Jasper is long forgotten at my tall, leggy sister telling me I have a good ass. "Thank you! That made my entire day. I do enjoy yoga and I used to hike a lot—"

"No! You do have a great ass, but I don't want to hear about workouts." Elsie cuts me off again, her stern voice back in full effect. "If you don't want to talk about Jasper anymore, I guess I can deal. But I only came today because you promised me brunch and mimosas. Yoga has been over for thirty minutes and I still don't have food. I want carbs."

"Ooooh! Nobody told me about brunch." Daisy is thrown off topic again. She must get that from her mom. I don't like claiming much from my dad, but focus that cannot be broken is one of the things we share. "I definitely prefer brunch talk to workout talk. Who needs a good ass when you can have hollandaise sauce?"

"Yes, girl!" Elsie lifts her hand to high-five my sister. "I'm glad at least one of you Young women gets me. I only have a few more hours of not having a small human latching on to my arm, leg, breast, or all of the above. I need waffles. Stat."

Elsie knows this argument can't be beat.

I might not be getting the recommended eight hours of sleep a night, but that's because I have a genuine disdain for time and my overall well-being. Elsie loves her sleep but cannot get it because she's changing diapers or acting as a human pacifier for the whole-ass baby she's created. After this is over, I will go home and take a long shower by myself. She has a bouncy seat in front of her shower so that Finn can sit and watch her like a little baby Peeping Tom. These two reasons alone mean the mom card wins every time. Thankfully, she only pulls it out when it's for something extra important . . . like champagne and carbs.

"Fine." Between waiting for my dad to make his next move, the

Dirty Birds, and now dinner with Jasper, I could really use booze and hash browns anyway. I roll up my yoga mat and tuck it beneath my arm before inhaling the fresh mountain air deep into my lungs and taking one more look at the view around me. "Brunch it is."

"And while we're there, we can come up with a plan for your night with Jasper." Elsie hops up with more energy than she had during the entire class. I was hoping she had moved on from Jasper, but I should've known better. "Because what kind of friend would I be if I let you blow this."

"Yes!" Daisy claps her hands together and drops her mat in her excitement. "I'll plan your outfit! Even though I don't start work for a few weeks, my employee discount is already in full effect. I'll be your private shopper slash stylist. It'll be great."

I'm not sure I'd go all the way to *great*.

I know this thing with Jasper is nothing more than a favor to the Dirty Birds. But it will still be nice for me to spend some more time with my best friend and my sister—whom I'm starting to really enjoy—instead of moping around my apartment all day. Even if it means trading my Birkenstocks for a pair of stilettos for a night.

# CHAPTER 7

ELSIE AND DAISY ARE NEVER ALLOWED TO BE AROUND EACH OTHER ever again.

Like ever.

They're terrible influences on their own, but together they melded their powers like some fashion-crazy supervillain, out to make me wince in pain and cry for mercy more than once. I practically had to grease my body to squeeze into the dress they forced me to wear and I'm going to need pliers (or scissors) to get out of it at the end of the night. That is, if I don't end up in the ER thanks to the shoes Daisy strapped onto my feet before shoving me out of my apartment.

My body was made for a lot of things, but wearing four-inch stilettos is not one of them.

I have trekked up mountains and crossed through rivers courtesy of the suede and cork footbed of my beloved Birkenstocks. But one short jaunt across the dining room of a steak house? I nearly died. Thrice.

If we had gone to the burger place across from the Book Nook, none of this would've been an issue.

I mean, sure, I'm the one who recommended this place to Jasper. And yeah, he just followed my lead for the night. But to be fair, it's not my fault that I'm complete trash for a fancy overpriced drink, and this place has an entire menu of floral cocktails. Do they taste good? Who knows! I had the opportunity to have one or two rose martinis with roses frozen into a globe ice cube (for free!) and jumped at it. Me nearly breaking an ankle and a rib tonight is what Gran would have called a case of karma. And she wouldn't have been wrong.

On the bright side, at least I was lucky enough to make my grand, wobbly entrance before Jasper was there to be a witness. This might not be a real date, but nobody wants the hotness that is Jasper Williams to see them struggle across a five-star restaurant looking like a newborn giraffe. I don't know how I'm going to sneak out without him seeing, but I'm hoping I'll have enough booze in me that I won't care.

"Thank you so much." I take the martini from the waitress much like I used to take Elsie's newborns from her, that is to say, gently and cautiously. Treating it like the precious creation I know it to be.

"You're so welcome. Can I get you anything else while you wait?" Janet, the lovely waitress who looks way better than is fair in her work uniform of plain black slacks and a white button-up, asks.

"No, thank you, this is perfect for now." I gesture to the martini glass in my hand.

She smiles and nods. "Wonderful, I'll be back to check on you soon."

I watch her walk away and greet another table, wondering if she thinks I'm being stood up. And then I wonder if I'm only wondering that because I'm afraid I'm going to get stood up.

It's not that I think this is an actual date to get stood up for. I'd just be pissed if I squeezed into this dress for no reason. Also, I made a really great list of places for him to check out, and even though there's only a 0.03 percent chance I'll read his book, it'd be a shame for his readers to miss out on the destinations I picked out for him.

I pick up my martini glass, admiring the perfectly preserved rose before bringing the peony-infused sugar rim to my mouth. It takes every ounce of self-control I have not to throw my head back and moan. I've had a little bit of a dry spell of late, but even if I hadn't, this drink is damn right orgasmic. It would be a good idea not to get drunk tonight, but with the way these cocktails are set up, I'm not sure that's an option anymore.

I try to take small, slow sips as I wait for Jasper to arrive. I pull my phone out of my purse and glance at the time when my glass is nearing empty. He's not late; I just really like getting places early. Especially when I'm feeling nervous. Having the opportunity to survey the land and get comfortable helps ease my anxiety. I slide my phone back inside my purse, refusing to doomscroll and instead being present in the moment.

The low whispers of business partners schmoozing clients and couples celebrating anniversaries hum throughout the restaurant. The delicate sounds of piano keys float from the corner of the room, playing just loud enough to both disguise awkward lulls in conversations and set the mood. It may be a Wednesday night, but that hasn't prevented every table from being filled. Waiters glide through the room, almost as if in a dance, replacing the empty martini glasses with full ones and setting plates covered with mouthwatering food in front of patrons.

I'm trying to eavesdrop on the couple in the booth behind me, something about the babysitter not respecting boundaries, when the energy in the room shifts.

I don't even know how to describe it, the subtle shift in the air. It seems as if all conversations come to a sudden hush; the only sound is the buzz of excitement bouncing from table to table. Goose bumps trail down my arms and the hair at the nape of my neck rises. My breathing speeds up, and if everyone around me didn't seem so thrilled, I'd wonder if this was my adrenaline warning me to get the freak out of Dodge.

And that's when I see him.

If I wasn't positive he was an author, I'd think he was a master of disguise. He looks different than both of the times I saw him at the Book Nook. Unlike the wholesome author with glasses and an affinity for tweed blazers, tonight he's wearing a perfectly tailored navy suit. Fitted close to his body, it showcases the lines of a man who dedicates time to take care of himself. His hair—I can't decide if it needs a haircut yesterday or to never be touched—is slicked back. He looks like a movie villain you shouldn't root for, but do anyway.

I'm sure if someone from the book signing saw him tonight, they wouldn't even recognize him.

But I do.

Because even though the hair and suit changed, there's no denying the blue-green eyes staring right back at me. Or the way when they focus on me, I feel like I'm the most important person in the room. In any room. I wish I could, but it's not a feeling I'll ever forget. And the bitter irony of being this attracted to the one person I know things would never work out with causes me to reach for my martini glass.

"You're here!" His voice carries over the silence of the room, spurring the diners back into action. "I was afraid I was going to get stood up."

"I was thinking the same thing." Whereas I've had to deal with the mortification of sitting alone in a restaurant until I couldn't weather the pitying gazes of the people around me anymore, it's hard for me to believe that Jasper has ever been stood up. "It's a good thing you didn't, though; you only saw the Dirty Birds on their best behavior. You don't want to get on their bad side."

Going against the Dirty Birds is like launching a special ops military operation. Months of planning and strategy go into it. Jasper doesn't have enough intel to get out of a situation like that unscathed.

"I'm sure I don't." He slides into the booth across from me, his large body still managing to look at ease even with the awkward movement. "But I was really looking forward to getting to know you a little better. And learn more about Colorado, of course."

*He makes up things for a living.* Elsie's words from Sunday rush unwelcome into my head, squashing the butterflies that had barely managed to take flight.

"Of course," I repeat after him before draining the dregs of my drink.

Between my dad and a few boyfriends—fine, all my boyfriends—

who cheated, it's safe to say that my expectations of men aren't on the ground level. They aren't even in the basement.

No.

My expectations are in an elevator that crashed through the floor and is now taking the direct route to hell.

I go into every relationship with people who identify as male assuming they're either a liar, a cheater, an asshole, or the grand trifecta of all of the above. Jasper seems nice enough, but who's to say this isn't one big act to see what will work for his next novel. I can see it now: famous romance author, moving from city to city, leaving a trail of broken hearts in his path. Hundreds of women all over the country, weeping into their morning coffee after a night spent dreaming about his gorgeous eyes and deep voice telling them how special they are.

*What a scumbag.*

"Is everything okay?" he asks, snapping me out of my thoughts.

I realize I'm glaring at him as I try to school my expression. I tend to wear all my thoughts on my face, and that is not always a good thing.

Actually, it's almost never a good thing. Resting bitch face has put me in some very tenuous situations over the years.

"Yeah, totally." I paste a smile onto my face, trying to think of anything to talk about that won't make me sound like a raving lunatic. "I'm just surprised you'd think anyone would say no to dinner with you."

The concerned look on his face is replaced by a gentle smile. Flattery easily erases any doubts he may have had. Not to pat myself on the back, but that was some A-plus deflection if I may say so myself.

"I think that most of my readers would like to come to dinner with me. I'm sure they'd like to ask me questions about my past work and what I have planned for the future. A few would undoubtedly ask if I'd be interested in writing their life story for them." He pauses and takes a small sip of water from the glass Janet filled up for him when I was first seated.

I take advantage of the pause in his story because he has officially piqued my interest. "Okay. Now I have a question."

"Shoot." He leans forward and aims a finger gun my way, losing approximately one thousand points on the cool scale.

"People ask you if you're interested in writing their life story? As in this has happened to you more than once by more than one person?" It's not that I think he's full of shit as much as I can't believe that multiple people think so highly of themselves that they would ask a famous author this question.

He nods. "All the time. I'd say I get at least ten emails every week with offers and detailed timelines of their lives. There was one that was pretty interesting. He was abducted while traveling through Europe, but it turned out to be a setup by his wife and her professor— who wanted insurance money."

As Elsie painted my lips with the fourth shade of red lipstick for tonight, I was warned—*threatened* would be more accurate—to be on my best, most ladylike behavior tonight. I gave her my promise I would be.

I just didn't expect attempted murder to be on the docket for the night, and it's almost impossible to remain calm and quiet when talk of hit men and affairs is happening.

"Shut the fuck up!" I lean forward and ignore the way the old man at the table across from us glares at me. "You're messing with me, aren't you? That's a plot of one of your books and you're testing me to see if I really haven't read them."

He throws his head back, his loud, deep laughter sounding better than every note of music played by the pianist. I watch with no small amount of wonder as his Adam's apple moves up and down in his throat for a moment. The small, normal movement I've never noticed on another human entices me in a way that's almost obscene. I wish I could put my finger on it—and smother it—but for some reason, everything about the man in front of me is deceptively sexual.

When he finally stops laughing, he swipes his large hands beneath his wet eyes. "You've really never read my books, have you?"

"Ummm . . ." I draw out the word, not sure what to say. There's no way to make this less awkward. "I haven't, but it's not you. I'm not a big reader. I'll watch the occasional movie, but I'd much prefer a good serial killer documentary to anything fictional."

His thick eyebrows touch his hairline and I make a quick mental note to add *mentioning serial killer fascination* to the list of topics to avoid while at dinner.

Before he can ask what the fuck is wrong with me and why I'm not in intensive therapy, my girl Janet approaches the table. She looks happier than I've seen her all evening. And while it can't be proven, I think it might have something to do with the man in front of me.

"Hello. I'm Janet and I'll be serving you tonight." Her voice has a sultry rasp to it that wasn't there when she greeted me, and I'm more than a little insulted. "Can I get you a drink other than water, sir?"

A drink.

Yeah. Sure, Janet. Is that what the kids are calling it these days? You're not fooling anybody!

"Hi, Janet." Jasper repeats her name, the same way he did with all the people who introduced themselves to him at the Book Nook. "I'd love an old-fashioned, please."

"One old-fashioned." Janet's smile gets even larger and I think Jasper passed a test neither of us knew he was taking. "I'll get that right to you."

"Thank you, Janet. I appreciate that." He aims his bright, perfect smile her way and her cheeks flush bright red beneath the power of it.

Gran always told me there were three types of people we should avoid at all costs:

1.  Someone who doesn't return their grocery cart to the cart corral.

2.  A person whose voice doesn't change when talking to dogs or babies.

3.  Anybody who is rude to the waitstaff at restaurants.

"Doesn't matter what they do with the rest of their time. They do any of those three things, you run for the hills because they're a jerk who cannot be redeemed," she would tell me. I took her word as law and it hasn't failed me yet.

I just wish she told me what to do with someone who is so nice to everyone that it borders on sketchy . . .

"So," Jasper says once our waitress walks away. "All jokes aside, I really do want to thank you for taking the time to meet with me and help me get to know Denver. I don't know why I was expecting it to be so much smaller than it is, but between the city and all of the mountain towns, I'm having a hard time pinpointing the setting."

"It's not a problem. As a Denver native, it's my birthright to tell people how wonderful this city is. Now that we have so many transplants it's expanding really fast, too fast in some areas, but I love that people are starting to understand how great it is here." I reach into my purse and pull out the pages I stapled together before I came. "I started with Denver. I broke the city down into my favorite neighborhoods, a brief history, and a quick rundown of the overall demographics. I didn't know what you needed, so there are restaurants, local shops, nighttime hangs, daytime activities, and even schools. Then as you go, I've made a travel guide of sorts depending on the direction you're leaving Denver. There's a quick rundown of the popular places, your Aspens and Vails, before getting into the hidden gems. I included pictures of my favorite lakes and mountain towns. Little stories I have from when I've visited them so you can get an idea of the lay of the land, and then activities you can do in each place . . . depending on the season. Of course."

I slide the packet across the table, trying not to jerk my hand back when his fingers graze across mine. There's an expression on his face I can't quite read as he starts to flip through the papers.

"Wow. This is . . . wow." His gaze flickers between me and the packet I painstakingly organized. "Really, Drew, I'm not a person that's ever short on words, but I don't even know what to say. This is so great. I can't believe you had the time to do all of this. Thank you."

Warmth blooms in my stomach at his praise. Most days, I feel like I'm struggling to tread water, barely staying afloat. Everything feels hard. But when I was doing this, I remembered not only why I loved what I did so much, but also how good at it I was. Like really, really good.

"It wasn't a problem at all." I wave off his gratitude. "I had a lot of fun doing it. I should be thanking you."

"Well, still." He flips through the pages one last time before carefully moving them to the side. "I have to do something to thank you for this."

"You really don't. I promise. I had fun. Before . . ." I let my words trail off. Jasper is so nice, it's easy for me to forget that he's still a stranger—a very attractive, very attentive stranger—who doesn't need me unloading all my issues on him. "You know what, never mind. I'm just glad I was able to help. Truly."

"No." He shakes his head and a small strand falls free from his slicked-back locks. My fingers itch to reach across the table and tuck it behind his ear. "What were you going to say?"

"It was nothing." I look around for Janet, realizing I forgot to order a new martini . . . something I could really use right about now. "Trust me, the last thing you want is to hear about my old life."

"And you trust me, there's nothing I'd rather hear more." He unfolds his hands and reaches across the table. I watch in slow motion as they approach my hand, and when they engulf my hand in a quick but tender squeeze, my nerves light up like the flash of my camera.

I'm sure he meant for it to be a friendly or reassuring gesture, but my stupid body, which hasn't been touched in way too long, goes haywire. I wish I could blame the rose martini for being stronger than I thought or even say the peony sugar was really infused with magic . . . or psychedelics, but I can't. It's all Jasper. With his eyes focused on me, the feel of his touch still lingering on my skin, I'm unable to think straight.

So I do what I haven't dared to since the day I walked out of the lawyer's office as the new owner of the Book Nook.

I forget every lie I've told, every excuse I've made, and I word-vomit all over the table.

"So it all started when my dad cheated on my mom and left us for his new, rich family in the mountains when I was in kindergarten."

Bring another one, Janet, this is going to be a long night.

# CHAPTER 8

I KNOW THAT GETTING BLACKOUT DRUNK IS BAD. HOWEVER, I really wish I had gotten blackout drunk on my date-not-date with Jasper.

Would my hangover have been worse? Maybe. Would not remembering with vivid detail the way I spilled my entire life story to him over wedge salads and steak be worth hugging the porcelain throne? Abso-fucking-lutely.

I told him about my college boyfriend. How I thought we were going to get married until someone reached out to me on Facebook with pictures of his girlfriend back home showing off her engagement ring. It was like a knockoff version of *Legally Blonde*. I was Elle Woods minus the money, dog, and Harvard. How tragic.

I cried.

When I woke up the next morning, my cheeks were still stained with black mascara. It was the saddest, most accurate visual representation of my life.

And as much as I'd like to never think of that night again, like ever? It's burned into my freaking brain, and every time I have a moment of quiet, I remember something else that I told him. Like the fact that I was glad he made money off writing lies since I would probably never be able to afford a down payment on a house trying to sell them.

On the bright side, at least for the last couple of hours, the Book Nook has been relatively busy. Since Jasper's signing, traffic in the store has picked up quite a bit. Not mortgage big, but pays-bills and buys-organic-occasionally big. Friday nights can be hit-and-miss and I was worried I was going to spend my night standing next to Jasper's books, wishing I could go back in time. But tonight customers have been drifting in and out, skimming our inventory, and getting cozy in the nook. It's nothing like Saturday-morning craziness, but it's enough to keep me busy and to keep my tears out of the crisp pages of his books.

Small wins.

The bell over the front door rings and I look over just in time to see a couple holding hands walk in. They're locked in conversation. His focus is devoted to her as she gestures with her free hand, her wide eyes and smile taking over her beautiful face.

"Welcome to the Book Nook," I call to them across the store. "Let me know if you need help finding anything." *So I can get Dani to find it for you.*

"Thank you," they say in unison, and then the woman's smile grows brighter before she shouts, "Jinx! You owe me a pop!"

Her giggles float through the store and her partner looks down at her like she's the most amazing person he's ever had the pleasure to be around. It's adorable.

I bet she reads Jasper's books.

It's rude the way I can't seem to forget about him. The way his name is fighting to stay at the forefront of my brain while he's probably tapping away at a keyboard somewhere, content to never think about me again. Not that I blame him. I was the crazy lady who blubbered about her dead grandma and then wistfully droned on and on about lost dreams of photography and travel. And again, I cried! A groan of embarrassment gets lodged in my throat and I want to bang my head against the counter thinking about the way I unloaded on poor, unsuspecting Jasper.

To be fair, though, part of it is definitely his fault.

*Trust me, Drew, you can tell me anything. Look into my beautiful eyes and spill your heart out to me.* Who can say no to that? He practically begged for it.

Okay. Fine.

He didn't say all that, but he might as well have. Holding my hands and looking at me like he did. I don't have a defense for that. Nobody has a defense for that!

But even as I felt his hands tense on mine and saw his eyes widen with shock—and maybe a small amount of horror—as I told him about the way my dad has been fighting me or how I've ignored the camera tucked in the back of my closet for months, I could not stop talking.

It was a fucking nightmare.

Such a nightmare, in fact, that when I got home and noticed the five missed calls from Elsie and two missed calls from Daisy, I just let my phone die and haven't charged it since. Is there a chance I will be stranded on the highway because of my nearing-on-ancient Jeep? Sure. Is that worth plugging in my phone and having to rehash the night in great detail with my sister or best friend? Nope. I'd rather hitchhike and try my hand at avoiding a serial killer. Honestly, anything other than getting scolded for my terrible social skills and scaring off a man who is, perhaps, the most eligible bachelor in all of America sounds like a goddamn picnic.

I piddle around the register, putting the pens away and throwing away mysterious scraps of paper that always seem to clutter the space, until I can't stay back here any longer. I weave through the tall shelves, making sure the books are where they're supposed to be and moving the ones that aren't, before I end up in the travel section.

I avoid this section as much as possible and it shows. Books are scattered all over the place. Travel guides are mixed up with photography books. Books on Australia are beside ones about France. I make a pile on one of the lower shelves and begin to reorganize the section. I'm lost in the task, mindlessly dancing to whatever song the local radio station we always have on is playing, until my fingers skim the spine of a book I remember Gran showing me.

She was so excited when she got it in, said she ordered it specifically so she could give it to me. Hundreds of heart-stopping photos of hiking trails across the world. She knew how much I loved that stuff, and told me she thought I could make one even better, even more beautiful than the stunning book in my hands. She meant it; her belief in me was never-ending. And I believed her.

I flip through the book, still breathless as I look at the pictures of trails from all over the world, many of which are on my bucket list and have still gone unchecked. I pause on the pictures from the Fitz Roy trek in Argentina. It's at the top of my list. I even started planning a trip not long before Gran passed. I still dream about the jagged mountain range, the glaciers, and the turquoise lakes, which are stunning in photos, but which I know deep down to my bones are life changing to see in person.

I'm lost in the book, my mind running away from me, drifting off to dangerous thoughts of what-ifs and maybes, when a hand on my shoulder startles me back to reality. I drop the book and it just misses my toes before landing on the old carpet with a heavy thud.

"Sorry!" a voice I didn't think I'd hear again so soon says. "I didn't mean to sneak up on you."

I turn around and look up into eyes that rival the lakes I dream of visiting. The small lines creasing around them aren't like the smile lines I've seen on his gorgeous face before. He looks tense, concerned. Probably worried I'm going to unload on him again.

"Oh. Hi! No need to apologize." I infuse way too much peppiness into my voice and sound slightly demented even to my own ears. "What are you doing here?"

I realize, after the words leave my mouth, that they sound much ruder than I intended . . . especially since I didn't mean for them to sound rude at all.

"I mean. Not that . . . I just—" I stumble over my words as my cheeks begin to heat. Embarrassment seems to be unescapable when I'm in Jasper's presence. I close my eyes and take a deep breath, hoping it will help me string words together in a coherent sentence. "I wasn't expecting you."

Jasper's full lips tip up into a small smile, but I still get the distinct feeling that he's trying not to laugh at me.

"It's fine. I know what you meant," he says. And as I expected, his voice is vibrating with laughter. "I've been trying to get in touch with you since Wednesday, but your phone's been off. I started to get worried. I wanted to make sure you were okay."

God. He's just so damn nice! This would all be so much easier on me if he was a fuckboy like pretty much every other person I've been attracted to.

"Oh, I'm fine." I tell him something he's very aware of now that he's standing in front of me. "My phone died and I haven't charged it again. Sometimes it's nice to disconnect for a little bit." I semi-lie about my reasoning, but I've word-vomited all over him once already and I don't plan on doing it again.

"Disconnecting can be nice; it can be a lot always being available." Shadows drift over his face, but they're gone before I can really take them in. "I hope you don't mind me stopping in like this."

"Not at all." I bend over and pick up the book I dropped, slipping it back on the shelf before turning my full attention back to Jasper. "I'm sorry I disappeared. I didn't think I'd hear from you."

He jerks his head back an inch as his thick brows knit together behind the thick-rimmed glasses he wears so well.

"Why'd you think that? I had a great time."

He can't be serious.

I inspect his face for a moment, trying to decipher whether or not he's messing with me and playing deliberately obtuse. I'm not the best at reading people, but I think he's genuinely confused.

"I just . . ." I pause, trying to figure out how to word what I want to say without getting flustered. "You know, I kind of unloaded on you at dinner. It was a lot. I'm sorry about that, by the way."

"Why would you apologize?" He takes a small step toward me and closes the small space between us. "I asked you to tell me. I hate that you've gone through some of that stuff, but I loved learning about you."

I open my mouth to speak, but I don't know what to say. So instead of making an ass out of myself, for once, I close my mouth and choose silence.

"I've been trying to call you because I have an idea to run by you." He reaches into his pocket and pulls out a familiar piece of paper. It's no longer stapled to the rest of the stack I handed him at dinner, but it's definitely one of the lists I gave him. "I've been looking up a lot of these places and the internet does a great job at filling me in. It's just that . . ." He trails off, looking uncertain for the first time since I met him.

"Just that what?" I ask, my curiosity reaching unparalleled heights.

He looks at me for a moment longer before rushing out his next words. "I was thinking you could be my travel guide. You sounded so passionate about seeing all of these places, I think my story would be so much stronger if I visit some of these places with someone who really loves them."

I freeze.

I didn't know what I was expecting him to say, but it was not that.

Conflicting thoughts race through my mind as I consider his offer. Part of me wants to jump at it. To jump at the opportunity to pull my camera back out, lace up my hiking boots, and settle into my Jeep, ready for adventure. But the other part of me is so scared to get a taste of it again and to do it with Jasper at my side. It's all so temporary. What will it be like when Jasper finishes his book and I have to pack my camera away again? Could I handle that?

I don't think I can. But then Jasper keeps talking.

"But I was thinking, it wouldn't be too fair to have you show me everything you love and me only going along for the ride. So I figured it could be a swap of sorts."

"A swap?" My refusal dies as my interest spikes. "What do you mean?"

He lifts up the list I made for him, and behind it is another one with names I don't recognize.

"You say you don't like books, but I think you just haven't read the right ones." He hands me the sheet of paper, and when I look at it, I realize it's filled with book titles. "You turn me into a Colorado lover and I'll turn you into a book lover. You read a book and I'll take you on an adventure that reminds me of it. I'll pick a place on your list, and you'll take me on an adventure to explore it."

My heart rate kicks up, excitement and fear battling for supremacy, and I don't know which one will win. Fear starts to edge excitement out as my self-preservation begins to kick in.

"I don't know—" I start, but stop when Jasper's hand latches on to mine.

"Don't answer now," he says. It's hard to hear him as blood rushes between my ears. All my attention is laser focused to where our skin is touching and the way my body begins to tingle. "You're busy and this is a big ask. I promise, if you say yes, I'll make it worth your time. Please, just think about it."

I nod in response, unable to speak.

"Okay." He lets out a long, deep exhale. "Good. Thank you."

It's in this moment, watching the smile I'm positive has left a trail of broken hearts in its wake spread across his face in happy relief, that I realize he was nervous. Jasper Williams, Author, was nervous to ask me, Drew Young, Mess, to spend time with him. How is this even possible?

"Um, you're welcome." I don't know what for, but I say it anyway. I'm not convinced this isn't some kind of weird simulation. I half expect to see Neo come around the corner and tell me that I've been sucked into the Matrix or something.

"Well." He lets go of my hand and steps away, plunging me back into reality. My hand feels cold without his around it. I miss the contact immediately. "I'll let you get back to work. I'm sorry I interrupted you."

"No worries. It wasn't a big deal at all." I brush off his apology and hold up the sheet of paper he handed me. "And thank you for this. I really will consider it."

"I hope so." His voice drops to a whisper. "I would love to get to know you more."

After that, he aims one more panty-dropping smile my way before turning and disappearing behind the bookshelf. I stand frozen, hearing him call out a quick goodbye before the bell above the front door chimes and he's gone.

I leave the pile of books I have yet to put away and run through the store, ignoring Dani's confused stare as she watches me go. I twist the doorknob on Gran's office so hard, it's a miracle it doesn't fall off, and sprint straight to her desk. I rip open the top drawer, finding the phone charger I keep there in case of emergencies. I untwist it with clumsy hands and it falls to the ground more than once before I plug it into the wall, impatiently tapping my foot as I connect it to my phone and wait for my screen to light up.

It feels like centuries before the white apple appears on my phone. Nerves take over my brain and I type in the wrong passcode four times before I get it correct. But as soon as I do, I go straight to my text messages, pulling up the number I didn't even bother to save before I type in two small words.

I'm in.

It's not even seconds later before the bubble indicating Jasper is typing pops up. And it's even less time before I get his response.

Thank freaking god.

No wonder he's an author.

Because three words have never made me happier.

I pull out the list he gave me and recognize the title of a book I've been asked to help find more than once. I leave Gran's office and head back into the store to do something I haven't done in ages: find a book that I'm going to read and actually feeling excited about.

Jasper Williams, Author, is a certified miracle worker.

# CHAPTER 9

AFTER I AGREED TO THE CRAZIEST PLAN IN THE HISTORY OF PLANS, I pulled my tail from between my legs and fired off a text to Elsie and Daisy.

It wasn't easy, but I did it because, let's be honest, I'm in way over my head with this mess. I'm not sure either of my reinforcements knows what they're doing either, but strength in numbers. Right?

Maybe.

Probably not at all.

All I know is if the group text I added them to is any indication at all, they've formed quite the alliance over the last couple of days and I'm screwed.

I'm putting the finishing touches on my charcuterie board when there's a knock on my door. Elsie had to skip story time this morning because her mother-in-law signed the twins up for soccer and they had their first game. And even though Elsie isn't thrilled with me, she still sent me a copious number of pictures and videos of the entire event. Including three videos of Wren scoring goals and one video of Willow modeling the grass crowns she made as she sat on the sideline, protesting having to wear cleats.

I freaking love those girls so much.

I hurry to the door, not wanting to leave her waiting for long, since I already did that once this week.

I swing open the door, and even though I've known Elsie for almost my entire life, I'm still knocked back by how freaking beautiful my friend is. She's sleep-deprived and has a diet that consists of whatever food her kids didn't eat, but she's never looked better. She has the glow of a well-loved woman.

"Hey!" I gesture her into my essential-oil-infused apartment, which is supposed to smell like Zen. I don't know, I just saw it at the natural grocery store when I was grabbing cheese and crackers and figured what the hell, anything could help. "You look great! I love your hair. When'd you get those done?"

Instead of the mom bun she's been rocking, her hair has been parted and braided into long box braids falling to the top of her butt. It's a great look on her.

"Well, you would know if you answered your phone, wouldn't you?" she shoots back, and I wonder if I should just go ahead and dump the entire bottle of Zen into my diffuser since the eight drops aren't working.

This is gonna be fun.

Not.

"I told you I was sorry and I know I messed up. It was a disaster and you and Daisy went out of your way to make it amazing. I felt terrible. I needed time to process before I could call you."

I think this will soften her up a little bit, but it doesn't. Not at all. In fact, it might make it worse.

"Time to process? Are you kidding me?" She twists around and her long braids fan across the room, narrowly missing the framed picture of me and Gran on my console table by the door. "We don't process it alone, we do it together." She holds up her hands and begins ticking them away. "The twins, the grand surprise that turned out to be Finn, Alice, the Book Nook? We got through all that shit together."

Of course, she's not wrong about any of this.

When she found out she was pregnant with the twins, she called me from inside the ultrasound room, and she did it before she called Brandon. I'm still not sure if she was laughing or crying as she told me the news. She was definitely crying when she found out she was pregnant with Finn the week before Brandon was scheduled to get snipped. It's still kind of a blur, but I vaguely remember dialing her number from the hospital—my phone had no service—to tell her Gran had died. And then I called her again from inside the lawyer's office when I was told I was the new owner of the Book Nook.

"I know. You're right, it's just . . ." I trail off, not knowing what else to tell her, since I'm not sure even I understand my decision, before I let it all loose. "Listen, I'm a fucking mess, okay? I'm sorry I didn't call you. I don't know why I didn't. I cried at dinner with Jasper. Like, real, fat, ugly tears. Not cute, dainty ones you dab away with the corner of a tissue. He asked me to tell him about my old life and instead of holding on to a modicum of self-respect, I launched into it all. Dad, Gran, my photography, I mentioned it all."

"You . . . you told him about your dad and photography? And

you cried?" All the anger in her face has fled and instead she looks as horrified as I feel. She knows I'm not a pretty crier. I'm the poor version of Kim Kardashian, ugly crier.

"Yes to all of the above." I walk to my kitchen, not waiting for Daisy to get here before I pour my glass of wine. "Now do you see why I needed some time?"

"Wow. Condolences." She falls onto my couch before leaning forward and attacking the salami I spent way too much time arranging into little meat rosettes. "This is beautiful, by the way."

And just like that, it's all behind us. I know Elsie will never bring it up again. She won't hold it against me, no more apologies needed. We talked, we figured it out, and now it's over.

"Glad you like it. I wanted it to feel fancy even though we'll just be on my couch."

My pour was a little too heavy. The crimson wine flirts dangerously close to the edge of the glass with every step I take. I place the glasses on the coffee table and three loud knocks on my door disguise my sigh of relief for my unscathed rug.

"It's your favorite sister!" Daisy singsongs from the hallway. "And I have vodka!"

Unlike Elsie, Daisy wasn't fazed by my phone being off after the dinner. She's living her best, single, financially secure life, where she can eat out every night without bothering to check her bank account. I don't think she even noticed that I hadn't returned her calls. She sounded confused when I called to apologize last night.

"It's open," I call over my shoulder, and that's all the prompting she needs before the door swings open and Daisy makes her grand entrance.

Her long legs make quick work of my small entryway. She kicks off her heels, which take her from tall to taller, and tosses her long blond hair over her shoulder. Her red-painted lips and winged eyeliner are giving me serious Taylor Swift vibes. I know I invited them, but standing between my gorgeous best friend and fabulous sister, I feel woefully underdressed in my plain tank top and tattered jeans.

"Oooh! Wine!" Daisy puts her bottle of vodka on the counter before grabbing a wineglass, filling it up, and joining us on my couch. "Soooo . . . what's new?"

Each time I'm around Daisy, I regret the years we spent apart. She fits so naturally in my life, it's been great having her around.

"Yeah." Elsie reaches for her wineglass and taps it against Daisy's before taking a small sip. "This is the second time you've called for reinforcements. Something big must be happening if you've planned an official sit-down with wine and snacks."

"I'm not sure *big* is the right word." I've been trying to decide how to fill them in on the new arrangement between me and Jasper since I texted him back last night. But now, with Elsie's and Daisy's full attention on me, I don't know what to say. "So as I've told you both, the date was a bloody disaster."

"A bloody disaster?" Elsie repeats after me, amusement thick in her voice. "What the fuck?"

"I've been watching a lot of *Love Island UK*, okay? Now, focus," I scold her. She raises her hands in surrender but doesn't even attempt to stop laughing. "I didn't think I would hear from Jasper again, but I did."

Elsie's laughter dies on her lips as both she and Daisy lean in closer.

"He called you?" Daisy asks. "What did he say?"

"Did he ask you out again? Are you still thinking he's only doing this because of the Dirty Birds? What did—"

"Elsie!" I cut her off when I realize this line of questioning isn't going to come to an end otherwise. "Do you want me to tell you or do you want to keep guessing until you get it right?"

"Oh wow." Daisy raises her eyebrows and looks at Elsie. "She's a little testy when she's stressed, yeah?"

"Oh yeah." Elsie looks straight through me. "This one time, in middle school, we had a pop quiz in a class and she—"

"Whoa, whoa, whoa," I cut her off. "That feels like a very unnecessary story to tell in the middle of me explaining to you that Jasper has proposed I play tour guide for him while he's here."

That gets their attention.

"Wait. I'm sorry." Elsie turns back to me, blinking more times than I've ever seen a person blink. "What did you just say?"

"You know how I gave that list to Jasper with different places for him to use for his book?" I ask, even though I know they both know what I'm talking about. "He came by the store last night to tell me he appreciates the list, but he thinks it will be better for his story if he were to visit the places instead of just googling them. And since he knows I used to be a travel photographer, he asked me to be his travel guide, if you will."

"Ho. Lee. Shit," Daisy breathes out. "You said yes, right?"

"Well, that's not it," I say, and try not to laugh at both of their hisses of breath. "He knows I'm busy and didn't think it would be fair for me to work to show him all this and him to just get to go along for the ride." I scoot forward and grab the folded-up list of book titles he gave me from beside the charcuterie board. "So he gave me this list of books. He said that for each book, he'll pair it with an activity that will convince me to be a book lover."

"Oh my goodness!" Daisy screeches, jumping off the couch, her long hair flying all around her at the same time Elsie collapses into my couch, her body slowly sliding down.

"And you said yes!" Daisy is still jumping up and down and clapping her hands. But when I don't answer right away, she stops jumping and narrows her eyes as she repeats herself, just a little bit louder. "You said yes, right?"

I nod. "I said yes."

Elsie, bless her beautiful heart, with her body half on my couch, half on the floor, looks at me and whispers, "Thank freaking god."

"But now I'm kind of regretting it and I don't know what to do. Hence"—I gesture to my living room—"this meeting of the minds."

"Well." Elsie pushes off the ground until she's nestled into the cushions. "I'm glad you called us before you made some crazy mistake like backing out of this."

"But what—" I try to interrupt, but Elsie doesn't let me.

"No." Elsie points a short, unpolished nail in my face. "No buts, no what-ifs. You are doing this. If nothing else, you'll spend time with a nice person, getting back outdoors and exploring like you used to."

"I just—" I try again, but don't get any further.

"No!" she says, louder this time, and I realize I might've accidentally woken the sleeping bear. "You're doing this. For reasons I will never understand, you need the great outdoors to really connect with who you are. You haven't been okay in a long time. I don't know if you'll be ready to take your camera with you, but you can do this. Taking over the Book Nook was a shock, and I know you're dedicated to helping it succeed, but you don't have to give up everything that brought you joy to do it. There's no reason you can't go to the mountains for a day or even a week. Dani's completely capable of holding down the fort without you. Mona would help. I could help."

"I could help too," Daisy pipes in, and I almost forgot she was witnessing this entire scene. "I know I only have secondhand knowledge about the store, but I'm great at retail, and now that I'm here, I want to be there for you. For Gran."

Alone in my apartment, at the Book Nook, not picking up my camera and doing the one thing that made me feel at peace with the world, I've felt really lonely. Right now, though, I feel anything but. My vision blurs with unshed tears. The gratitude I have for the two women in my living room is overwhelming. I beat back the urge to cry as the familiar sting behind my sinuses builds to a full-out burn.

"I do not appreciate you both being all supportive and caring." I fan my face, refusing to let a single tear fall because thugs don't cry.

"You know there's nothing I love more than tears of happiness." Elsie reminds me of a fact I know all too well. She might be the best gift giver in the entire world. After Gran died, she reached out to my mom, the Dirty Birds, and some sources she still hasn't revealed. She collected pictures and stories and made me the most beautiful scrapbook. I cried for hours. And she'd never looked so pleased with herself.

"I have ulterior motives," Daisy says. "I'm really hoping I'll get some personalized Jasper Williams swag. Oh!" She claps her hands together, her eyes tripling in size. "What if you two end up falling in love and getting married? This would be like watching his books in real time."

"I'm going to need you to relax." I grab Daisy's still-clapping hands and pull her back down to the couch. "That's not going to happen for many reasons. One being we have so little in common that he's having to challenge me to read a book. Another being he doesn't live here. Logistically, it could never work."

Daisy and Elsie look at each other and I know they've read too many books with happily ever afters to listen to me. They're lost in a fantasy of this turning into some grand adventure romance when I know it will most likely resemble some horror tragedy. I also know telling them this is a waste of breath.

I do it anyway.

"Seriously, you two, stop looking at each other like that. Jasper is a very nice guy, I'll give him that, but that's all this is. I'm helping him out, he feels the need to do something for me in return. It's just . . ." I close my eyes and fall back into my couch, my fears about this whole arrangement rearing their nasty heads again. "I'm worried."

"About what?" Daisy asks. "It's just reading a few books and being a tour guide, right? Or am I missing something?"

She's missing something.

She's missing a lot of things.

I know it sounds ridiculous and I joke about being a book hater, but I really don't know if I can do this. I read an article once about brain science—I was in college and pretending to be an intellectual, sue me—and it said how when you're reading a book, your brain can't differentiate between the character in the story and you. In your mind, you are this character; you're living their experiences. This left me feeling both horrified and vindicated. Because herein lies my issue with books: escapism leads to denial and denial leads to heartbreak. Roaming my favorite places with Jasper, reading stories about good guys and happily ever afters? It's the one book I have read and the ending sucks. I'm afraid I'm going to get sucked into the fantasy. Into the lies. And I'm not sure I have it in me to get back up after the inevitable fall.

Getting to know Daisy has been a very pleasant surprise. She's fun and hilarious and we have more in common than I could've ever dreamt. But, because we're about twenty years late on the sister-bonding train, she wasn't there a few months ago when I didn't know if I was going to be able to recover from the back-to-back blows that kept knocking me down. She didn't see me trying to pick up the pieces when I lost two of the biggest parts of myself within weeks of each other. First Gran, then photography. I'm just now settling into a rhythm where I don't feel like I'm moments away from crumbling.

"It was . . . it was difficult to walk away from my life when Gran died." I tell Daisy the understatement of the century. "Photography, I don't know how to explain it. It was my passion, but more than that, it was my safe place. It set my soul at ease. I love it in a way I can't do it halfway. When I walked away, I needed a clean break or else I wouldn't have been able to focus on keeping the Book Nook running." *And out of our scumbag father's hands,* though I definitely do not say that.

I think a big reason things have been so nice between me and Daisy is because we haven't discussed dear old Dad at all. I'd very much like to keep it that way.

"So you're nervous that playing travel guide for a hot author will put you back in a dark place." She summarizes my worries perfectly.

"She's afraid it will be worse." Elsie speaks up, and she is not wrong. "Your sister is so terrified of losing anything or anyone else, she's put herself in a self-imposed purgatory."

"Purgatory? That feels a little dramatic." I mean, seriously? So I haven't gone on a real date or a vacation or pretty much left my apartment for something other than work. Is that really purgatory?

"It feels accurate and you know it. And as much as you're trying to deny it, you like Jasper. You're freaking out because you're afraid you're not only going to remember how much you love lacing up your ugly hiking boots, but you're gonna like doing it with Jasper even more."

"You know, it's very, very rude the way you attack me unprovoked all the time." The audacity. I didn't ask for that! "You were just supposed to tell me not to do it."

"You better fucking do it." She points her finger so close to my face that I flinch. "I'm not letting you back out of this. Read some fucking books, go outside, take some pictures, and flirt with the fine-ass man or else."

My head snaps back and I feel my eyebrows try to kiss each other. "Or else?" I repeat her ridiculous threat. It should make me laugh, but with the look on her face, it makes my blood go cold a little bit. "Or else what?"

"You don't want to know." She stands up and crosses my small living room, grabbing my phone off the charger. "Here." She throws me the phone. "Text Jasper now. Tell him the first place you're taking him and what time he should expect you on Monday."

"Monday?" My voice is so high, I don't even recognize it. "That's in two days! That's too soon. I can't plan a day trip for his book in two days. What about next weekend?"

"Monday," she repeats, and Daisy giggles. "I have four kids who think they can play me all day, every day. I can smell the bullshit,

Drew. You knew exactly where you'd take him and had an itinerary worked out in your head the second he suggested this and don't try to convince me otherwise. Text him. Now."

"I would listen to her, she seems pretty serious." Daisy sides with Elsie and I try not to glare. So much for blood is thicker than water, I see.

"You're both traitors and this is the last time I ask for your help." I throw out the empty threat but they see right through me. Extremely pleased smiles light both of their beautiful, jerky faces.

Both women sidle in close to me, watching as I type out a text to Jasper.

**Hey. This is Drew.**

"He knows it's you." Daisy offers her constructive criticism. "Get to the good stuff."

I roll my eyes and huff out an annoyed breath before deleting and starting over.

**If you're still up for me showing you places, would Monday work? If it does, I'll come get you around 8 am. I'm thinking Seven Falls.**

"Eight? Geez. You're an intense travel guide." Daisy is still reading over my shoulder, but at least she doesn't make me delete it this time. "What's Seven Falls?"

"It's this place in Colorado Springs, so not too far, and it has waterfalls and hiking and great views. It's a good place to start."

"See. I knew you already had a plan in place." Elsie sounds smug.

One quick glance in her direction shows she looks it too. "Now hurry up and hit send so we can be done with this and I can destroy this board you made. There's a new episode of *Housewives* and I want to watch it without a child crying every five minutes."

I hesitate, my finger hovering over the send button for a second, still not convinced this is a good idea.

"Oh hell. I'll do it." Daisy snatches the phone out my hand and hits send before I can even process what in the world just happened. "There. Sent."

"Oh my god!" Elsie shouts even though we are all within inches of one another. "He's already writing back!"

All thoughts of *Housewives* are forgotten as we stare at my phone. Nerves settle in my gut like a pile of rocks. Now that the text has been sent, I realize how much I want to do this. How much I want to play pretend with a master of it, making believe, even for a little bit, that I can have my old life back. Well, parts of it.

The longer the bubbles linger on my screen, the more I'm convinced he's backing out of this absurd plan.

Finally the phone buzzes in Daisy's hand. We all let out a collective screech when we read his text.

I was hoping we'd get started tomorrow, but I can wait until Monday . . . I guess. ☺ I'll have breakfast ready for you, let me know your coffee order. I'm so excited to explore with you. Thank you for agreeing to this.

Before we can even finish reading the message, another one pops up, this time with a pin to his location.

All the nerves and anxiety I was feeling disappear in a flash. And even though I know I shouldn't, I feel excited. The vaguely familiar feeling of anticipation starts to bloom deep inside me as I remember the thrill that comes with fresh, cool mountain air filling my lungs as I chase the perfect shot.

And doing it with Jasper Williams at my side.

Maybe my luck is finally beginning to change.

# CHAPTER 10

My luck is not beginning to change.

I'm starting to think I committed some seriously heinous acts in my past lives.

When I woke up this morning, I did it bright-eyed and bushy-tailed. I was like a little kid on Christmas waking up an hour before my alarm was scheduled to go off. I got ready, pulling my wild curls back into a bun so they'd stay out of the way, and applied a healthy amount of sunscreen to my skin. After much internal debate, I pulled out my camera and tucked it away in my backpack. I even filled up an extra water bottle for Jasper.

In fact, I was in such a good mood and this morning was going so well, I used the spare time I had to sit and read some of the first book from the list Jasper made me. I wasn't sure what I was going to think of this book, but so far, so good. It's not a "typical" book. The format is different; it's like someone put the transcript from a documentary into book format. I know it's why Jasper put this first on the list; it's the perfect way to ease me in. Plus, the concept is really cool. It's about a band from the seventies and the characters are all messy, messy, messy. Which is my favorite aesthetic. I appreciate that the characters have real flaws.

Of course, after the perfect morning and ready for the perfect day, I walked outside to find my Jeep with not one, but two flat tires.

Bright side? At least it didn't happen in Colorado Springs?

But two hours and four hundred dollars later, that's all I can come up with.

I pull to a stop in front of an adorable bungalow in Washington Park. It's my dream neighborhood. Gran lived not far from here and I spent more time at her house than I did my own. My dad sold it for seven figures thanks to an overabundance of Denver transplants and skyrocketing housing prices. I doubt I'll ever be able to afford anything over here, but who cares? Not me. Why build equity and own something when I can just throw my money away every single month to a landlord who raises the rent every other year but doesn't do anything to improve the building?

Living every millennial's dream.

The huge, beautifully stained wood front door swings open and Jasper steps onto the front porch complete with two planters framing the door and lots of Adirondack chairs. Even from this distance, I can see his bright smile as he struggles to wave to me while holding two cups of coffee. I wave back, feeling some of the day's earlier frustrations begin to drift away, keeping my eyes on him as he locks the door. I absolutely do not stare at the dark gray basketball shorts he's wearing or the way they cling just so to the curve of his ass.

No.

I definitely do not do that.

He turns back toward me, a skip in his step as he hustles to my old Jeep. I unstrap my seat belt, leaning over the center console to open the door for him.

"Thanks." He catches the bottom of the door with the toe of his tennis shoe and pulls it open the rest of the way. He leans in, stretching his long, muscular arm across my car, and hands me the plastic cup dripping with condensation. "One iced coffee, light on the sugar, heavy on the half-and-half." He recites the order he insisted I tell him.

"Thank you. I really appreciate this." As much as I told him this wasn't necessary, after the morning I had, extra caffeine is very much welcome. "And sorry about this morning."

I sent him, like, I don't know, a hundred texts informing him of my tire situation, updating him on said tire situation, and, of course, apologizing. Not only do I not like being late to anything; I had a plan in my head and I wanted to stick to it.

Also, it's July in Colorado. I know most people think of snow and cold weather when they think of my state, but we're close to the sun and it gets hot in the summer. I love hiking. It's one of my favorite activities in the world, but nobody wants to be a gross, sweaty, miserable mess when they're trekking along a trail. Plus, while Seven Falls isn't a super-well-known spot, it's close to a big hotel in the Springs, so by default there's tourist overlap. I was hoping to avoid the blazing afternoon sun and the even bigger nuisance: crowds.

"Like I told you after all of those texts, it's not a problem at all." There's a smile in his voice and I can tell he thinks I'm ridiculous. Which isn't wrong. He sets his cup in the drink holder between our seats before reaching over his shoulder and buckling up. "I'm glad you still wanted to go. I know car trouble can ruin an entire day."

This is big facts.

"It probably would've been more upsetting if I had to back out." My cheeks heat at the unexpected burst of honesty. I keep my attention on the road as I start to navigate my way out of his temporary neighborhood. "I haven't hit any trails in months. I'm looking forward to this, though be warned, there's a staircase that will kill your hamstrings."

"Hopefully CrossFit has prepared me," he says, and his deep laugh fills every inch of my Jeep when I groan.

"Wow! Already going there." I take one hand off the steering wheel and give his shoulder a light shove. "I hope you know that I will turn this car around if you start talking about WODs."

"I had to get one in since I know how much you love it." His voice is still vibrating with laughter and I decide I have to risk a quick glance his way. Just one second to indulge in a close-up view of his perfect smile. But when I turn to see him, I have to fight to regain my breath when his stunning eyes are staring back at me, all his attention focused on me.

Holy crap.

*Nobody should be this good-looking.*

"So . . ." I struggle to think of something to talk about that doesn't include me waxing poetic about the way his eyes rival oceans. "I started the first book on your list."

"You did?" He sounds surprised even though it was part of our deal. "How are you feeling about it so far?"

"I like it." I don't tell him that I'm only a quarter of the way through the book. It's good so far, but this could change when their problems magically disappear by the end. "I like the main characters. They're a mess . . . which is relatable."

"It is relatable, but you're not a mess." There's a seriousness that has crept into his tone and knocks me off guard a bit.

"That's very nice of you to say, but I'm a certified hot mess. I mean, I was two hours late for this, you saw me at the Book Nook when I couldn't even find your books, and we won't even talk about the way I broke down at dinner." I list off a few examples he's been witness to, realizing in the moment that reminding him of these events is just more proof of me being a total freaking disaster. "I'm okay with it though. I think everybody's lives can be a bit messy at times. Some people get hot-girl summers, I have hot-mess-girl summers. It, too, shall pass." *Hopefully.*

He barks out a laugh and I'm relieved to hear it. "Did you just say *hot-mess-girl summer?*"

"Me and Megan Thee Stallion are basically the same person . . . minus the rhythm, body, and bank account." I name some of our differences.

"And that's all?" he asks, and I appreciate that he's encouraging this ridiculous line of conversation between us.

"Well, those and probably our taste in footwear." I don't know that for a fact, but I do know that I haven't seen any pictures of Megan in Birkenstocks and there are no pictures of me in heels. So it feels like a safe assumption.

"Good to know." His chuckle is deep and throaty and I swear I can feel it caress my bare arm. "I'm learning so much about you already."

I don't have many expectations about this deal between the two of us. I know he needs my help to write his book, and I also know that in a few months, he'll be long gone. I'm taking it one day at a time, indulging in the opportunity to get out on the trails again, to feel the spark of excitement I thought died along with Gran. But it doesn't hurt that an unexpected perk is getting to wrangle as many smiles and laughs out of this man as possible. Looking at a Colorado sunset from a mountain is my favorite view, but it will far from suck having Jasper by my side as I do it.

We settle into my car, a comfortable silence surrounding us. I hop on I-25 and start our drive south; the traffic isn't bumper-to-bumper, but there's still more than there should be at this time of day.

"But really." Jasper's voice pulls me out of my inner screaming as the asshole in front of me taps on his brakes again. "You do know you're not a mess at all, right? You have it more together than anyone I've met in a long time."

This is nice of him.

Really nice.

Total bullshit, but still nice.

"Then I really feel for the people you've surrounded yourself with recently." I decide to live on the edge and take my eyes off the road for a millisecond to aim my teasing smile at him full on. "Thank you though. It's been a lot and I don't know if I've gotten a handle on everything yet, but I'm getting there."

And I am.

Our numbers aren't horrible, but they aren't going to send me to an early retirement. Gran had a system that worked for her and it's been a bit of a journey to adapt one that works for me. Thanks to the growing popularity of story time on Saturdays, the constant panic I was feeling is beginning to fade. Jasper's event also brought in so much business, it forced me to get over my fears and start reaching out to more authors to come in. I don't know if I'm going to move forward, but I've called some contractors to get estimates for installing a coffee/wine bar.

"Not sure how much this will mean to you," he says, and I keep my eyes focused on the bumper-sticker-covered car in front of me. "But I've been to a lot of bookstores in my day, and the Book Nook is already one of my favorites. A few friends told me how great it was, so I had high expectations, but you still managed to surpass them all."

While he was talking, my heart did this really weird thing. It started pounding in my chest, harder than it ever has before, even skipping a few beats before winding me so tight that I'm pretty sure it's lodged in my throat. As much as I want to thank him, it's preventing me from saying anything at all.

I don't know what it is about his words, coming out of his mouth, in the deep, thick tenor of his voice, that makes them feel so important. Elsie and the Dirty Birds (minus sweet old Collette) often tell me I'm doing a great job. I know they mean it, but I also know that they love me and are extremely biased. When Jasper's friends visited, Gran was in charge. Hearing his gracious compliments quiets the anxiety and fear I have about disappointing people because I'm not her.

I bite my bottom lip and fidget with the steering wheel for a moment before getting my shit together enough to say thank you.

"I really appreciate you saying that, thank you." I still don't look at him because if he happens to look back at me, with that soft look he gets on his face, his eyes sparkling with sincerity, I know I'll cry. I'm not wearing any makeup that will get ruined or anything, but my face will still get all blotchy and my eyes will get swollen. Plus, I've already cried in front of him once and I will not allow it to become a regular occurrence.

"You're welcome. And I promise I didn't say that because Mona forced me to." He's joking . . . or at least I think he is. You never know with Mona, and now I might have to give her a call when I get home this evening. "Or because I like the owner with not-so-great book knowledge, but who's turning out to be a fantastic travel guide."

Even if the car in front of me flipped over and burst into flames, exploding in midair, it still wouldn't have stopped me from turning my head—and complete attention—to the man next to me, who I think said out loud and in real life that he likes me.

Or maybe I have finally lost it.

The former seems way more plausible.

"What?" I forget any semblance of manners as I stare wide-eyed and slack-jawed at the gorgeous man next to me.

"Drew, the road." His eyes crease around the sides, the lines I've spent hundreds of dollars on creams and potions to avoid only making his face more enjoyable to look at.

"Right." I nod once, closing my mouth and blinking a few times to relieve my dry eyes. "That's probably a good idea."

Lucky for my car—and our lives—we're past the stretch of highway that's most congested and the car in front of me is still a safe distance away. The views out the window are less suburb-mini-mall realness and more hills-and-trees scenic. I try to think of anything else to say, but when a sign from the universe comes in the form of the opening notes of my favorite song playing from the speakers, I take it as the gift it is. I turn up the radio and focus on the road in front of me.


UNLIKE A LOT OF OTHER places on my list, Seven Falls is run through the Broadmoor—a super-swanky hotel in Colorado Springs that people love but I have a personal vendetta against because of an experience in high school, and have I mentioned that I'm a grudge holder? So there's not only dedicated parking and a shuttle, but also a ticket booth with an entrance fee.

I don't love a tourist destination, but considering Jasper is a tourist and it's only a short drive from the city, it is a perfect location for our first outing. I'll be able to gauge his interest in hiking so I can further plan the rest of our trips.

"Two, please," I say to the uninterested teen behind the plexiglass barrier and reach into my backpack for my wallet.

"Oh no. I got this." Jasper's huge, warm—and soft, but who noticed that?—hand halts my progress. He slides in front of me, wielding his credit card like a magic wand. I can only see his back now, but I can see the teen who was zero percent interested in me. By the way she perks up and her entire demeanor changes, it's safe to assume he's aiming his toothpaste-commercial-worthy smile at her.

He slides the credit card beneath the barrier and she reaches for it but misses twice. She's unable to rip her eyes off Jasper Williams, Author, and apparently hero of teenage girls who hate their jobs. Good for him, I guess.

"He-here you g-go." The poor thing can't even say a simple sentence without stumbling over her words. She should've tried driving with him sitting beside her. The heat of his gaze damn near burned a hole through my skin. I had to pretend to love every song that played for the last forty minutes.

She slides the tickets out with his credit card, and I swear, she's swooning so hard, her hand is trembling.

"Thank you." He takes the tickets and angles toward me, giving me a perfect view of the way his eyes sparkle and his megawatt smile takes over his entire face. "I hope you have a fantastic day."

Giggles burst through the plexiglass and the girl's pale cheeks turn a deep shade of scarlet. He doesn't seem to notice as he slips his card back into his wallet and hands me my ticket.

I take the ticket from him, way too fascinated by the way that little scene played out to focus on anything else.

"You're like . . ." I look back to the still-reddened teen who's staring at Jasper's back despite helping another person. "A teenage-girl slayer."

"Oh god." He cringes. "Please never say that again. I'm pretty sure if an officer was nearby and heard you say that, I'd already be in cuffs. I don't want to be a teenage-girl slayer of any kind."

Since Gran passed away, I have picked up a new habit of listening to podcasts about serial killers. This is wonderful because they're super interesting and give me something to listen to besides my own thoughts. It's the worst because I'm a certified scaredy-cat. There have been more than a few nights when I slept with all the lights in my apartment on. I'm pretty sure there was one about a teenage-girl slayer.

"Yeah, you're right. I didn't even realize how that sounded until you said something." I agree with him as we enter the park. "But you did get her very worked up."

The wording was wrong; my point still stands. I don't know if teenage girls these days still have physical diaries or if they just type all their feelings onto Beyoncé's internet—a thought that makes me feel as old as some of the fossils found in the mountains surrounding us—but she's for sure going to write about Jasper somewhere.

He looks over his shoulder to the girl in the booth and his thick eyebrows knit together. "Did I?" There's genuine confusion in his voice.

I blink at him, unable to speak because there's no way he didn't notice how he affected that girl. Imagine being so hot that over-the-top reactions to your physical perfection are so common, you don't even notice when they happen.

What must it be like to not even be aware you wield such power? He seems completely unaware to the havoc his smile wreaks on all of those who cross his path. I have to force myself to remember this because after spending the morning with him, it's easy to fall prey to the fantasy of Jasper saving all his smiles for me.

Before I can unpack this any more, shuttle buses appear in my line of vision and allow me to change the subject.

"Okay, so here are the options for this part." I point to the shuttles lined up not too far away. "We can hitch a ride and it will bring us pretty close to the waterfall, or we can walk."

"How far is the walk?" Mr. CrossFit asks.

"Not too far." I try to remember what I read about this part. "I can't remember the exact distance, but I do know it's under a mile. And the view on the walk is amazing. Some people like to call it 'the grandest mile of scenery' in all of Colorado." I don't tell him that while I do agree with it being a spectacular freaking view, I think the people who came up with that title might be the marketing department for the Broadmoor.

"Well, if it's the grandest, a word in the English language I don't think gets as much respect as it should, then we have to walk. Taking in the views is the reason we're here, after all."

I was planning on teasing him for his grand feelings about the word *grand*, but then he said that last bit and my mind went blank. Not because he's so excited to walk up this first stretch of road, but because when he said he was here for the view, he looked directly at me. Like I'm the view he's here for. Like a day spent looking at me would be a day well spent.

Maybe I imagined it, but nobody has ever made me feel like that before.

Especially not a man who turns teenage girls and elderly women alike into giggling messes.

No.

Not ever.

And all of a sudden, even though we haven't started on our hike, I feel a little light-headed and out of breath.

How come nobody ever warned me that being with a person like Jasper Williams would do things to my body that nature could never?

# CHAPTER 11

I GUESS WHEN I ACCOUNTED FOR WHAT NATURE CAN DO TO SOME-
one, I did so as a person who has been acclimated to the high Colorado altitude for all my life.

Jasper, on the other hand, can't say the same thing.

"I'm so sorry." He groans from where he's lying on the rock,
using my backpack as his pillow. "This has never happened to me
before."

"I should be the one apologizing." I kick some leaves and twigs
away and plop down onto the dirt beside him. "Here, drink some
water."

It's a good thing that before the madness hit this morning, I
filled up an extra water bottle, and Jasper brought one as well.
Without them, I probably would've had to leave Jasper alone up here
while I ran back to the base of the waterfall to buy a few. He reaches
out his hand, his olive skin practically translucent with how pale
he's gone.

"Just open your mouth, I'll squirt some in for you." I feel terrible for him. He's lying on a rock and unable to move without his nausea ratcheting up about a hundred notches, but I'm so freaking grateful he can't see me. Because if he could, there's not a doubt he would be able to read my mind after what I said—with very pure intentions—made me think some filthy fucking thoughts.

Instead, he keeps one arm limp at his side while the other rests over his eyes, blocking what little sun the trees above us haven't filtered out already, and opens his mouth.

We sit here for a little while longer. I force him to drink every few minutes until his color begins to gradually return.

Thank god.

"Fuck. Talk about embarrassing." Jasper uses his elbow to help him sit up. "I thought I was going to impress you with my CrossFit strength and outdoorsy skills."

"Stop it." My tone is gentle but firm. "There's nothing to be embarrassed about. I should've thought about this before taking you on a hike that requires a steep incline spike up stairs when you're not used to the altitude here. This could've happened to anyone. If anything, now you know how to write about altitude sickness in your book if it comes up."

He groans again, squeezing his eyes shut and letting his head fall back. "No way am I writing about this. I'm going to do everything I can to forget this ever happened so I have no recollection of today's events."

I know he's joking and that even if he wanted to, he couldn't just forget about our day. But still, the idea of it makes my heart twist, because even though he ended up vomiting once or twice, our time leading up to it was the most fun I've had in months.

"Don't do that." I lean forward, handing him the water bottle so he can take another small sip. "Because if you can write what I experienced walking to the waterfall and up the stairs with you, it's bound to be a bestseller."

"Yeah?" The cloudiness that has dulled his eyes for the past hour begins to lift. "You mean that or are you just trying to make me feel better so we can finally leave?"

"Well . . ." I pretend to ponder this question when the reality is I wouldn't mind staying up here, enjoying the peace and quiet and stealthily snapping pictures of Jasper's perfect profile—like a creep!—forever. "Kidding! I hate that you got sick, but even with a minor bump in the road, I've loved this. I just hope it hasn't scared you off of the rest of the excursions I have planned for you."

I push off the dirt and my body aches as my muscles try to remember the last time they were put to such use. Yoga is great, but not much compares to the steep stairs and rocky trails of Seven Falls.

"If anything, I'm more determined than I was before. I can't go out like this."

Because he was sick, I tried very hard to be a decent human and not gawk when he ripped his T-shirt off and was left in nothing but a tank top and his basketball shorts. But now he's seeming to feel a little bit better and my self-restraint is slipping. I can't help the way my eyes drop to his biceps and forearms as the muscles flex from his wrist to his shoulder when he pushes his palm against the stone beneath him for leverage.

He's an author, for goodness' sake, not a freaking sports star. There's absolutely no reason his body should be set up this way. It's rude and unnecessary.

"I made it!" His whoop of excitement drags my attention—

kicking and screaming—away from his lean body and up to his face. He's beaming with pride and not even a little bit green.

I don't know why I do it, but I tip my imaginary hat and curtsy before saying—in a very terrible Irish accent, by the way—"And congratulations to ye, sir." Any self-respect I had for myself swan dives into the waterfall.

"Drew." Jasper stares at me, open disbelief written across his face. There's no doubt he's wondering how I was able to out-embarrass him after he threw up multiple times. "Did you just curtsy?"

"You know . . ." I try to think of an excuse that will leave me with even a shred of dignity, but come up empty. "I did. It felt right in the moment but I do have regrets. Let's leave it alone."

"Sorry." He closes some of the distance between us, showing no signs of the dizziness that hit him hard earlier. His steps are no longer wobbly or unsure. "I can't let it go."

I groan and look to the heavens. First I cry, then I curtsy. I have zero game. "I was so close to having the upper hand."

"You still have the upper hand." I don't think he meant to say that out loud. His whisper rises just above the sounds of the water rushing downstream.

But instead of following proper social protocol, I don't drop it. Oh no, no, no. I push. I'm a pusher. "I do? How so?"

"Well, you know." His hands fidget at his sides and he kicks a pattern into the dirt with the toe of his sneaker. He's nervous. I forget all my self-preservation and for a moment, I let myself dream that he's nervous because of me. "You're doing me such a huge favor by showing me around, I'm really at your mercy. I was hoping to keep up and maybe even impress you, but I failed at both."

I feel so ridiculous for even allowing myself to hope it could've been for something more. Even though I know Jasper Williams, Author, and I have almost nothing in common and could never last, for a second, I wished it could be more.

"Well, to be fair." I try to keep the disappointment out of my voice and only halfway succeed. "I've never seen someone throw up so much without alcohol being the cause. It was very impressive how fast you turned and ran so you could do it off the main trail."

Poor guy. It hit him so fast and so hard. It was like watching a cartoon. First he went white as a ghost, then turned green, before he spun on his heels and darted behind a tree to let it all out.

"I don't know if that makes me feel better or worse." He pulls his lips into a straight, thin line.

"Better, definitely better," I tell him. "Altitude is no joke and can get the best of anyone. This is why Olympians train here, and no offense to your CrossFit routine, but I don't think it holds a candle to Olympic training."

"You're never going to let me live down the CrossFit comment, are you?" His tone is slightly annoyed, but the huge smile on his face lets on to the act.

I smile back at him before giving him the god's-honest truth. "Literally never."

Again, another reason why this could never have been anything more than the small exchange we're having. Even if I could let the author thing go, I can never get behind CrossFit.

"That's what I thought." His rueful smile tugs on my heart-strings. It takes all my restraint not to launch myself at him, kiss it off his face, and possibly be arrested. "Should we head back down before I get hit with another spell?"

"Yeah, probably a good idea." Plus, it's getting late, and even though the park will be open for a while longer, I cannot hit traffic in the Springs and in Denver. I don't have the patience for that. "We can take the shuttle back to the ticket booth this time, let you get some more rest after the stairs."

I tighten the straps of my backpack, and when my hands fall to my sides, one grazes against his. Just a brush, the barest swipe, but it lights me up in places I thought would be dark forever. I have no idea what it is about this man, but when I'm around him, it's as if I'm not in control of myself anymore.

It sounds so silly because I'm a grown woman who's had sex with multiple partners in my life, but in this moment, all I want to do is wind my fingers through his and hold his hand. I want to know what his touch would feel like. Would it be sweet and unassuming like he is or would it feel firm and possessive? I have a feeling I would love either, that my body would cry out for him in any form. Just the thought of it alone causes my stomach to perform flips that would blow all those Olympians nearby out of the water.

I tuck my hands in my pockets, not trusting myself as we walk in silence along the trail. I try to soak in the beauty of this moment, back in the great outdoors, exploring it with someone who might be even more fun to look at than the nature around us. We start across a bridge over the stream leading to the first of the seven waterfalls when Jasper comes to a stop, taking in the scenery in front of us.

"You were right." He stops, but never lets his eyes move to mine. "This is the perfect setting for a romance book."

I try to remind myself of the poor ticket girl stunned silent by Jasper's beauty and how obtuse he seems to be about the charms he possesses. However, my heart wants to hear none of it. Standing beside Jasper, looking at a view I didn't think I would allow myself to ever witness again, my camera in my backpack, the dangerous spark of hope begins to burn. In this perfect moment, why couldn't I be the person Jasper wants to be with? What if, for just a moment, I were to turn to face him and feel his lips brush against mine?

"I hoped you would like it." I pretend not to notice the breathiness in my voice that wasn't there even during the steep climb up the stairs. "I'm not the best at romance, but this felt like a safe bet."

"Well, as the creator of many romance couples, I have to say, I'm not sure anything I write will hold a candle to this. I don't know if I'll be able to create something that compares to this trip or a character as patient and kind as you've been today."

Okay. Wow.

That was sweet.

Like really, really sweet.

I rock back on my heels. I don't trust myself not to lean in closer and see exactly how romantic this day can become.

"Nice of you to say I'm patient after you witnessed my car rage firsthand, but I appreciate the compliment nonetheless."

My mom always told me I had an unnatural obsession with receiving compliments and she wasn't wrong. Words of affirmation is my love language, and Jasper Williams, Author, a skilled wordsmith, is unknowingly turning me on with every sweet word leaving his luscious lips.

"Everyone gets a free pass in the car," he says. "Nobody can help an expletive or two when the person in front of you slams on their brakes for no reason."

"Thank you!" I shout, and my voice bounces off the rocks.

"Nobody was in front of them. I swear they saw me in their rearview mirror and decided to choose violence."

Jasper turns to me, his deep, throaty laugh washing over me like the light breeze. The sun shines down on him as if he's God's chosen one, each ray highlighting the gold flecks in his skin. The blue of his eyes shimmers like sapphires and my fingers itch to grab my camera. I'm positive if I were to take his picture in this moment, it would be hung on museum walls until the end of time. I don't know if it's my imagination or not, but I swear his eyes drop to my mouth, and for one glorious second, I let myself believe he's having the same thoughts about me.

I should've said no to this agreement.

I thought the worst that could happen was I'd have to read a few books I hated. I didn't realize I'd turn into this pathetic sack, waxing poetic and lusting after a man who only sees me as a glorified tour guide.

"Drew?" Jasper pulls me out of my sad thoughts. "Where'd you go?"

"Oh, sorry." I wave off his concern. I attempt to replace whatever forlorn expression I was wearing with one that I hope reads easy, breezy woman who absolutely does not want to kiss him. "I just re-membered what comes next and I'm hoping you don't hate me for it."

Although part of this is a lie to cover for my sad, lusty thoughts, it's also very, very true.

His eyebrows furrow together and his back straightens. "What are you talking about?"

"You'll see." I start walking in the direction we initially came from and don't stop until we're standing atop the very steep set of stairs leading us back to the base of the waterfall.

"All right." I point to the first of 224 steps. "Sit."

His head snaps back and he looks at me, an incredulous stare marring his gorgeous face. "Sit? What?"

"You spent over an hour with your vision spinning. If you think I'm going to let you try to walk down these stairs, you're delusional." I may not be the most responsible person in the world, but I can't be held accountable for his death.

"But I feel fine now. What do I have to do in order for you to deem me well enough to walk down the stairs like an adult?"

"Let me think about it." I tap my chin with my pointer finger, pretending to ponder his question. "Nothing. This is a safety thing. You cannot walk down these steps when you've been showing symptoms of altitude sickness. The Dirty Birds would kill me if I let anything happen to you."

"But—" He starts, but that's all he gets out.

"Nope. This is it. I'll stand here all day, but the only way you're going down these stairs is scooting on your ass."

He opens his mouth and closes it just as fast. His eyes dart back and forth between me and the steps before he lets out a very resigned sigh and plops his firm behind on the top step.

He points a finger at me. "We will never speak of this again."

"Cross my heart." I draw an X across my chest. "This is between you, me, and anybody who happens to walk past us on our descent."

"Geez, thanks." He rolls his eyes and I have to swallow my laughter, seeing him not only going down the stairs like a toddler, but now acting like one too.

"You can be mad now, but you'll thank me later when your brain is still in your skull and not all over the ground."

I meant what I said about not sharing this detail with anyone else, but that doesn't stop me from taking out my camera and taking one picture to remember this by.

Because as much as I should try to ignore everything that happened today, I never want to forget a single second of it.

Not ever.

# CHAPTER 12

GRAN'S OFFICE NEEDS A WINDOW.

Numbers are stressful and I need some vitamin D to balance me out. I enter in another contractor's information on the spreadsheet I'm creating so I can start the interview process for the coffee/wine bar I want to install and add another column with "Window????" as the header.

Professional.

"Drew?" Dani's voice pulls me from the task at hand as she pushes open the door to the cave I've been in for the last hour and a half.

"Hey. I'm glad you're here." I close my computer and spin my chair to face her. "Have you ever had a sun lamp? And by that, I mean do you think I would benefit from some light therapy?"

"Ummm . . . maybe? I don't know." Her usually peppy voice is off and her hands are fidgeting in a way I only saw when I first interviewed her.

"Are you okay?" I come out of my seat and make my way around the desk. "What's going on?"

"Yeah, I'm fine, sorry. There are two men in the front who are super insistent on talking to you." She tries to force a smile, but it's very unconvincing. "One said he's your dad? I'm so sorry, I didn't know. I would've got you right away if I would've known."

I was already pissed someone was giving her a hard time, but finding out that it's my dad? My vision turns red.

The nicest way to describe him is a jerk. He's the most insecure human who has ever graced this earth and proves it by talking down to almost every person he crosses paths with.

I can deal with it when it's aimed at me, but no way in hell am I okay with him walking into this store, the one Gran left me, and being a dick to the people who have stood by me while he made my life a living hell.

Absolutely. The. Fuck. Not.

"Wait back here, you know where I keep my snacks." I gesture to the file cabinet that houses all my pop, chips, and Sour Punch Straws. "I'll handle him."

I don't wait for a response before I push out of the dark office and go in search of Andrew Young. I should've known it was too good to be true, Daisy being close by without him coming down and taking at least one opportunity to jack me around.

Since we are a bookstore, most people who come in do so with a library-like mindset. Their voices are hushed and conversations are kept quiet to respect the other patrons who are in search of their next great read.

But not Andrew Young.

Oh no. My father has never been aware of anybody but himself.

Which is evident by his booming voice echoing across the entire damn store. When I find him, I have to stop and take a deep breath in order to not launch myself at him.

He's in the nook section, sitting in Vivian's chair, with his loafers—which I'm sure cost a mint despite them being the ugliest effing shoes I've ever seen—resting on the coffee table Gran and I spent a week refinishing.

How he shares genetics with me and Gran will be a mystery I never solve. Truly one of life's cruelest jokes.

"Drew!" He kicks his shoes off the table and aims his bright, wide smile, which has tricked so many people, my way. "There you are. I'd like you to meet my friend Connor Walsh. Connor, this is my daughter Drew."

Some of my anger dies with the shock of his cordial greeting. Even if he were to ever make a phone call to tell me happy birthday, there was always a thread of indifference in his voice. I've always been an obligation, never a priority. When I'd visit him, I learned to ignore the sting that came with being an afterthought to the rest of his family.

"Drew." Connor, who to my knowledge had enough common courtesy not to have his shoes on my furniture, unfolds his body from Ethel's rocking chair. "It's so nice to meet you. Your father has told me so much about you."

He crosses the space and I can't help but give him a once-over. He's a good-looking man. His skin is fair in a way that makes me think he spends more time indoors than out, and his blond hair is slicked back in a professional but still attractive way. He's tall, but not as tall as Jasper. Not as built either. He's cute in a boy-band way where Jasper's hot in a superhero way. His brown eyes sparkle with humor, but not with warmth. And even though he's only said a handful of words to me, I don't trust him.

He's a good liar, I'll give him that. It's just that my father couldn't have told him much about me because my father doesn't know much about me. But how was he supposed to know that?

"Connor Walsh?" His name sounds so familiar, but I'm unable to place it. "Have we met before?"

"I don't think we have." He stops a few feet in front of me, outstretching his suit-covered arm to shake my hand. "I'm pretty sure I'd remember you."

I don't want to be flattered. If this is a man my dad considers a friend, acquaintance, or business partner, that's all I need to know to want to stay far away from him. I don't need to know specifics to know this visit to the Book Nook does not bode good things for my future. But even understanding this, I still feel the all-too-familiar sensation of a blush rising in my cheeks.

What can I say? I'm a sucker for a good compliment.

I'll take "Daddy Issues" for six hundred, Alex!

"That's nice of you." I place my hand in his, frustrated that I can't remember where I know him from, but letting it go for now. "Now, what can I do for the two of you?"

I don't actually care. However, I've dealt with Andrew Young enough in the past to be aware of how this is going to work. Playing along only makes this annoying process move a little faster.

Connor opens his mouth, but my dad speaks over him.

I watch in fascination as pink tinges Connor's ears and his eyes narrow on my dad.

*Hmmm . . . maybe I do want to know this Connor guy. An enemy of my enemy and all that jazz.*

"I wanted to show him around the store. You know, see the space in person and how we've set it up." His gaze sharpens on me and I read the unsaid warning loud and clear. "Before any talks get serious, I thought it was imperative for us all to be on the same page about how we can all benefit. Not only is this property worth quite a bit, I wanted Connor here to see what the Book Nook is and how it could fit within his portfolio."

"It is a wonderful space." Connor turns his attention away from my dad and focuses on me. "You've both done a wonderful job. I know keeping a small business up and running is no small feat."

Now, while I was able to read Dad's warning look, that doesn't mean I'm going to proceed with caution because, well . . . because screw him.

"Thank you so much." I keep my tone light, friendly even, as I smile at the look of relief on my dear old dad's face. "The Book Nook has been a lot of work, and excuse me if this sounds like a silly question, but what has my dad told you about this property? Because I keep hearing him say 'we' as if he's had any part of this store, when that's not true at all." I do nothing to beat back my grin when I hear Dad's enraged hiss of breath. "He's never helped, and, in fact, after my grandma passed away, she made it very clear that the Book Nook was in no way, in any capacity, my father's. I'm the full owner and I have no interest in selling or partnering. This store was my gran's pride and joy and she has entrusted me to keep the vision she had for it up and running. Unfortunately for whatever Andrew told you, this does not include you, no matter how kind you seem to be."

"Oh, for fuck's sake, Drew!" Dad snaps, dropping the father-of-the-year facade for Connor. "Her will was a crock of shit. She was starting to lose it months before it was signed and there's no way it will hold up in court. If you would stop trying to ice me out for some make-believe vendetta you and your mom have against me, you'd see this is best for everyone."

His lips are still moving, but I don't hear him over the sound of blood rushing through my ears. It's not news to me that Andrew Young is trash. I doubt it's news to anyone who's spent more than ten minutes around him. And usually I can ignore it, but usually he's not in my place of business insulting the two women who did everything for me.

He's still ranting and raving, but now his feet are moving just as fast as his mouth.

"If you keep this shit up, you'll end up with nothing!"

"Whoa, whoa, whoa." Connor steps in front of Dad and places his hands on his chest. "Why don't you take a breather, Andrew."

"Yeah, Dad. Take a breather." I step around Connor, appreciating the gesture, but not needing protecting, and definitely not needing it from my jerk of a father. "Just do it outside."

I point in the direction of the front door. I've seen this show before and I don't need to watch it again.

"I'm not leaving!" His whiny voice rises to a roar, and out of the corner of my eye, I see customers beginning to take notice of this pathetic little scene. "She was my fucking mom, not yours! This is mine, and when I get it, I'll make sure you never see a dime from it again."

"Real novel idea from you, Dad, making sure I don't get any money from you. How much child support did you owe before Scarlett started writing the checks? And fun that you're so worried about your mom now that she's gone when she hadn't heard a peep from you in months while she was still here." Unlike my dad, I don't need to raise my voice to get my point across. He's damn near vibrating with rage, and I'm not sure he wouldn't hit me if it weren't for Connor watching. "Now, I'm going to tell you one more time, whatever you're trying to do? Do it somewhere else and do it fast. Because if you don't, I will call the police and get you removed."

He stops straining against Connor and all the color he was so valiantly building up drains from his face.

*Interesting.*

"You wouldn't call the police. I'm your goddamn father!"

The fucking audacity of this man!

I lean in this time, my unpolished nail getting so in his face I almost scratch his nose. "Then fucking act like it for once in your life."

My voice doesn't sound like my own. All the acid of a sad little girl turned into an angry woman drips from my words. The hurt and betrayal I've felt all these years is finally beginning to seep out, and to my total mortification, it catches my sinuses aflame.

Without waiting for him to respond, I spin on my heel, needing an escape. I will not let him leave here thinking he got to me in any way. I will not allow him to mistake my fury for sadness. He doesn't get that.

Not now.

Not ever.

"If you aren't gone in three minutes, I'm calling the police." I keep my tone even as I throw that parting line over my shoulder, giving him exactly what he's given me my entire life—not one fucking thing.

I'm walking to the front desk, ignoring the concerned looks of customers who overheard our lovely father-daughter reunion, when the front door swings open and the Dirty Birds start to filter in.

Freaking fabulous.

"Drew!" Mona shouts my name as soon as she sees me and hurries across the floor like she's not a seventy-year-old woman in three-inch stilettos. "You'll never guess—" She stops talking and her hazel eyes narrow on my face. I guess I didn't do as well as I'd hoped at giving nothing. "What in the world? What's wrong?"

Those words are like a homing signal to the rest of the ladies, who all scurry across the store and crowd around me like a bunch of mother hens—even Collette. Which is how I know I must look terrible.

In the combination of genetics from my Black mother and white father, I got my fabulous curls, full lips I was teased for in school by the same girls who are now overlining theirs and paying thousands for fillers, a great ass, and golden skin that still shows the red splotches that appear all over my face when I cry.

They're all talking at once, trying to figure out what happened to me by talking to one another and not asking me anything, when Collette's hoarse smoker's voice rises above the rest.

"Well, shit. I guess we know the answer now." She steps away from the group, no hesitation in her steps as she walks up to my dad, who is being led out by Connor and looking anything but happy. "What hole'd you crawl out of? Ignoring your poor ol' ma wasn't enough? Now you gotta come harass your daughter?"

He rolls his eyes and now I wonder if he has a death wish. "Nice to see you, too, Collette."

"It's Mrs. Wagner to you," she snaps. Part of me just wants to drown my worries in a milkshake or two and maybe a glass of wine, but the other part is finding immense pleasure watching my dad flinch as he gets scolded. "Knew your mom since I moved here from

Chicago. Knew your dad too. Both of them good people. Solid. Always willing to help me when I needed it. And to this day, it's a fucking mystery how they got a crap kid like you outta the deal. Guess that's why Alice loved Drew so much; our Drew here gave her everything you couldn't."

*Our Drew here.*

Up until this very moment, if someone were to ask me what Collette Wagner thought of me, I'd tell them she hated me. She dealt with me because I came with the package of Alice Young and the Book Nook. But right now, hearing her stand up for me against the man who has made my life hell since what feels like my very first day on earth? Tears start to build again, but this time they're good tears.

Thankful tears.

"Ummm . . ." a deep voice I've only heard on the phone for the last week says from behind me. My body doesn't need to see him in order to react. Goose bumps race down my spine as those butterflies I've been trying to rid myself of take off. "Is everything okay here?"

"Oh yes." Mona's eyes drift over my shoulder. "That's what I was trying to tell you. We ran into Jasper outside."

Jasper.

Of course it is. Because why couldn't this get any worse?

## CHAPTER 13

I DON'T KNOW IF I SHOULD FEEL THRILLED OR MORTIFIED WHEN I turn around and see Jasper's concerned gaze laser focused on me.

I haven't seen him since I dropped him off at his place after our hike last week. He had to go to some book conference thing in California and was supposed to get back tomorrow. Just in time for him to take me on our first bookish excursion. I was hoping when I saw him next, it'd be with my hair and makeup done after an Issa Rae mirror pep talk or even makeup-less and unprepared. Anything other than the current domestic dispute I'm embroiled in.

When I accidentally word-vomited about my life during our first dinner, he found out a little bit about my relationship with my dad. But hearing it and seeing it are two different things. Dark, messed-up family relationships should be saved for—I don't know—forever? At least, that would be ideal. But for some reason that I refuse to investigate further, instead of profound embarrassment, I feel beyond

grateful to see Jasper taking my back . . . both literally and figura-
tively.

"Jasper, hi." I swipe a hand across my cheeks before I move to
him. His eyes follow the movement and I take a sick pleasure at the
way they narrow in concern. "What are you doing here? I thought
you weren't getting back until tomorrow."

"They didn't need me for the last day of the conference so I was
able to leave early." He glances over my shoulder, but when he looks
back at me, it's as if everyone else disappears and I'm the only person
he sees. "Are you okay?"

"Just a little drama with my dad, nothing new." I go for noncha-
lance and force a smile onto my face. However, when Jasper's frown
deepens, I realize my efforts were for naught. "He's leaving now, so
no worries."

"Your dad? I thought . . ." He looks behind me again, but this
time when he does, his entire demeanor changes. His shoulders snap
back and the lines around his mouth tighten. It's a version of Jasper
I've never seen before. Even when he was throwing up and miserable,
there was still a light, happy-go-lucky vibe about him. And now
that's gone.

"What's wro—" I begin to ask, but stop short when Jasper speaks
over me.

"Connor." There's a nervousness to his voice that I've yet to hear
from him. "What are you doing here?"

Connor?

All right. This is too much now. What the fuck is happening?

"Jasper! My man." Connor either doesn't hear the anxiousness
in Jasper's voice or he ignores it. He leaves my dad standing there

with a still-irate Collette in front of him. "Long time. How've you been?"

Connor grabs Jasper's hand and does one of those man hand-shake/hug things where he slaps Jasper on the back. I wasn't wrong, Connor is a couple inches shorter and his frame is noticeably thinner than Jasper's when they're standing beside each other. It's almost hard to focus on anything other than the extreme handsomeness in front of me. If I had my camera with me, I'd be snapping away. But beneath the general optics of two hot guys, one in a suit, one in shorts and a tee, something else is happening. None of the rigidness leaves Jasper's frame as Connor bombards him with this gesture. If anything, he becomes more tense.

"I've been fine." Jasper keeps his answer short and sweet, not giving anything away. "I didn't expect to see you here."

"Andrew brought me in, he wanted me to meet Drew." Connor looks away from Jasper, and when he spots me, his eyes soften as if he regrets this scene as much as I do. I don't want to think it's sweet . . . but it is. "Unfortunately, he didn't clue me in on the full situation, so now we're leaving. Aren't we, Andrew?"

"Yeah." My dad looks anywhere but at me as he answers. "We're going."

His shoulders slump and the lines on his face deepen as real-ization sets in that his plan didn't only fail; it backfired. He shoves his hands in his pockets and heads to the front door, not uttering a single word as he goes.

"Not the best circumstances, but it was nice to see you, Jasper. We'll have to catch up soon." Connor slaps him on the back once more but doesn't wait for a response before moving toward me. "Again, I'm very sorry about today, Drew."

"Not your fault." I wave off his apology. "I know firsthand how convincing Andrew can be."

"Well, still." He steps in a little closer and his voice drops. "I hope one day we'll be able to chat under different circumstances."

Social awkwardness is one of my key personality traits. I doubt I'd know how to respond to this in the best of situations, but I definitely don't know how to with my dad skulking about, a flock of Dirty Birds watching, and Jasper fidgeting beside me.

Lucky for me, he doesn't wait for me to say anything before aiming one more nod at Jasper. He turns on his heel and walks out the door with my father dearest in tow.

*Good riddance.*

"Geez," a woman with a stack of books in her arms says after the door slams shut. "I thought a trip to the bookstore on a Tuesday would be drama-free, but—and no disrespect—that was the most entertaining thing I've seen in a while. I'm gonna have to come here more often."

"Hate to break it to you"—I turn to face her—"but that show is not going to have a repeat performance."

She shrugs, a smirk on her face as she heads to the register. "We'll see about that."

It's unfortunate, but I know she's not wrong to be hopeful.

I know my dad will be back. I can only hope he'll be stuck licking his wounds for a little bit longer this time and I'll be able to catch my breath before his next sneak attack.

"Drew, dear." Ethel taps me on the shoulder and startles the heck out of me. I forgot she was so close during everything. "Why don't you bring Jasper here back to your office and take a break. Mona and I can handle things out here for a bit."

"That'd be great. Thank you." I don't hesitate to take her up on that offer. I turn to show Jasper the way to my office and it's only then I realize he's holding something. My eyebrows knit together as I nod toward the grease-stained paper bag in his other hand. "Did you have that the entire time?"

"Yeah." For the first time since he walked in, the tension falls off his face and the lines around his eyes deepen as his smile grows wide. "My magic skills aren't that good yet."

I stop and turn to him, preparing to ask a question I'm not sure I want the answer to.

"Does that mean you do have some magic skills?"

I once dated a guy whose hobby was magic, and it wasn't great for me. But admittedly, it also wasn't terrible? He was a hit at parties and it was cute how excited he was when he learned a new trick. I might be a little bitter because his best act happened to be how he disappeared at the end of our relationship.

Not that Jasper and I are dating or anything.

"Unfortunately, no. My only talent is writing, though if you go on the internet you'll see that even that is debatable."

I have gone on the internet and that is not what I found. I don't tell him that though. Gotta keep my creepin' ways to myself.

"You're ridiculous." I laugh, appreciating the way he's trying to lighten the mood before I remember something. "Hey, what's with you and Connor? You didn't seem yourself around him."

I might've been pretty focused on my own mess, but Jasper is always so confident, it was strange to see him falter.

"It's nothing." He brushes off the question. "We worked together a long time ago. I was surprised to see him."

His words tell one story, but his body tells another. The lines of his shoulders go rigid and his eyes avoid mine. I can't put a finger on it, but something about his casual tone is off.

"Wow, such a small world." As a person with many sore spots in my life, I understand when someone doesn't want to talk about something. So I drop it even if I'm more curious than before. "Let's go free Dani. She's been in the office this entire time."

His relief is palpable at the change of subject. I lead the way to my office, navigating bookshelves and customers while trying to ignore the tingling feeling wrapped around my spine, knowing Jasper's following so close behind.

"He's gone," I tell Dani when I push the door open. "I hope he won't be back anytime soon, but if you do see him, don't interact with him. Come get me and I'll deal with him."

Dani pulls the Blow Pop she grabbed from my candy stash out of her mouth. "I'm so sorry. I didn't know he was your dad. I feel terrible."

"Do *not* apologize." I motion for Jasper to come in and try to avoid running into a box—or three—to get to Dani. "He's the worst. His default is awful, nothing you could've done would have changed that. Please promise not to quit after having to deal with him."

"I promise." A weak smile tugs on the corners of her mouth and she looks as relieved as I feel.

"Thank goodness." Because I swear, if the Book Nook's most knowledgeable employee quit because of Andrew freaking Young? I might've had to go all Taylor Swift, "No Body, No Crime" on him. "Mona and Ethel are working up front with Jess. I know what it feels like to be on the receiving end of an Andrew Young attack, so why don't you take the rest of the day off to recover?"

Bubbly Dani is back in full force. She giggles like I told a joke.

"You're wild. I'll go relieve Mona and Ethel." She rolls her eyes and stands up from the lumbar-supporting chair. "Oh! And hey, Jasper. Nice to see you again."

"Nice to see you too." Color rises in her cheeks, but as usual, Jasper doesn't seem to notice.

"Sooooo . . ." The door clicks shut and I'm alone with Jasper again. I wish it was with the same ease we had when he climbed into my Jeep last weekend, but thanks to my dear old dad, a heaviness tinges the already stale air of Gran's office. "That was only slightly mortifying. I'm sorry you had to see that."

I'm not completely sure he isn't going to cancel our entire deal after seeing the madness up close and personal.

"No need to apologize." He moves deeper into the office I'm convinced served as a closet at one point. It only takes him a few steps before he's right in front of me, his large body blocking out the rest of the cluttered space, and he sets the bag on the desk. "I'm sorry you had to deal with it."

I want to tell him he's wrong, that I do need to apologize. Explain how I've let my dad get away with his shit behavior toward me for so long, I've allowed it to spill into every aspect of my life.

"Thank you," I say instead, savoring the way his eyes soften around the edges and his smile warms. "I appreciate you saying that."

"Well, it's true. It sucks, but we don't get to choose our parents." He pulls his hand from his pocket, and time freezes as it nears my face. My breath catches in my throat as his fingers graze across the shell of my ear to tuck a defiant curl back into place.

His touch is lighter than the summer breeze rustling the leaves at sunset, but I feel it in every part of my body. It's nice.

It's *more* than nice.

I've never had that before. My friends have told me about it, but I always thought they were full of it. I've spent nights with men who never elicited a fraction of the feeling Jasper caused with a brush of his fingertips.

Jasper is just supposed to be a friend, but knowing that doesn't prevent my body from reacting. The hairs on the back of my neck rise, and chills shoot down my spine. My stomach clenches and my legs spasm. I try to keep my eyes open, I try my hardest, but I can't. They fall shut and I lean into his hand, not wanting to lose his touch. Maybe Jasper is a magician after all. Because with the barest hint of contact, I'm not in control of myself anymore. This is Jasper's body now.

When I open my eyes, the few inches separating us before have ceased to exist. And so has the sweet, understanding Jasper who touched me with such gentleness. This Jasper is new and it's like a siren call I couldn't resist even if I tried.

"Jasper?" I try to say his name, but it comes out as a whisper. A moan.

I know this is a bad idea . . . the worst, actually. If I was smart, I would send him out of my office and cancel this entire ridiculous deal between the two of us. I've never been this affected by another person before and I'm sure I'm going to send him running for the hills.

"Do you know how hard it was for me to control myself at Seven Falls?" His hoarse voice sends another shock wave throughout my body, like the frequency of his tone is affecting me on a cellular level and I'm not sure I can even comprehend what he's saying. "I've wanted to kiss you from the first time you turned around and I saw your face. I don't know what it is about you, but I can't make myself walk away."

His words have my world spinning. None of this makes any sense and I'm still not sure I'm not imagining all of it.

But on the off chance this is real life, I don't hold back. "I don't want you to walk away."

Nothing about Jasper is right for me and yet I can't find it in myself to care. This has a definite end date, but I already know that nothing lasts forever—not the bad and definitely not the good. All I can do is indulge in the now and appreciate every beautiful second it lasts.

"I shouldn't want to kiss you right now. I should wait, give you space, but I can't." With every word, his mouth moves closer to mine until our heavy breathing is the only thing separating us. "If you don't want this to happen, I need you to tell me now."

I never imagined kissing anyone in a depressing, musty office space after getting in a fight with my dad. I'm not a romance writer, but even I know this scenario is lacking. But would I rather wait for a better moment instead of feeling Jasper's mouth on mine right now? Absolutely fucking not.

All of the need I've been trying to suppress breaks free. My breasts are heavy and a need builds between my thighs to heights I've never felt before. I'd kiss him behind a dumpster with my dad standing next to it if I had to. I'm desperate for it.

Instead of telling him any of that, I rest my hands on his hips and clutch the loose fabric of his T-shirt in my fists, and hope I don't wake up from this dream I'm living. I angle my head toward his and roll onto my toes until my hardened nipples brush against his chest. A gasp falls from my parted lips, but that's the only sound that escapes before his mouth is on mine and the world around me implodes.

I don't know what I was expecting.

Maybe that Jasper's kisses would be like him? Soft and gentle, patiently exploring until I gave him the sense I was ready for more.

But for once, reality is so much better than expectations.

The Jasper I thought I knew transforms into somebody else the moment his full, pillow-soft lips push against mine. His light touch turns frantic as his fingers flex into my neck and his free hand finds my ass, pulling me so impossibly close that I'm half-convinced he can feel my heart beating against him.

His impatient mouth works mine until he can't wait any longer. His teeth nip at my bottom lip—the unfamiliar sting only adding to the need building between my legs—before his tongue replaces them, tracing the sting away. The sudden switch between soft and hard, frenzied and patient, undoes me. I have no idea what Jasper's going to give me, but I want every drop of it.

I'm desperate, on the verge of begging for whatever he's going to do next.

My lips part, giving him the access he's so nobly earned, and he doesn't hesitate to take advantage of the silent invitation. Twisting and tasting, his tongue tangles with mine as he ravishes my mouth. A hum of appreciation rips from the back of his throat and the vibrations send shock waves throughout my entire body. My skin feels like it's crackling with need and every touch shoots off another charge of electricity. I've never felt so attuned to my body. I thought this kiss would sate my need for him; instead, it's only made it stronger.

If someone were to ask me my name right now, I'm not sure I could answer. I only know one thing and it's that I never want this to end. I would gladly spend the rest of my days in this windowless room surrounded with nothing but the musty scent of old books and Jasper's cologne if it means he'll kiss me forever.

But like we already know, all good things come to an end.

Jasper's grip on my ass lightens as he begins to pull away, dropping featherlight kisses against my mouth to lessen the blow.

"Wow." He looks down at me with hooded eyes when we're done. "That was . . . wow."

"That about sums it up." My lips are tingling and my pulse is still racing. I feel like I'm floating. Jasper is a drug and this is one high I'll never stop chasing.

"Sooo . . ." His hand leaves my neck and he wraps my ponytail around his fingers, giving it a light tug so I can't look anywhere but at him and the cocky smile he's wearing. "Wanna do it again?"

My smile widens at the same time my stomach flips. "Oh yeah." And that's all I say before his mouth is back on mine.

I was right, the smart thing to do would've been to turn him away and stay in my nice, warm comfort zone of average men with average abilities.

You can't miss what you've never had.

But after this? There's no turning back.

Not ever.

# CHAPTER 14

I DID IT.

I managed not to beg Jasper to stay and fuck me on my gran's desk when we broke our second kiss.

Alas, this was not a testament to my ironclad self-control. Jasper reminded me about the bag he brought in with him and then he showed me what was in the bag: burgers from my favorite hole-in-the-wall burger joint in town. And after the afternoon I had, plus the very strenuous make-out session, I was pretty freaking hungry.

Oh. And I also finished a freaking book.

I'm sure this doesn't sound like a big deal to the average human, but for me—a person who has actively avoided reading a book since I was forced to in school—it was huge. It was such an accomplishment that I had an adrenaline rush when I closed the book.

The wildest part is that I enjoyed it.

I only read it because I made a deal with Jasper and was curious about what he had planned. But as I got into it, I realized I didn't only like the story—I enjoyed the act of reading. It encouraged me to turn off my phone rather than endlessly scrolling before bed. Instead, I began to settle beneath my comforter and read until my eyes were too heavy to leave open. Even my sleep has gotten better. My Apple Watch is no longer shaming me with my sleep quality.

Plus, I loved all the characters. They had real problems—some I could relate to and many I'm grateful I couldn't—that weren't magically resolved by the end. Instead, each character had their own ending, some happier than others, all with growth and understanding. There was no Prince Charming who swooped in and solved everything. Maybe it's another of my never-ending list of issues stemming from my childhood, but I don't want to watch someone get saved. I want to watch them save themselves. I want to know they can live a fulfilling life with or without a love interest.

My phone buzzes on the counter and I hit ignore when I see the name on the screen. It's not that I'm mad at Daisy. I'm not. It wouldn't matter if she begged Dad to leave me alone; he'd still do whatever he wanted. I don't want to put my problems with Dad on her and I'm still too raw from yesterday's scene to talk about it. I also have to acknowledge that Daisy has a different experience with him. I'm glad she does, but I don't know how I'd feel hearing her stick up for him.

It's just too bad this had to happen before my night out with Jasper. I really could've used her styling expertise. Elsie couldn't help because the twins caught the stomach flu and she's "up to here in fluids." Add that to the long list of reasons procreating is low on my to-do list. I feel terrible for her, but I also warned her not to take her kids to a place where the mascot is a mouse. That alone promises bad things.

I spritz my curls with a few more pumps of olive oil spray and paint on a final layer of the deep plum lipstick I picked up from Sephora on my way home from the store today. I don't know where Jasper is taking me, but curls and lipstick are good for any occasion. Dani told me skinny jeans aren't in style anymore, but I'm wearing them anyway. They make my ass look fantastic. I zip up my shiny patent leather Dr. Martens, which, while they aren't my beloved Birkenstocks, come in a very close second, and check myself out in the mirror. Forgive my ego, but good for me. I look fantastic.

I'd do me, but fingers crossed I won't have to because Jasper will.

I grab my keys and decide to go wait outside. My place isn't the hardest to find, but it's not the easiest. There are so many new complexes being built, it's kind of like a maze.

I lock the door behind me, and I'm walking down my well-lit hallway when the elevator dings. The doors slide open and Jasper steps out.

"Jasper? Hey." My pace picks up and I look at my phone again to see if I somehow missed his text, but there's nothing from him. "I must've missed your call somehow. Were you waiting long?"

When you don't live in my building and have access to the underground lot, parking is a bitch. It must've taken him ages to find a place to park.

"I didn't call," he says. "I wanted to come up and get you."

"Oh . . ." I stop short, not knowing how to respond.

Now, listen, I'm not saying I've only dated assholes in my life—because that wouldn't be true. What I *am* saying is that even in high school, guys would honk their horn or call to tell me to come out. I'm not sure coming to my front door is a chivalrous act worthy of knighthood, but it sure as hell feels like it.

The sales rep assured me my lipstick wouldn't smear, but I'm not willing to risk it this soon after applying it. So instead of biting back my smile at Jasper's sweetness, I let it fly. When I do, I'm rewarded as a matching smile spreads across his face and his eyes drop to my mouth.

My stomach clenches as memories of yesterday flood my mind. The feel of his mouth on mine, the slight ache on my scalp after he pulled my hair, the way his eyes sparkled as he laughed when I told him my best dad jokes over burgers.

I let him take me in and I return the favor.

Since meeting Jasper, I've seen a lot of different looks on him. He's been a DILF, a professor, an outdoorsman, and casually cool. But he's never looked like this before. Good thing, too, because if he had, I can say with great certainty that yesterday wouldn't have ended with a kiss. As it is, with him in my hallway, only steps away from my apartment, I want to grab him by the collar and drag him to my bed.

If someone had told me that Jasper would show up at my door wearing a pair of black trousers and a silk floral-print shirt only buttoned halfway, I'm not sure I would've believed them. I also don't think I would've thought that outfit would make my mouth go dry.

Yet here we are.

"Wow." I use every ounce of self-control I have to pry my eyes away from his exposed chest and back up to his eyes. "Serving some Harry Styles realness, are we?"

He nods, and his smile changes in a way I may not understand, but do like. "Just hoping for a little watermelon sugar."

My jaw drops open.

I don't know what I was expecting him to say, but it was not that. It feels like a small miracle I don't fall to the floor, my clothes evaporating into thin air so he can have his wicked way with me.

"If you want, we can just stay here." I ignore all social norms and go for it. Sure, we've only kissed a couple of times, but YOLO or whatever.

"As much fun as that sounds, and it does sound fun." He leans in and drags his hand up my back until he's cradling my neck and it's like I only have nerve endings where he's touching me. "We have a concert to get to."

I stop thinking sexy thoughts.

My eyes go wide and I start jumping up and down, my heavy rubber soles shaking the hardwood floors. "Oh my god! Really? A concert?"

Whereas books have never been my favorite, music has been a dependable confidant for as long as I can remember. There's just something about concerts, the music overpowering any thoughts you might have had and the bass vibrating throughout your body. It forces you to live in the moment and feel. Swaying with the person next to you as you sing along to the lyrics, which mean something different to every person in the crowd.

It's the best.

And now I get to go to one with Jasper Williams on my arm.

What a treat!

"You didn't guess? I thought it might be pretty obvious from the book what the activity would be." He looks so pleased with himself for pulling off a surprise that I decide not to tell him I'm notorious for being a terrible guesser.

He's very, very cute when he's happy, and it's something I realize I'd do many things to see as often as possible.

"I had no clue. I was a little worried you were going to take me to a book club and make me discuss what I read."

"No offense." He warns me that he's about to say something offensive. "But I'm not sure you're ready for that yet. I love doing book clubs, but most of the time they're smarter than me and notice things I didn't even realize I wrote into the story. Right now my only goal is for you to enjoy reading. We can work on analyzing the text down the line."

Oh good. That didn't even need the forewarning. I know I'm not at book-club level yet. Sometimes the Dirty Birds will force me to sit in on their meetings and I have no idea what they're talking about half the time. If I hosted a book club, the only question I would ask would be the same note I passed around in sixth grade.

*Do you like me?*
*Circle one.*
*Yes. No. Maybe.*

The end.

Then we'd eat, drink, and have a jolly time.

Which may be why Dani and Mona have worked with book clubs on the occasions when they—besides the Dirty Birds, obvi—come to the Book Nook.

"No offense taken, and anyways, a concert is a lot better." I tuck my phone into my crossbody bag and push the elevator button. "I'm just glad I wore my rocking shoes."

While I know they aren't the high heels I'm sure the women in his books wear, when his eyes travel the length of my body, landing on my clunky Dr. Martens, he looks at me like I'm the sexiest woman on the planet.

And then he acts on it, leaning forward and dropping his mouth to mine.

"Sorry." He pulls away. "I couldn't wait any longer."

Oh yeah.

This is going to be a good night.

For once, I didn't jinx myself with early cheer and excitement for the night. Not only was there no traffic, but Jasper must have a button that controls the stoplights, because we didn't miss one, not even an arrow.

It was witchcraft.

But even better was that after he found a great parking spot, we held hands as we navigated the crowded sidewalk on Colfax to get to the Fillmore Auditorium.

Now, it must be said that Red Rocks is obviously my favorite concert venue in Colorado. Maybe even the world—but I haven't been to many concerts outside of Colorado, so this could change. However, the Fillmore is my number two. I love a small standing-room-only venue. I appreciate the level of artistry it must take to entertain an entire stadium, but there's something so intimate and fun about bumping shoulders with strangers all night long, bonding as you belt your favorite songs at the top of your lungs.

"I can't believe you got tickets to see Red Autumn! How'd you know I love them?" I try to remember if I told him about them in passing or if maybe the Dirty Birds knew, but nothing comes to mind.

"I didn't, I just hoped." Even beneath the moody lighting of the auditorium, his smile shines so bright it takes my breath away. I know I'm not alone when the woman walking past us looks at him and then proceeds to spill her fresh drink all over the floor.

*Solidarity, sister.*

"Well, you hoped right. I'm low-key obsessed with them. I've been to a few of their shows and they're great live."

He tightens his hand around mine. "I'm excited to hear them."

Back when I used to have a life outside of stocking bookshelves and getting well acquainted with accounting software, I tried to hit as many concerts as I could. Didn't matter the genre—although I did have to cut back on rock shows after I sprained my wrist because I'd had one too many and got a little overexcited when I saw the mosh pit get going. I just loved getting out and meeting new people and hearing new music. My favorites were the small bands I stumbled upon while in random towns to take pictures.

I first saw Red Autumn on a whim. They're a group of four women—two sisters, and the other two are friends they made while gigging around Colorado. I don't know how they categorize their music, but they're like if your favorite pop girls decided to go alt rock, with a hint of folk. They can sing, dance, and play the crap out of their instruments. They're the shit, and if I had any musical talent whatsoever, I'd audition to be the fifth member of the group. Until I can do something about my tragic singing voice, I get to be a fangirl. Something I take immense pride in.

"Ooh!" I spot the merch booth in the back corner of the auditorium. "We need T-shirts!"

Jasper doesn't resist as I pull him through the crowd, weaving in and out of people and narrowly avoiding slipping on the beer-splattered floor. Unlike women who spend money on silk and lace nighties, my pajamas drawer consists of worn-out concert tees that are no longer appropriate to be seen out in public. My last Red Autumn shirt has seen her final day and I need a replacement to wear to the store.

There's no line when we get to the merch station and we're early enough to have our choice of styles and sizes.

"Can I get two of the black T-shirts, one in a medium and one in a—" I turn and eye up Jasper, not only to figure out his size, but because I like to eye him up. "And one in double XL, please." The man behind the makeshift counter nods but doesn't speak as he grabs our requested sizes while bopping his head to music playing over the speakers.

"How much?" Jasper asks, reaching into his back pocket to grab his wallet.

"Oh no you don't." I slap his hand away. "I'm buying the shirts. You got the tickets, I get the shirts. No objections."

Even though I said no objections, it's clear Jasper doesn't agree.

"You got everything the other day, this time it's on me. It's only fair."

Considering all I bought on our trip to Seven Falls was my gas, this doesn't feel comparable. But I can see that this is a fight I'm not going to win, so I try one last bargain.

"Fine, but if you get these, then you have to at least let me buy the drinks."

One side of his mouth pulls up into a smirk. "Deal."

When we look back at our T-shirt salesman, he looks none too impressed with our squabble or our negotiating skills. He spins the iPad around, mumbling, "Fifty-two dollars," and gesturing to where Jasper should insert his card.

Glad to see he loves his job.

Jasper signs the screen and I take the shirts, slipping mine over my head and probably ruining the curls I took way too long to perfect.

"What do you think?" I point to their name scrolled across the shirt in the signature script of their band name with an illustration of their beautiful faces beneath it.

"Love it." His cheeks go a little red and it's only then that I realize I asked him to check out my boobs. "It looks great on you."

"Thank you, I'm definitely wearing it to the Book Nook this week." If there's one perk to owning a business, it's being in charge of the dress code. I can't imagine having to show up to work each day in pantyhose and a blazer. Talk about hell on earth.

"Speaking of the Book Nook," Jasper calls above the building noise as the crowd around us begins to grow. "I was thinking you could do something like this there."

My eyebrows knit together as I look up at him. "Something like what? A concert?"

I'm not an expert by any means, but I think concerts need . . . I don't know? Space and some kind of equipment to perform or something. All things I do not have.

"Not a concert, no." He shakes his head and his unruly waves fall across his face. My palms itch to tuck his hair behind his ear, to see if it feels as soft as it looks. "Have an open mic night. Display your poetry books and let local artists perform in the nook. It might be something you and your customers enjoy."

I let the idea simmer for a minute before I realize he's right, I would like that. Just like I love story time, I love the idea of forming a more adult evening. It's surprised me how much I enjoy planning out the details and building community through the store.

But even though it sounds fun, I don't know if I'll act on it. I'm in charge at the Book Nook, but it still doesn't feel like it's mine. Every day I walk into the store, I do so trying to preserve the vision Gran had for the space. I need to make sure it evolves, but in a way I know she would be proud of. I would love an open mic night, but would she? That's something I'll have to think about a little longer.

"I really do like the idea. I'm going to think on it, see how it would fit in the store." I tell him the truth but leave out all the extra junk. For one night I want to have fun and live in the moment. I don't want to think about what tomorrow might bring or what happened yesterday—well, maybe the kiss, but def not my dad—only this exact moment. One where I'm a normal woman on a kick-ass date with the hottest, kindest guy I've ever met. I want to be a character in a book who doesn't live in her head and makes the most out of her life. "Now let me buy you a drink. If I'm going to dance, I'm going to need to be well lubricated."

I can tell he wants to say more about the open mic night, but he goes along with my subject change.

"I'd love a drink." He takes my hand again, but before we start walking to the bar, he pulls me against his chest, dropping his head to mine. "But I want to kiss you more."

I don't answer.

Well, not with words, anyway.

I loop my hands around his neck and pull his smiling face to mine, the entire world falling away the moment his lips hit mine. I drink him in, not at all worried about what the people around us might be thinking, and realize that I don't need a drink anymore.

I'm already drunk off of Jasper.

# CHAPTER 15

"Are you sure none of the kid germs are hiding under your fingernails or something?" I eye Elsie with suspicion as she dips her chip into the salsa. "I can't get a stomach bug. You know I can't handle throwing up."

It's been a few weeks since my concert date with Jasper and things have only gotten better. I've been dying to tell Elsie about everything, but she's selfish and had a life of her own to tend to.

"First of all, you're rude. Do you really think I don't wash my hands on a regular basis and go crazy when my kids are sick? My hands are still raw from how many times I've washed them and bleached the house." She holds her unpolished hands in front of my face like it's proof of anything other than busy mom life. "Second, bitch, how long do you think that stuff lasts? The kids haven't been sick for like three weeks and you know if there was any chance I could spread the hell I lived through to anybody, I'd be at home."

This is true. While Elsie can be a major asshole—like the one time she forced me to go on a double date with her cousin who got accepted into an Ivy League college and spent the entire night telling me all the reasons the schools I applied to weren't up to par—she wouldn't put my health at risk.

"Fair." I show my faith in her and decide not to ask for another basket of chips and salsa. "I'm glad everyone is on the mend in your house."

"Girl. You have no idea." She takes a sip of the giant margarita she ordered. "When you have as many kids as I do, when one gets sick, you try to fight it, but it's really a waiting game until it filters through the entire house. It's the saddest game of dominos ever played. I've never seen so much vom—"

"Nope!" I cut her off, not needing to hear that word while we're at lunch. "No details. I didn't want them on the phone and I don't want them now. Not ever, actually."

She rolls her eyes to the back of her head.

"Whatever." Even though we've been friends for ages, she still doesn't love my dramatics. "All I'm saying is that I'm glad it's over too. I was losing it. And apparently, I missed out on a hell of a lot with you. Daisy told me your dad showed his entire ass a while ago and now you're not taking her calls."

I fall back into my chair, regretting the moment I introduced Elsie and Daisy to each other.

"It's not that I'm ignoring her as much as I'm trying to figure out what I'm going to say to her." Which is also making me not take her calls, so I guess, technically, I am ignoring her. But whatever. "It's not like I'm planning on never talking to her again. Things have been going really well between us and I'm afraid I'm going to screw it up by calling Dad a fucking asshole in front of her. I don't want to fight with her about him."

"You do realize that she thinks your dad is a jerk, too, right?" Elsie narrows her eyes on me like she does when she catches her kids sneaking fruit snacks from the pantry. "She grew up with him; maybe she was looking forward to having someone she can also confide in. I know you had different experiences, but from what I've heard, your dad being a dick isn't an insular experience."

Blah. Having smart friends sucks.

It's really hard for me to keep my perspective when it comes to Andrew Young. Even though I'm glad we had a few mountains between us, part of me still wishes he had been around to go to my soccer games and school concerts. I wish I hadn't had to come up with excuses about why I couldn't go to the father-daughter dance or why he missed my graduations. I don't like to think of myself as an envious person, but sometimes it pisses me off that Daisy got all of that. Even if it was from our jerk of a dad.

"I guess you might be right." I grab another chip and chomp down on it with a little too much gusto. "I'll call her tonight."

"I have an even better idea." Elsie looks beyond smug as she puts her margarita on a paper coaster and pulls out her phone. "Why put off for the future what we can accomplish today?"

"You better be fucking with me, Elsie Kamille Cooper." My voice drops to a whisper so the nice couple across from us won't have to hear my foul mouth over their lunch. "You're a mom now, and I would hate to fight you in public."

She finishes typing on her phone and looks me dead in the eye. "Try me, Drew. You know you could never take me."

I can only hold her stare for a few seconds because she's right, I do know that. Yoga keeps me in shape, but Elsie has a natural scrappiness I could never compete with. Plus, she's been carrying children or car seats for the last four years; her upper-body strength is incredible.

"Fine." I pout and fall back into my chair. "You win, but I'm not happy about it."

"Well, you better get happy because here she comes." She looks over my shoulder and I think she's lying until she stands up, shouting, "Daisy, hey! We're over here!"

Friends are overrated. There really is something to be said about living that recluse life. But I can only wallow in my poor life decisions for a moment before the chair beside me is pulled out and Daisy's long body folds into it.

"Daisy! Um, hey." I sound every bit as uncomfortable as I feel. "How are you?"

"I'm okay." She sounds as awkward as I do. The usual pep and excitement in her voice are missing. "I'm sorry if this—I mean, Elsie said it would be fine, but I know everything with Dad and . . ." She trails off, closing her eyes and taking a breath so deep that I feel it. "I can leave if this isn't okay with you."

"No," I answer without hesitation and grab her hand in mine. "I'm glad you're here."

"Really?" Hope sparkles in her blue eyes and embarrassment causes the margarita I've been sipping on to sour in my gut.

As much as I try to tell myself that my dad doesn't control me, here I am, letting him dictate my relationship with Daisy. I've given him so much power without even realizing it. And that ends now.

"Yes, really." I tighten my grip on hers, anxious to say what needs to be said. "You know my relationship with Dad isn't great, and I don't see that ever changing. I know he does what he wants without ever considering anybody else. I don't hold his actions against you, but I know you have a different relationship with him. I was worried about offending you because there's a one hundred percent chance I'll call him an asshole in front of you at some point. I thought a little distance would be better than fighting over him."

"Oh my god. I think Dad is an asshole too! You should hear my sessions with my therapist." She pulls her hand out of mine and tugs me into a tight hug. "I'm embarrassed it took me so long to understand how he left you, but I want you to know that I would never judge you for your feelings toward him. I've given you so much space because I didn't want to force you into a relationship where you felt uncomfortable."

"Wow. Look at this." Elsie leans into her chair, looking mighty smug for someone who was knee-deep in bodily fluids not long ago. "Who would've thought that a simple conversation would've fixed everything? But now that you've kissed and made up, is it time to talk about Jasper yet?"

"Oh yes!" Daisy drops her arms around me like I'm a bad habit. "I'm super far behind on everything, I need all the details. Last I heard you were going on a hike?"

"They went to Colorado Springs to see some waterfalls and she got Jasper sick and he spent the entire time throwing up." Elsie sums up my date with brutal efficiency. "Which is what she gets for thinking exercise is an acceptable date. But now Jasper has taken over and they've been doing book stuff, which I've been MIA for, thanks to sick kids."

I've been acting like I didn't mind not talking to Daisy, but with her not around and Elsie out of commission with her family, I haven't had anyone to talk to about all the developments in my relationship. It's been killing me. I almost bought a notebook at Target the other day and started journaling.

"Oh my god. You two." I lean in and drop my sunglasses on the black steel table. "I have so much to tell you!"

"Hurry up and spill!" Elsie follows my lead, taking off her sunglasses even though the Colorado sun is high in the afternoon sky and shining in her face. "I didn't ask my mother-in-law to babysit to not to get all the details."

Because Elsie has been with Brandon for what feels like centuries, she missed the hell that is dating apps and the casual hookups of adulthood. She's been trying to live vicariously through me for years; it's just that—unfortunately for both of us—my dating life sucks. I've had a handful of exciting one-night stands that left her sated, but otherwise it's been a depressing cycle of jerks who are selfish and mediocre at best in bed. So me going on dates with Jasper Williams, the man who apparently writes her favorite romance novels, is a dream come true for her.

"Seriously." Daisy cosigns. "I've been dying to know what has happened between you two. I almost started writing fan fiction about it."

I try not to but I can't help but laugh at that. Jasper showed me some fan fiction sites the other day. I was telling him about my favorite show that was canceled after one season and I fell into a deep rabbit hole of short stories shipping my favorite characters. I guess you could say my stance on happily ever afters is beginning to shift because I almost burst into tears when one story ended with Ginny and Mike having a little baseball team of their own.

"Okay, okay. So we all know about Andrew Young busting into the store, right?" Even though most diners opted to sit in the air-conditioned restaurant instead of on the patio, I still drop my voice to a juicy gossip-worthy whisper.

"Yesss . . ." Elsie is also whispering as she draws out the word, and Daisy nods along.

"Okay, well, that sucked, obviously, but Jasper showed while it was all going down."

Daisy sucks in a sharp breath. "Oh, wow. Dad left that part out of his story."

"I bet he did." I don't bother to bite back my grin. "Anyways, after he left, Jasper walked me back to Gran's office—"

Elsie cuts me off to correct me. "You mean your office."

"Fine, my office." Now I'm the one rolling my eyes. "If you two keep interrupting me, we're going to be here all day, right?"

"Honestly? That's what I'm hoping for." Elsie picks her glasses off the table and slides them back on her stunning face. "Did you not hear my story about being stuck in a house with four sick children?"

That seems fair.

"Whatever." I hide my grin by taking another sip of my drink. "So Jasper comes with me to *my* office and ends up asking if he can kiss me."

Across the table, I watch as Elsie actually, physically swoons. Her eyes flutter closed as she slides down her chair until I can only see her sunglasses and the top of her head.

"Oh my god." She pushes herself up, and when she takes her glasses off again, I swear I see hearts in her eyes. "He asked if he could kiss you? That is so Jasper."

One of the things I love most about Elsie is that she's the total optimist to my pessimist. She can find the best in any person she meets, even the totally shit ones. She's the first person I turn to when I have a problem because her brilliant mind—literal rocket-science smart—can attack any problem with logic and reasoning, but in the next breath she can point out all the bright spots and how I can overcome whatever challenge is plaguing me.

And she's a total romantic.

"You've only met him once. How can you say that's so him?" I pretend to be annoyed by her statement of fact, but she can see through my lies.

"Because we've read his books," Daisy answers for her.

"His *fictional* books." I remind them both of something they should be well aware of, since out of the three of us, they're the only two who have read his work. "But whatever, he's an amazing kisser. Top tier, actually."

"Oh yeah he is." Daisy nods, a shit-eating grin spreading across her face.

"I knew it! That man is way too fine to be a bust!" Elsie forgets about the conspiratorial whispering we were doing and shouts. The couple sitting four tables away turns and stares at us with open curiosity.

I smile at them before narrowing my eyes on my oblivious best friend.

"Can you not?" I hiss beneath my breath. "People are staring now."

"Well, let them stare, girl." She's still yelling. "You made out with Jasper freaking Williams! You're the one who should be screaming from the mountaintops."

"She's not wrong." Daisy cosigns and high-fives Elsie across the table.

*Why, oh why did I introduce the two of them again?*

"Are you two finished or would you like me to continue?" I try to sound snooty but suck at it.

"Hmmm . . ." Elsie cocks her head to the side and taps her chin with her pointer finger. "I guess I'll let you finish."

"Geez. Thanks, Kanye." The sarcasm is heavy in my voice, and even though I know she doesn't miss it, she def ignores it. "So now we kiss . . . a lot, which is fun. But we're also going on our book dates."

"Oh! This is what I've been dying to hear." Daisy rests both of her elbows on the tabletop. "Where did you go?"

My stomach does its best Simone Biles impersonation as I recall the amazing dates we've been on. It's like Jasper is singlehandedly changing my thoughts on dating. I'm certain no other person on this earth puts as much thought and care into planning a date. Nobody has ever made me feel so special and I've had to constantly remind myself that this isn't a forever thing.

"The first date, he took me to see Red Autumn." Even though it's a hot, dry day in Denver, it doesn't stop the shivers from racing down my spine as I remember the way he stood behind me with his arms wrapped tight around my waist, swaying with me as I belted out the lyrics to all my favorite songs. "Then he took me to the Renaissance Festival, which was so much fun that I can't even tell you."

The last time I went to the Renaissance Festival, I was like eight and Gran took me because my mom had to work an extra shift on the weekend. All I remembered was flower crowns and riding elephants—which I'm against now that I'm an informed adult. It was a fun day, but it has nothing on going as an adult, when you can indulge in booze, shout "Huzzah" at the top of your lungs, and the man on your arm looks as if he could play a prince in any production.

Also, the flower crown was still top-notch.

"Oh really?" Elsie asks. "I was thinking about taking the kids this year. Do you think the twins will like it?"

"I think I have no idea what mini humans enjoy, but I did see a lot of children who were smiling, so maybe?" This might be why Elsie doesn't ask me to babysit often. And I'm okay with that.

"You're the worst." Elsie rolls her eyes, but she's smiling, so I don't take too much offense.

"Did you do anything else?" Daisy gets us back on track and I appreciate her focus.

"Not anything big." I grab my previously frozen margarita and take a long sip. "I've taken him to a couple of my favorite restaurants and to see an art show at Abend Gallery. He's been working and I started the next book on the list."

It's been dangerous, because it almost feels like we're a normal couple and not virtual strangers with a definite end date looming.

A couple of weeks ago, Jasper started coming into the Book Nook on days I work, bringing his laptop to work on his next great novel. He sits in the same rocking chair every morning with a large cup of coffee and a breakfast burrito from a restaurant around the corner from his place. I try to leave him alone, but I can't help the way I gravitate toward him, always checking the shelves around him and jumping at the opportunity to answer any question about Colorado he may have. I love watching the way he leans into his computer and pecks away at the keyboard. When he gets stuck, his eyebrows furrow together and he glares at the computer screen before reaching into his snack-filled backpack and pulling out a Red Vine to munch on.

"That's fun and cute. But I think what we really want to know is if you've seen the man naked yet," Elsie says, and I choke on my spit at the forwardness of her question.

"Oh my god." I take a giant sip of my margarita to try to calm my coughing. "I can't believe you asked that."

"Why?" Elsie asks. "You know I live vicariously through you and this is the first time in our adult lives that you're actually serving. I need details . . . and lots of them."

Daisy says nothing, but she nods so hard that her topknot comes loose.

"There are no details." I hold back my laughter when they both look like I've kicked their puppies. "But I have been thinking of our next adventure and I could use your help."

"Ughhhh." Elsie throws her head back and her sunglasses slip off her head, hitting the concrete beneath the table with a crack. I'd be surprised if they survived. "You know I can't help with outdoorsy crap."

"That's why I need your help." I explain what I thought was obvious. "The first time, he got sick. I need to show him what I love about Colorado, but in a way he can enjoy. You're the best person to ask for help."

"I guess you're right." She perks back up but doesn't bother to grab her glasses.

"Oh!" Daisy slaps my arm. "What about a mini road trip? Nothing too far, maybe something two or three hours away so you have uninterrupted talking time."

"Yes!" I hold up my hand for a high five this time. "Now you're thinking. Let's build on that."

We sit around the table, planning my date, only stopping when our waiter brings us food and/or new drinks.

And by the time we're finished, Jasper should be worried that he's not the only person who can plan a book-worthy day out. I just hope mine has something of a happy ending as well.

# CHAPTER 16

"Want another licorice?" Jasper waves a Red Vine in my peripheral. "We're starting to run low, but we still have popcorn and jerky left."

You'd think after spending so much time with Jasper over the last few weeks, I'd be over that butterflies-in-my-belly feeling by now. I know I'm not a relationship expert or anything, but there's no way this is a sustainable feeling. It has to fade away at some point. But for some reason, every time he says "we" with such ease, my insides go wild.

"I can't say no to Red Vines. It's one of my fatal flaws." I snatch it from his hand and rip off a bite before I can think better of it. I always steal them from him when he's at the Book Nook; he's started bringing an extra pack just for me.

"Death by licorice isn't one I've seen before; it should lead to an interesting obituary." There's laughter in his voice, but he's kind enough to keep it under control.

"Did you know that black licorice can be toxic in large amounts? It messes with your potassium levels, gives you high blood pressure, and fucks up your heart." Do I know anything that can come in handy and help me turn my business into a cash cow? Absolutely not. But I do know random facts about licorice, and who is to say which is greater? "Plus, it's disgusting. So there's also that."

"It really is awful." He tosses the bag I stuffed full of junk food in the back seat. "I can't imagine liking it so much you poison yourself."

The drive to Salida is a little under three hours, but you wouldn't know with the amount of crap I packed for us to eat. Good thing, too, because Jasper already demolished the peanut M&M'S, more than half of the Red Vines, and all the Chex Mix . . . and we still have the ride home tonight. Thank goodness the car doesn't affect Jasper like the altitude did because I wouldn't even want to imagine the horror that could happen.

"Thanks for clearing your schedule for today." I keep my eyes on the road in front of me. Not looking at him makes it much easier to say the things that make me feel more vulnerable than I'm comfortable with. "I know this is further than we've gone before, but I'm really so excited to show you Salida. It's one of my favorite places."

It's been so much fun showing Jasper the local things that I've let this part of the plan fall behind. Plus, it's much easier to go out for an evening than it is to take an entire day. Luckily, Dani needed to pick up an extra shift and I was able to slip away.

The best thing about Salida is there's so much more than hiking that—hopefully—we can avoid any altitude issues this time around. I have the entire day planned and I can't wait to see his face when he sees what we're doing.

"I don't know why you're thanking me; you've done all of the work." His hand drifts over the center console like it has done a few times during the drive, and he rests it on my bare knee. It's such an innocent touch, he never moves it any higher, but the way his thumb draws circles on the sensitive skin on the side of my leg makes it hard for me to focus. "I'm lucky enough to sit back and enjoy this beautiful ride."

I wanted the entire day to explore, so I forced Jasper into my Jeep before sunrise. It was so early, in fact, that for the first time since I can remember, I didn't hit any traffic as we left the city behind us. It might be the first time Jasper didn't hear me swearing like a sailor behind the wheel.

The Colorado mountains sat in front of us, and as the sun rose, the dark sky brightened into the blue that sets my heart on fire. When the trees grew nearer and the boulders rose around us, breathing came easier as we rose and fell with the road.

A lull in conversation falls over the car. It's not uncomfortable— it's never uncomfortable between us—but there's been a question that's been nagging my mind for the last few days. I didn't know if I was going to ask him, but now seems like the perfect time.

"So, no pressure or anything if you don't want to say." I preface my question in case I'm overstepping. "Are you ever going to tell me what this book you're writing is about?"

"Do you want to know?" He sounds surprised I'm asking, and I guess I can't blame him. If I haven't made an effort to read the books he's already written, why would I care now?

"I do, but being up-front, part of my curiosity is purely selfish." So sue me, I want to know what my travel guide expertise is going toward.

He squeezes my knee and his deep chuckle touches all the places his fingers don't. "That's fair. I'd want to know what I was helping with too."

He makes my nosiness seem more noble than it is, but I won't argue with him.

"It's about this guy, Eli, a thirty-three-year-old accountant who moves to Denver to start over after a divorce. He was always a romantic, but the nasty end of his marriage left him feeling pessimistic and out of sorts. He's disappointed with the way his life has gone so far. He's always played it safe in life and decides to start taking some risks in his new city."

"An angry man with a chip on his shoulder? Two points for a realistic character." I joke, but I'm also intrigued.

"I do what I can." Amusement laces his words. "So in order to do what he promised himself, he signs up for a wilderness survival course. He goes to weekly classes that end in a weeklong camping trip in the mountains. Of course, when he gets to his first class, he realizes his instructor, Ash 'the Griz' Pelman, is in fact not the bearded giant he assumed he'd be meeting, but a beautiful woman with eyes as dark and haunting as the forest they'll be exploring."

"Oh! As a woman named Drew, I appreciate this confusion a lot." Nothing romantic has ever happened from the countless real-life misunderstandings I've dealt with, but I appreciate his spin on it.

"I'd be lying if I said your name didn't have anything to do with it," he admits, and my stomach somersaults beneath my seat belt. "I always knew it was going to be a book exploring the outdoors with a fish-out-of-water approach, but when I met you, this idea popped into my head, and it's worked out so well. So please thank your mom for me."

"Next time I talk to her, I'll be sure to mention it." It's been such a nice change of pace to be able to talk to my mom about things that don't make her worry. I haven't told her about Dad's latest antics because why would I do that? But she's living for Jasper Williams, Author, updates. "How far into the book are you? Do you still have a lot left?"

"I'm a little past the midway point. The weekly classes are finished and they're about to go on the camping trip. Their relationship hit a high point and now I get to create chaos and rip them apart."

I chance a look at him and he looks as excited as he sounds.

"Should I be concerned by how happy you seem to be about ripping these fictional people apart?"

"I'm only excited because it means I get to put them back together at the end." His voice drops a decibel or two. "I'm not in the habit of overlooking a good thing when I see it."

I know we're talking about a book—and maybe Elsie, Daisy, and all the fictional characters I've been reading about are beginning to get to me—but I can't help but think he's talking about us.

Us.

Because as much as I've been trying to guard my heart around him, my defenses are crumbling. When I'm with him, it feels like there is an "us" to be had.

"Well, maybe I will finally pick up a Jasper Williams book and not just because I better be in the acknowledgments either." I try to make light of how deep I'm falling. "It sounds great. I'm excited for you."

"Thank you." He lifts his hand from my knee and tucks the one stinking curl I can't keep out of my face behind my ear. "That means a lot to me."

I don't know what to say, so I say nothing. A new song plays through the speakers; Taylor's voice singing about broken hearts and second chances settles around us as the road begins to flatten. Salida spreads out in front of us and the familiar view never fails to take my breath away.

"Welcome to Salida!" I turn down the radio and check the clock. "We don't have to check in for our activity for another hour. Do you want to stop in town and grab some real food before heading over?"

And by real food, I mean coffee. It's been hours since my first mug and I'm desperate for more.

"Sounds good to me." Jasper peels his gaze away from the picturesque town in front of us and aims his perfect smile my way. "Are you going to tell me where we're going? I mean, I already know it has something to do with water since you forced me to buy a swimsuit."

Not only am I terrible at guessing surprises; I'm even worse at keeping them. The fact that I've been able to keep the details of this trip to myself is a minor miracle. I'm convinced the only reason Elsie's kids like me is because I give them their birthday presents weeks before their actual birthdays and then buy more so they have something to open on the day from me. Elsie calls it the parade of presents, but hey! Gotta win them over somehow.

"And that's the only hint you're getting." I glance over at him, still not used to how gorgeous he is or that he's spending all this time with me. "But you can swim, right?"

"Yeah, I can swim." The tone of his voice doesn't match his answer and I can't figure out if he's telling the truth or not. "I'm not going to the Olympics or anything, but my mom put me in lessons when I was a kid."

*That should be fine . . .*

"Okay, as long as you know the basics, I guess."

"Why? You're not making me do extreme water sports, right?" He sounds almost panicked and grips my knee so tight, I think I might have finger-shaped bruises in the morning.

"I mean . . ." My eyes shift from the road to his nervous face and back to the road again. "How extreme is extreme? Let's just say you might come away with a great new experience for Eli to try out in your book."

"Oh god." He lets go of me and leans into the back seat, grabbing the almost empty bag of licorice. "I think this might call for another Red Vine."


THE LAST TIME I WENT white water rafting was at least three years ago. I was trying to make some new friends and signed up for this photography clinic in Steamboat Springs. One of the activities was shooting while on a raft. It was amazing.

Some Coloradans might shun me, but I'm not into winter sports. I love taking pictures of the snow-covered mountains, but strapping wood to my feet and speeding down the side of a mountain? No, thank you, not interested. I much more enjoy a leisurely hike when it's warm outside or kayaking across one of our beautiful lakes. White water rafting is a little more adrenaline spiking than I'm used to, but I love it.

And I thought Jasper would too.

But I think I might've been wrong.

"Are you sure you're okay?" I ask him again. His skin is still looking a little pale and the flash of terror that shone in his eyes when we checked in hasn't quite disappeared. "We don't have to do this if you don't want to."

I hope he doesn't want to cancel because not only do I think he'll end up having an amazing time, but he looks very hot in his sunglasses and helmet. I was hoping to hold on to him when the rapids got rough. Though now, seeing how anxious he seems, he might be the one holding on to me.

Whatever.

I just want as much physical contact with Jasper Williams, Author, not outdoorsman, as possible.

I can see his mind working as he weighs all the different options. It isn't until a family of four with their two children in tow joins us that he speaks up.

"Let's do it." He snaps the clasp of the helmet beneath his chin before turning very serious eyes my way. "But if I die, I'm putting you in charge of finishing this final book."

Oh good.

Even the idea of having to write a book makes me break out in hives.

"Then thank goodness you're going to be fine, because if that were to happen, I'd have a lot of very angry Jasper Williams fans on my hands." And after seeing how intense they are live and in person, that's the last thing I'd ever want.

"All right, rafters!" A man with long, wavy blond hair and an unclasped life jacket and helmet claps his hands together, gaining the attention of the group. "Welcome to Salida Rafting. I'm Jason, this is Rex, and over there with the tie-dye helmet is Georgia, and we're your guides for today. We're going to be taking an all-day rafting adventure down the Arkansas River, though beautiful Browns Canyon, stopping about midway for lunch and some splashing around. Are you ready?"

The kids from the family standing in front of us raise their arms in the air, shouting out whoops of excitement, and I whoop along, nudging my nervous partner to join in.

"Woohoo!" My loud shout draws a quiet chuckle out of Jasper. "Let's do this!"

The kids in front of us turn around and we exchange high fives as their amused parents look on.

"That's what I like to see!" Jason points to us before turning to the other guides. "I call dibs on that group."

There's a lot of laughter and the not-so-quiet rush of the river filling the air, but I can still hear Jasper's groan through it all.

"Don't worry." I turn to face him, forcing him to lean over so I can wrap my arms around his neck. It's much more difficult with the bulky life vests between us. "I promise this is going to be fun. You've spoiled me with a concert and trip to the festival; it's my turn to give you an experience you won't forget."

"You don't need to try hard for that." He leans in closer, looking at me over the rims of his glasses and giving me the perfect view of the way his eyes sparkle from the reflection of the sun and the water hitting them. "Every time I'm with you is an experience I won't forget."

My heart spasms in my chest.

It's times like these when I wonder if this is all too good to be true. If this is the real Jasper and not some character he's portraying. I don't know how somebody could possibly be this perfect. How he can make me feel the way he does.

I want to figure out a way to hold on to him forever.

"All right, lovebirds, enough of that." Jason brushes past us, high-fiving our preteen group members. "Let's go over the rules and regulations so we can get out on this water and have the best day ever."

We all climb into the raft, Jasper and me in the front, the brothers behind us, and their parents in the third row, with Jason and a solo rider at the rear. We aren't in the water yet, so it's easy to focus as Jason shows us how to secure our feet—which are encased in rented booties—into the raft. He hands out oars and makes us complete a dry run as he shouts out different commands. We all catch on quick and our paddles slice through the crisp air, which is already starting to warm up. By the time we drag our raft to the mouth of the river, Jasper's nerves seem to have disappeared.

"I can't believe we're doing this." His grin is practically taking over his entire face as he looks at me from across the raft. "Thank you for planning this."

"I figured what better way to learn about Colorado than to experience it?" I'm so relieved he seems excited for this. I would've hated it if he only did it for me. "Plus the views from the water are so different from the views of hiking. I wanted you to get them both firsthand."

"I can't wait." Something shifts on his face. His smile gets smaller, but not any less dazzling.

I want to ask him what just happened, what he's thinking, but our little rafting partners who aren't really little—one is definitely an inch or so taller than me—pull our attention to them.

"This is going to be so awesome, Jasp!" Oliver, the younger brother, who's sitting behind Jasper, shouts. I don't even try to hold back my giggle at the nickname.

"Yeah, you're going to love it. I went with my summer camp last year and I loved it so much that Ollie got so jealous and made Mom and Dad take us this year," Sawyer, the older brother, sitting behind me, says. "Except this is going to be better because last summer we only got to do it for one hour and this one is all day. It's going to be epic!"

I look across the raft at Jasper, his golden skin pulled taut across the bulge of his biceps, and realize that Sawyer is one hundred percent correct.

"You're so right." I tap my oar to his. "This is going to be so totally epic."

The river currents pick up the raft and we start down the river. It's a smooth ride at first, enough to trick anyone into thinking this will be a relaxing afternoon jaunt on the water. But soon the water picks up, and the choppiness below us splashes water into the raft.

"Four two!" Jason shouts over the sound of the roaring river. We all dig our oars into the water, pulling hard against the current two times. "Great job!"

Our speed picks up and the brothers shriek with delight as the cool water hits them. The raft bounces along, jumping into the air as the water divots and swirls. Jasper's deep laughter rises above the noise around us and his joy wraps around me, keeping me warmer than the bright sun beating down on us ever could.

"Here comes the first drop," Jason warns the group. "Everyone prepare!"

I wiggle my feet, making sure they're secure, and tighten my grip on my oar. When I know I won't bounce out of my seat, I chance a look at Jasper to make sure he's okay.

He's looking right back at me, his smile so big I worry it might break his perfect face. "Best day ever!"

"THAT WAS AMAZING," JASPER CALLS across the raft as we help pull it ashore at the end of our eighteen-mile journey. "I already want to do it again."

"Right?" My cheeks hurt from smiling and my throat is sore from laughing and screaming so loud. "I'm so glad you were up for it."

I'm not ready for it to be over. I groaned like Oliver and Sawyer when Jason told us we were approaching the end. When I booked today, I assumed that after six hours, we'd be wiped out when it was over. I forgot about the way the adrenaline rush hits after a day like today.

A big yellow school bus is parked on the road and people from the rafts that got here before us are already filing on board. Staff members stand in different locations instructing us where to drop our oars and life jackets, and telling the people who wore wet suits to keep them on until we return to the base.

I was not one of the people who opted to wear a wet suit. The last time I went rafting, it was earlier in the season and they were required. Now, I'm not ashamed of my body. Do I have some bumps and curves some people might have an issue with? Sure. But they don't bother me. I enjoy eating and hate the gym, so it is what it is. However, no matter how confident I am with my body, there was not a chance in hell I was going to squeeze into a wet suit in front of Jasper—it's like putting on Spanx, but a million times worse. I would've vetoed the entire excursion if they made me.

I thought because I wouldn't have to flop around—my body completing head-to-toe jiggles—I was avoiding all issues pertaining to the body-ody-ody.

I thought wrong.

The problem is that while all the people in wet suits are still fully clothed as they board the bus, when Jasper took off his life jacket to place it in the proper pile, he also removed the wet tank top he had underneath it. So now he's standing in front of me in nothing but his swim trunks and chest.

Just chest.

Everywhere.

And I've forgotten how to human properly because I can't stop staring.

I knew he was in shape. He's mentioned CrossFit enough for me to know he actually does it and it isn't just a joke. But what I maybe wasn't expecting was how his skin would glitter like the skin of some kind of tan vampire who feeds off the lust of people around him. I didn't think he would have the perfect amount of chest hair—not too much that it's a coat, but enough that I know he doesn't wax—or that his abs would be rippling like he lives in the gym. You can tell he works out, but he likes beer and burgers. His body is hard and it's soft.

It's just like Jasper.

Perfect.

"Lunch was great and all, but I'm already starving again," Jasper says, forcing my attention from his broad chest to his gorgeous face. His cheeks are red from time under the sun and his dark hair looks even darker now that it's wet and curling at the ends. "What do you say we grab dinner before we head home?"

"Food sounds great." But Jasper sounds better.

I did a pretty great job of planning this day trip, but I totally underestimated how much I would want to kiss him in public. And while I loved our raft mates, Oliver and Sawyer were not the best wingmen. In fact, they were terrible, what with making all the kissing noises whenever Jasper and I would come close to having a moment and splashing us with water and yelling, "Cool it!" every calm moment we had.

Jasper links his fingers through mine before pulling me gently into his side and touching his lips to my forehead. "Then it's settled," he whispers into my ear.

Despite the scorching summer weather and being pressed into his warm skin, chill bumps cover my arms as we climb up the steps to the bus. Jasper's grip on my hand never loosens as we make our way down the narrow aisle. The group of women celebrating their friend's upcoming nuptials go quiet when we pass them, all their attention lasering in on Jasper. My skin tingles when their stares fall to me and I try not to imagine what's being said through hushed voices.

Jasper slides onto the vinyl seat, giving my hand a slight tug so I fall into place right beside him before his arm drapes over my shoulders.

We don't say anything as we sit and wait for everyone to board the bus. Instead, we let the silence say everything neither one of us is prepared to. I knew today was going to be fun, but I wasn't prepared for it to make me feel as close to Jasper as it did. I let my eyelids fall shut, trying as hard as I can to preserve this moment for the rest of my life.

It was the perfect day and it's not even over yet.

# CHAPTER 17

---

"I CANNOT BELIEVE THIS IS HAPPENING RIGHT NOW." MY HEAD FALLS against the white-painted cinder-block wall behind me as I wait for the mechanic to update us.

After the buses dropped us back off at the parking lot where our cars were, we hopped in and drove to downtown Salida. We parked along the street and wandered around, taking in all the Victorian buildings, which are still in peak condition. I took Jasper to my favorite restaurant on the river. We ate and talked as we watched the kayakers glide by, reminiscing about our time on the river. It was the perfect ending to a perfect day.

Then we climbed into my Jeep, ready for the long drive home . . . and nothing.

The car wouldn't start.

I called a tow truck, hoping a jump was all I'd need, but of course it wasn't.

I guess I was starting to get a little confident that spending time with Jasper could be nothing but wonderful and the universe needed to bitch-slap me back to reality. And props to her, because nothing says *bitch-slap* like your car breaking down when you're three hours from home.

"I'm so sorry." I close my eyes to avoid looking at Jasper. I mean, talk about embarrassing.

"You need to stop apologizing." His grip on my thigh tightens. "This isn't your fault."

While I appreciate the effort and the fact that he's not technically wrong, he's not right either.

My Jeep has been on her last legs for a few years now. I should've traded her in ages ago. But even though I try to deny it, I'm sentimental AF. I've had this Jeep since high school. All my adventures happened in it. I just couldn't get rid of it.

Until now.

The freaking traitor.

The second I get back to town I'm taking it to the chop shop.

"Drew?" An older Black man in oil-stained coveralls pushes through the door connecting the garage to the office.

"That's me." I step forward when I notice his eyes are trained on Jasper. "Please tell me you were able to fix it."

I'm close to begging, but I don't even care.

"I was able to figure out what's wrong. You're going to need a new fuel pump." His gravelly voice carries a thread of remorse and I brace when he continues. "Now, I can fix that, but unfortunately, the only place I can get the piece from closed about an hour ago and doesn't reopen until noon tomorrow."

My stomach falls to my feet and I think I might get sick.

"Okay . . ." I draw out the word, trying to process what this means at the same time I'm trying not to cry. "So what should we do in the meantime?"

"Well, there's not much to do. If you're going to want your car driving back to Denver instead of on the back of a truck—which would cost you a pretty penny—you're gonna have to stay close by. I'll do my best to get the piece over here and I'll work on your car soon's possible, but there's nothing I can do tonight." To his credit, the mechanic looks very remorseful as he breaks this horrendous news to me. "There's a hotel right around the corner. You can walk over there and see if they have any rooms. If you tell them Titus sent you, Cheryl will give you a deal."

I look up at the popcorn ceiling, blinking my vision clear. Out of all the days, all the places for this to happen, it had to happen here, with Jasper? What god is working so hard to smite me? I need someone to make it make sense.

"Okay, thank you." I nod when I'm convinced I'm not going to cry or punch the wall. "Could you give us a minute to figure out what we're going to do?"

"Course, darling." Titus's voice goes soft and wet hits my eyes again.

Dammit, Titus.

He heads back into the garage and Jasper steps in front of me when the door slams shut.

"Jasper. I am so—"

"Nope. Do not even think about apologizing to me." He cuts me off. "If you need to go back to Denver tonight, we can figure it out. But I don't have anything to be back for and am fine staying here for the night."

It's a struggle, but I try to think rationally.

As much as I want to throw my car away, I can't afford to buy a new one. I also can't blow the money on a tow from Salida to Denver on top of repairs. The Book Nook is closed on Sundays, so it isn't like I'll need to find somebody to cover for me if I'm not back tomorrow. As big of a pain in the ass as it's going to be, staying for the night will be the best in the end.

"Are you sure?" I feel terrible. He's already taken so much time out of his writing schedule for me, I don't want to take more of it. "I can stay and find you a car service to get you back to Denver."

"Do you really think I'd just leave you up here alone?" His eyes narrow, and for the first time since all this went down, he looks irritated.

"I mean, I've stayed in Salida alone before. It's not that, it's—" I stop and take a breath as I try to gather my thoughts. "I know you're busy. I don't want you to lose more time when you have deadlines and work to do."

"Don't worry about that. For once, I'm actually ahead of schedule." He steps in closer so I'm forced to look up at him. "But even if I wasn't, I'd choose spending extra time with you over that any day of the week."

Wow.

That was sweet.

"Okay, if you're sure." I reach out and take his hand, lacing our fingers together. "Let's go tell Titus we'll be back tomorrow."

He nods and his eyes soften in a way I don't understand, but like. "Sounds good to me."

Granted this isn't the way I envisioned today ending, I guess there are worse things than spending a little extra time with Jasper.

TITUS DIDN'T LIE: THE HOTEL was right around the corner from his shop.

We push through the heavy front door and it's like we step back in time. Dark wood vintage furniture is placed all around the space. Touches of the original architecture are evident everywhere, from the hand-carved crown molding to the antique chandeliers lighting the space. The casual click of my flip-flops feels completely out of place as we approach the front desk.

"Hello." An older woman with white hair curled and tucked greets us. Her eyes are warm and welcoming, a pleasant reminder of all the reasons I love this small town so much. "How can I help you tonight?"

"Hi." I return her kind smile, thankful that if my car had to break down, it did so in a town with a cute hotel and nice people. "Titus sent us over. We need two rooms for the night."

"Oh no." Her lips turn downward. "I love Titus, but it's never good when he has to send you over. Let me see what I can find for you."

"Thank you so much." All I want is to take the longest shower imaginable and go to sleep. The sooner that can happen, the better.

"Of course, dear. Let's see what we have here . . ." She looks away from us and stares at her computer screen as her red-painted nails make quick work of the keyboard. Her eyes narrow as she works, but when her frown deepens, my stomach twists into knots.

"Please don't tell me you're booked." I know they aren't the only hotel in town, but I really don't feel like walking to the other options.

"Unfortunately, this is our busy season." She stops typing and her eyes flicker between me and Jasper. "While we can't accommodate two rooms, we do have one open if that could work for you."

One room?

"Ummm . . ." I bite my bottom lip and look at Jasper, unsure of what to say. "What do you think?"

"That's fine with me if you're okay with it."

Am I okay with spending the night in a room with Jasper? Oh yeah. And mysteriously, I'm not so tired anymore.

"Okay, we'll take it." I reach for my purse to grab my credit card, but before I can, Jasper is handing her his.

"Jasper! No, you—" I start to protest, but he cuts me off before I can finish my argument.

"I can and I already did." He looks smug as the woman takes the card from his hand, swiping it without hesitation. "You worry about your car. I have this part covered."

I think about arguing some more, but for once, I don't. One of the things that I love most about my relationship with Jasper is that it feels even. I don't feel as though I need to prove myself to him. He's never made me feel as though I owe him anything and it's the first time in maybe forever that I feel safe enough to simply say thank you.

So I do.

"Thank you."

And then I get the encouragement to do it for the rest of my life when the lines around his eyes soften a millisecond before his lips touch mine.

He doesn't pull away before whispering against my mouth, "No thanks necessary."

"Here's your key," the woman I loved before this very moment interrupts. "You're in Room 203. Go up these stairs here and to the right."

I grit my teeth, forcing a smile as Jasper takes the key and thanks her.

Even though the walk to our room is short, it's still long enough for me to think of every reason sharing a room with Jasper could be horrible. *What if I snore? What if he snores? What will I do in the morning when my breath is awful and my hair is worse? What if I talk in my sleep and mumble how much I like him?*

By the time Jasper slides the key into the door, I've worked myself into a full-blown tizzy. I'm about to apologize for all the things I might do to embarrass myself while I'm sleeping when he pushes open the door and flips on the light.

And light speed fast, all my worries about snoring disappear.

In the book Jasper has me reading, the characters manage to get stuck in some crazy snowstorm. They find shelter in an abandoned cabin, but there's only one bed. I remember laughing at how ridiculous it all was. But as I look at the one and only queen-sized bed in the middle of the room, I stop thinking about how implausible it seemed and remember what came next.

All of a sudden my doubts and criticisms about books being unrealistic fade to oblivion and I hope beyond hope that I get a happy ending of my very own tonight.

# CHAPTER 18

THE ROOM IS VERY NICE.

The stuck-in-the-past look ends with the lobby. The room is comfortable and equipped with all the modern touches one could hope for. A flat-screen is mounted to the wall between what look to be original light sconces. A large rug protects the thin wooden-plank floors. There's a giant painting by the door, but unlike in most hotels, it doesn't look like a mass print made just for temporary spaces. Instead it feels just as unique as the space it's filling.

However, I can't focus on any of this.

Not when the only thing I can see is the single queen bed in the middle of the room. Can you say *awkward*?

"Ummm . . ." I pry my eyes away from the bed and try to keep some of the hope out of my voice. "Is this okay?"

After seeing him shirtless for so long today, it has to be okay. I don't know if it will be possible to lie so close to him and not make a move.

"Yeah, I mean, sure." He trips over his words in a very un-Jasper-like manner. "This is fine with me if it is for you."

*Oh, I am so, so, so fine with it.*

"Yeah, I'm okay with it." Trying to sound like you don't want to throw someone on a bed and rip their clothes off is much harder than I ever knew, but I think I'm succeeding. Maybe? "Is it okay if I hop in the shower first? I'll hurry so you can take one after."

I need to get away from him for a minute. I need to cool off and get myself together so I can act like a normal human being.

"Yeah, go ahead." He lets go of my hand and flips the latch on the door. "No need to hurry, though, I'm a bit of a night owl so I'll be fine."

He's a night owl? I've learned so much about him during our time together and each new tidbit feels like a gift. I love knowing this about him.

"Cool, thanks." I turn and rush into the bathroom.

I flip on the lights and lock the door behind me. I close my eyes and take a deep breath to gather my wits before I move to the deep shower and crank it all the way to hot.

I slip the straps of my dress off my shoulders, letting it fall to the ground before peeling off my bathing suit.

"Fuck." My change of clothes is in the back of my Jeep, and while I don't mind going to bed commando, I worry that might be a little bit too forward.

The steam from the shower billows around the curtain and the mirror begins to fog. I step in, avoiding getting my hair wet by instinct even though it was already soaked from the river. The hot water hits my skin and my muscles loosen, the stress washing away with the salty remnants of the day.

I think about the heroine in the book I'm reading. The way she takes charge of her wants and needs. When she was in this situation, she didn't sink into her head. No! She took what she wanted, and there's no reason I shouldn't do the same.

I love kissing him. It's pretty much all I've thought about all day every day since the first time it happened. I want more. I've wanted more, and maybe this is a sign for me to initiate it.

I grab the small bottles of hotel-issued body soap and lather the washcloth with renewed vigor. My car broke down? Who cares! I get to share a bed with Jasper freaking Williams. If that's not turning lemons into lemonade, then I don't know what is.

After scrubbing away all the dirt and sweat of a day spent exploring, I moisturize with the watery hotel lotion and try to twist my curls into something presentable. The mirror is still fogged up, so I'm able to convince myself that the shower worked miracles and I look sexy(ish). I take one last deep breath before unlocking the bathroom door and stepping into the room wearing nothing but my towel.

Jasper is sitting on the edge of the bed with his eyes on the TV when I walk in.

"Do you like—" He starts and stops when he gets a good look at me. "Wow . . . you . . . wow." The tips of his ears turn red. "Sorry. I don't mean to stare. It's . . ." He drops his gaze down my body, studying me like he'll be tested later. "You're really gorgeous."

At the beginning of our little arrangement, I thought his compliments were empty. Now I know that's not the case. From the way he kisses me to the thought he's put into each of the dates he's planned, I'm positive there's something between us. Usually, I don't think twice before going after someone I'm interested in, but he's different. He's dangerous. Because I know once I let all my guards down, I have no chance of ever putting them back up.

I just didn't realize until this very moment that Jasper felt the same way.

"Jasper." I take a small step in his direction and somehow my heart is beating harder than it did during the entire ride down the Arkansas.

His voice is a whisper of a breath when he speaks again. "If you want, I can—"

"Jasper," I cut him off, repeating his name a little louder this time. He hesitates for a moment before lifting his chin, looking at me beneath those thick lashes of his. No matter how much I want to look away—to close my eyes and jump—I don't. I hold eye contact and keep moving to him until my toes brush against his. "I want you to stay. I want . . . I want you."

Then I drop my towel.

The sound of the TV fades into the background and all I hear is his sharp inhale of breath.

"Jesus, Drew." His gaze drifts down my body, slowly taking in every dip and curve along the way. Goose bumps dance across my skin, but I'm not sure if it's from the cool breeze of the air conditioner or the feel of his eyes on me. "You . . . fuck."

I feel like I should be ashamed by how much I'm enjoying watching him struggle in front of me, but I'm not.

The opposite, to be honest.

If he never touched me, I think I'd still be able to get off on the memory of him in this moment. I love the way his voice is so hoarse, he sounds like a stranger. I never want to forget the way his muscles are so tightly corded as he twists his hands into the comforter to hold himself back. I'll dream about the way his eyes go black before he bites his lip.

But wow do I want him to touch me.

And I want it now.

I inch closer, sliding my leg in between his and putting my hands to the back of his head, tangling my fingers in his long hair like I've wanted to do all day. I pull gently, angling his head so our eyes meet again. I open my mouth to talk—to plead—but Jasper beats me to it.

"How are you real?" He lets go of the comforter, moving his hands to my bare back. "How did I get invited to speak at a book club meeting and end up getting to be here with you?"

"I don't know." My breath catches in my throat as his hands begin to move lower. "You're lucky, I guess."

His arms tighten around my waist and he pulls me into him so that I'm on his lap. I'm straddling his thighs with my chest pressed into his, our faces so close that I couldn't look away if I wanted to. So close that I see the absolute sincerity as his voice drops to a whisper and he says, "The absolute luckiest man in the entire fucking world."

Then the room flips and so do I.

I'm no longer on his lap.

I'm on my back in the middle of the bed, the antique chandelier only visible for a moment before Jasper is over me. His body fills my vision and I watch with acute focus as he pulls his shirt over his head, tossing it to the side, a cocky smile spreading across his face before he moves to all fours and crawls up the bed.

Holy shit.

After kissing him, I knew this was in him. But knowing something and seeing it are two completely different things. Watching him moving up the bed, seeing this wild and uninhibited side of him that he shields so well from the rest of the world, makes my mouth go dry.

I swallow hard, the air thickening around me as he hovers over me, trapping me between his arms and legs. He seems bigger than ever, his abs tightening as he drops to his forearms on either side of my body. He lowers his head and his soft lips touch my neck. He drops kisses, licking and nipping as he moves ever . . . so . . . slowly . . .

Until finally.

His mouth grazes the skin between my breasts. The light touch causes my entire body to clench with need. My nipples harden and my inner muscles clench as my back arches off the bed, desperate for more.

His tongue slips out between his lips and he draws a trail from the base of my breasts, nipping as he moves up my neck.

"I write dreams, but never, not in my wildest imagination, could I have dreamt up anything better than having you naked underneath me." His words send shock waves through my body. "You're everything I never thought I could have. And I'm never going to let you go."

I want to tell him I want that. That I never want him to let go. That I could lie here with him, savoring the sound of his voice and the feel of his breath against the shell of my ear, for eternity.

But then he gives me more.

So much more.

The weight of his body collapses on top of me, his mouth leaving my ear and slamming onto mine. His lips are firm against mine and any patience he had is gone. He pulls my lips between his teeth, pushing his tongue into my mouth the second he releases them. I'm meeting him exactly where he is, trying to tell him without words how I feel about him. How much I want— No. How much I *need* this.

His hands are frantic. Moving down my hips, one going beneath me, his fingernails digging into the flesh of my ass as the other doesn't falter before finding the wetness between my thighs. He doesn't miss as he deftly draws circles around the bundle of nerves currently in control of my entire body.

I tangle my fingers into the strands of his thick, wavy hair. My fingers tense against his scalp as I pull his head back, needing him to see me.

Needing him to witness the way he makes me completely undone.

"Oh my," I rasp as the pressure between my legs begins to build. "I'm going to—"

Jasper's hand disappears and he cuts me off before I can finish . . . in every way imaginable. "Oh no you don't."

But before I can even cry out in frustration, his mouth replaces his hand and the sound dies in my throat.

I don't know when the last time I've felt anything like this was.

I'm used to casual and meaningless. Easy and fast. But this? This is anything but. It's intimate and beautiful. Deliberate and monumental.

With a curve of his lips and dip of his tongue, Jasper exposes a piece of myself that I've been fighting for years to keep hidden. Laid out beneath him, I feel something I've never felt before. For once, I'm not worried about what's coming next or how to protect myself from the pain tomorrow might bring. In this moment, I can accept that things are good and for the first time in a really long time, I'm safe.

Jasper slides his arms beneath the back of my thighs, wrapping his hands around them, spreading me open.

"Eyes on me, Drew," he rasps, his voice deep and thick, before his mouth is between my legs.

I do as he says, our eyes locked together as Jasper watches. He toys with me. Switching between fast and slow, gentle and hard, until it doesn't matter anymore.

"Jasper." His name is a moan and no matter how hard I try to keep them open, my eyes flutter shut.

Pressure begins to build low in my belly and anticipation tingles up my spine. The sound of my breathing melds with my mews of pleasure as my back arches off the bed, as the sensation builds and builds until it finally explodes. The black behind my eyelids turns fuzzy and my lungs freeze, trapping my scream in the back of my throat as remnants of my orgasm ricochet until every nerve ending in my body is lit up.

Jasper never loosens his grip on me. He holds me tight, eating me as he draws out every last tremor until my body goes limp.

"Please tell me you have a condom," I whisper when my breathing begins to slow.

The light is still on . . . another first for me, and I get a perfect view when his eyes simultaneously soften and heat as he slides his hand into his pocket and pulls out his wallet.

I narrow my eyes in his direction. "You're still wearing pants?"

"I don't know if you noticed or not"—his smirk deepens and it makes my insides tighten—"but I was a little preoccupied."

Oh.

I noticed.

My cheeks heat, but not from embarrassment. Even though it just ended, I need more. His mouth was great . . . wonderful. But now I need to feel him inside me.

And I need it now.

He's taking his time, pulling the condom out of his wallet, but I can't wait any longer. I snatch the wrapper from his hand and tear it open with my teeth.

"Damn." Jasper's wide eyes are intense on me, lust and amusement written all across his beautiful face. But thankfully, as I'm learning, Jasper's a man of action. He only watches for a moment before his hands move the waistband of his shorts and he pulls them down along with his underwear.

And wow.

What a fucking treat.

From the bulge in his pants, I assumed he wasn't lacking in that department. But as it springs to life in front of me, I realize I didn't give him even close to enough credit.

He is a work of art.

It should be said that while I refuse to get a Brazilian wax—I did it once and just no, I'm not spreading my butt cheeks under fluorescent lights, absolutely not—I do take the time to prune my garden, if you will. And what a lovely surprise when I see that Jasper has done the same. Everything is neat and cared for and it only accentuates how blessed this man is. Large and thick . . . but not to the point that I'm scared for my vagina; it makes me want him inside me right this second.

I unroll the condom down his shaft, my stomach—and other parts—clenching when it twitches in my hand.

As soon as the rubber reaches the base, I push him flat onto his back.

"My turn to play now." I climb on top, straddling his hips and resting my hands on his chest for leverage before lowering myself onto him. Ever so slowly, I slide down, my eyes closing as I take him in one inch at a time. I don't rush it; I let my body expand as I take my fill of him.

"Jesus, Drew." His breathing is labored as his hands find my breasts. "Nothing in the world better than this. Feeling you. Watching you take me. Best in the fucking world."

I've never been into talking during sex before.

But I guess I've never had sex with Jasper before. Because hearing him snaps the little thread of restraint that I had.

Slow is a thing of the past. I push myself down, taking all of him and savoring the feel of him as my body struggles to adjust. I ride him hard and fast, taking all of him until the only sounds filling the room are our moans and the sound of our skin slapping against each other.

After what Jasper gave me, I didn't think there was any way I'd have another orgasm, and definitely not as huge as the one that almost wiped me out. But as I feel the familiar sensation begin to build low in my belly, I know it's not only possible, it's probable.

"Fuck, Jasper." My nails dig into his chest, needing to hold on to something. "I—I—"

That's all I get out before Jasper is out from beneath me and taking charge. He flips me onto my back, never missing a beat as he slams back inside of me.

"Don't hold back, baby." He grabs my ankles and spreads me

wide in front of him, never slowing his pace as he locks me in place, leaving me no option but to take what he's giving me. "That's it."

He lets go of one of my legs, his hand moving directly to where I need it, and that does it.

"Oh my god!" I don't care who hears me. In fact, I hope they do. I hope I wake up the entire town of Salida as the second orgasm rips me wide open. My vision turns Technicolor and my legs wrap tight around Jasper as his weight falls on top of me. His groan registers deep inside me and his pace slows with his final pumps of release.

He stays on top of me and I wind myself around him like a baby koala, clinging tight to him as our breathing evens out, both of our bodies slick with sweat.

"That was . . ." I try to think of any word that could accurately describe what that was but come up empty. "I don't actually know what that was, but I do know it was the best I've ever had."

I'm sure there are countless articles written advising women to say the opposite of what I just said. I bet most people would think I was crazy not to hold my cards close to my chest, not letting Jasper know how much he obliterated my freaking world. But I don't care.

Because as someone who has never had great before, I know exactly how hard it is to find. And now that I got it, I'm not going to hesitate to let him know how much I like it. If things go down between the two of us, it won't be because I played stupid games.

I like Jasper.

I more than like him.

And it's time I stop being afraid of it coming to an end and do whatever I can to make sure that never happens.

"The best." His lips touch my forehead and his happy, sated eyes take me in. "But I got you all sweaty again. I think it's only fair that I wash you off this time."

"I mean . . ." I bite back my smile, pretending to consider this offer. "I guess fair is fair."

He tightens his arms around me and takes me with him as he rolls us off the bed. My giggle fills the room as he runs to the small bathroom and only sets me on my feet when we're in front of the shower.

"Best day ever, Drew." He takes my hand in his as we wait for the water to heat up. "Every single second of it. Thank you."

I don't know what to say to that.

So I don't say anything at all.

Instead, my fingers find his hair again and I pull his mouth to mine. And I don't let go. Not when we're in the shower, and not after when we get dirty all over again.

And again.

# CHAPTER 19

---

THE WORLD IS A LITTLE BIT BRIGHTER WHEN YOU'RE GETTING IT good on the regular.

The air smells sweeter, food tastes better, sleep comes easier.

My skin is clearer.

This must be what people in musicals feel like. So happy that you have to burst into song at any given moment. It's just too bad I can't carry a tune.

Three weeks have passed in the blink of an eye.

"So I'm thinking the bar could go right here." I show Mr. Jenkins the spot where I want to install the coffee/wine bar in the Book Nook. "You can see that we don't have a ton of free space, so I'll need it to be compact and efficient."

He scratches a few things down on his tablet before snapping a few pictures of the space.

"I think this is the perfect space for what you want." He adjusts the stylish gold-rimmed glasses that look so good on his round face. "And your timing is great. We're finishing up a project now, but then we're free to get started within the next month."

After I talked to my mom about the coffee bar, she convinced me to take the leap. The store can't cover the cost on its own right now, so I am dipping into the money Gran left me. It feels right spending it this way. She would've liked it.

I interviewed more construction crews than I ever wanted to and finally reached the final two. I'm between Mr. Jenkins—who I know from when I went to high school with his son—and Henry, whose estimate was a little lower, but it would take him longer to get in here and get it done.

Either way, I don't think I can go wrong. They both had a ton of positive reviews and seem to think it will be a pretty easy project.

"That would be great, Mr.—" I stop and amend my sentence when he narrows his eyes at me. "Sorry, Mike. Old habits and all."

His straight teeth are a bright white against his dark brown skin. I wasn't the closest with his son in high school, but Mr. Jenkins was at every sporting event, cheering on the teams and donating to every fundraiser we had. He's a great guy and I'm about ninety-nine per-cent sure I'm going to go with him.

"You were always the most polite of Anthony's friends, but I al-ready feel old enough in here seeing you running this place. Calling me Mike is really doing me a favor."

"Well, you haven't aged a single day." It's the god's-honest truth. If I were to hold a picture of him from ten years ago to now, I wouldn't be able to tell the difference.

"You're trying to get me to knock the price down a little more, aren't you." He winks before patting me on the shoulder.

"That wasn't my plan." I drop my voice to a conspiratorial whisper and lean in a little closer. "But is it working?"

"Maybe." His deep, hearty laughter, which I always thought sounded like Santa Claus's, bounces through the store and makes my already good mood even better. "I'll get back to you with the final number tomorrow, if that works for you."

It's better than okay.

"That would be wonderful." When I first mentioned this idea to a few people, I was warned time and time again about how slow the process would be. Now that I have my heart set on the coffee/wine bar, I want it as soon as possible. I blame overnight shipping; I have zero patience anymore. "Thank you so much. I can't tell you how much I appreciate this."

"From where I'm standing, it's me that should be giving my appreciation." He takes a step toward me and drapes his arm over my shoulders, pulling me in for a quick side hug. "Tell your mom I said hello, will you?"

"Of course I will."

I walk him to the front door and we say our final goodbyes. The door closes behind him and I turn to find Dani, who's just as excited about this project as I am. But I barely get five steps in before the bell rings over the door.

Since getting back to Denver, Jasper and I haven't gone twenty-four hours without seeing each other. Even if we don't have time for a proper date, he sits in the back of the store, one of us grabbing food and turning the nook into our personal date spot.

Oh.

And then there's sex.

Lots and lots and lots of sex.

We're like horny teenagers. Only now it's so much better. Not only because we don't have to sneak around and have sex in the car—a terrible experience with a gear shift will haunt me forever—but because we both know what we're doing.

And by we, I feel like I mean Jasper.

I'm not saying I'm terrible in bed—far from it, thank you very much—but I am saying that Jasper is a wizard. Even when we go for a quickie, I still get mine at least once, but on more than one occasion, multiple times.

All this to say that I'm basically a fucking Pavlov's dog at this point. If my phone rings or a text comes through or the door to the Book Nook opens, my stomach clenches and my nipples get hard in anticipation of being with Jasper again.

I spin on my heel, prepared to launch myself at Jasper if it happens to be him, but come to a sudden stop when another handsome man fills the space inside the entrance.

"Connor. Hi." I greet him, beyond thankful I remembered his name. "How are you?"

I look behind him, bracing in case this is another ambush and my dad is hot on his heels.

"Don't worry. Andrew isn't here." He reads my thoughts. "I haven't spoken to him since that day in the store."

I'm sure there are people out there who are better humans than me who would feel bad hearing this. I mean, it did seem to be a business deal and I shouldn't wish bad things on anyone and their livelihood. Especially not my own flesh and blood.

But what can I say?

I am my father's daughter and I'm def not that good of a person.

"I'm a little biased, but that's probably for the best."

"You aren't wrong." His brown eyes sparkle with laughter and his smile widens. "I wish I knew that before I wasted all my time on the phone with him and giving you a bad first impression."

"Oh please." I wave a hand in front of my face. "You aren't the first and you won't be the last person who gets pulled into my dad's shenanigans."

As the offspring of Andrew Young, who very unfortunately shares his name, I know not to hold anyone else accountable for his selfish actions.

"Glad to hear that." He moves deeper into the store, a shy smile making his boyish features look even younger. "I wasn't able to look around like I wanted to the last time I was here and it would've sucked to get kicked out twice."

I already knew he was attractive, but away from the stench of my father, I can appreciate it a little more this time. He's still not Jasper—nobody is—but now I see the adorable little dimple pop out in his right cheek. He's in jeans and a T-shirt, but he's wearing them with the same confidence he wore his suit and tie with. There's a swagger about him that's a stark contrast to the good, preppy-boy persona he gives off, and I'd be lying if I said I wasn't intrigued.

"That would've sucked." I nod in agreement. "But I think you're safe this time."

His eyebrows reach for his hairline. "You think?"

"You might be a little bit of a troublemaker." I keep my tone light and teasing, but I can't help but remember the reaction Jasper had to seeing him. So even though my dad isn't with him, I haven't let my walls down around Connor Walsh. "But since you seem to be on your best behavior for now, would you like a tour of the store?"

"I'd love that." He catches me off guard with the intensity of his smile. "I really only saw the nook section last time, but I'm interested to learn more about it. Unfortunately, Andrew didn't know much about the store."

Shocker.

"He wouldn't. It's hard to know about a place you've almost never stepped foot in." I stop and take a deep breath, not wanting to let my dad get me worked up and ruin what was shaping up to be a fantastic day. "But enough about him. Let me give you the grand tour."

The store isn't very big, so the grand tour only takes about twenty minutes, with me pointing out all the projects Gran and I did together on top of the ones I've done since she's been gone. I tell him about all the trips to the flea market to nail the aesthetic of boho shabby realness that Gran was going for and how I struggled to keep the vibe cohesive when I created the kids' nook.

"And this is where the coffee/wine bar is going to be." I gesture to the space to the side of the cash register. "We'll get rid of these display tables to make space for the bar and add a few freestanding tables so customers can sit with their coffee. It's too small in here for a lot of tables, but we'll put a few more out front and then drop some poufs around the store so people can plop down and read."

I haven't been back to the flea market since Gran passed, but with the coffee bar coming, I'm going to have to get over that particular obstacle. It's the only place I can go to get tables and chairs for the space. Unfortunately for me, IKEA doesn't carry the same charm that Rosalie's booth does. It's going to suck, but I've been thinking of inviting Jasper with me. Maybe holding his hand while walking the grounds will help to ease the pain I can no longer avoid.

"And you're sure a coffee bar is the best investment for the Book Nook?" Connor's question knocks me off-balance. Throughout our little tour, he's listened intently and doled out an appropriate amount of compliments. He asked a few questions, but they were more about how I came up with the story time idea or how long it took Gran and me to complete our DIY projects.

This question feels loaded.

"I am." I try not to narrow my eyes as I answer. All of a sudden, his bright smile seems more deceptive than friendly. "I've done a lot of research on coffee being sold at bookstores, and I've talked to our customers. This is something they want. It's an investment we're prepared to make."

"And that's great . . ." He trails off. His eyes dart around the store and he hesitates for a moment, like he's not sure he wants to say what's about to leave his mouth. "Okay. Can I be straight with you?"

I didn't realize he wasn't already being straight with me.

"Um, yeah. Please." Knots form in my stomach as I replay our conversation and try to remember if I told him anything that I shouldn't have.

"I didn't just come here to see the store today. I came in over the weekend and looked around when you weren't here." He shoves his hands into his pockets and rocks back onto his heels. He keeps his eyes trained on the old carpet that I should probably also look into replacing. "I came in to talk to you."

"For what?" I slap my hand over my mouth because I most definitely didn't mean for that to come out the way it did. "I'm sorry. I'm not sure I understand what you need."

Because right now it feels like maybe he's hitting on me and that can't be the case.

"I mean, for the obvious reason, the day we met was a total disaster. I wanted to check and make sure you were okay after that." He looks up from the floor and his pale cheeks are tinged with pink. "But also, you're gorgeous and I wanted to see you again."

Okay now . . .

What in the Keanu Reeves hell is going on here? There has to be a glitch in the Matrix or something. Because really. I didn't go years and years without interest from anyone beyond a night of fun to two different but hot and smart guys showing interest in me.

"I . . . uhhh . . ." I try to remember what words are and how to use them. "Really?"

"Yeah, really." His smile shifts and I realize that he is nervous. "Andrew ambushed you in your place of business and you handled it like a total pro. As a person who's also dealt with a shit dad my entire life, I loved every second of it. I almost wish he stayed so I could see him get removed by the police."

"Honestly?" I drop my voice to a whisper despite nobody being near us. "So did I."

Connor throws his head back and laughs so loud that I see Dani peek her head around one of the bookcases to see what's happening.

While I wouldn't wish having a dad like Andrew Young on my worst enemy, there's an understanding that comes from people who've also had to deal with the emotional torment of a manipulative parent. A sort of kinship that allows you to feel seen and less alone. Like they won't judge you for daydreaming about your father being put in handcuffs.

It's really nice.

"Well, I hate to break it to you"—Connor swipes at the corners of his eyes—"but I think you might still be able to. Andrew's phone calls and emails to me have only increased in the last few weeks. I don't know exact details about what he's planning, but he seems pretty certain that he's going to be granted the rights to this property."

This isn't a surprise to me. I knew as soon as my dad walked out that door that he'd be back. He has it in his mind that he's entitled to the Book Nook and he does not like to lose.

What is a surprise, however, is why he's telling Connor about it . . . and why Connor is telling me.

"I knew he wouldn't give up that easily." I point toward the back of the store and Connor nods before I turn to walk to Gran's office. "I don't even remember when Gran bought the Book Nook; I just know I can't remember a time in my life when this building wasn't part of it. This is where I came every day after school until I was in high school. I spent weekends here helping Gran when business started picking up. I hung up streamers and spent hours assembling balloon arches decorating the nook for the surprise birthday party we threw her when she turned seventy. Gran loved it here. The Book Nook was a huge part of her life and nearly all my memories of her take place within these walls. My dad isn't in a single one."

Connor stays in step beside me. I can feel the intensity of his gaze on my face as we walk, but he stays silent, listening as we approach the office. I pause outside the office door and squeeze my eyes shut to fight the stupid tears that always want to fall when I think about Gran for too long. Once I know I have it together, I draw in a deep breath through my nose and plaster a smile on my face. I push open the door and gesture Connor into the tiny office.

"I'm sorry he's doing this to you," Connor says, and I think he really means it. "I'm sure you can guess that it's not exactly company policy to let you know what my client is planning, but something about this really isn't sitting well with me. You don't deserve to be blindsided by Andrew."

While I appreciate all he's saying, I'm still not understanding why he's telling me. It's hard for me to believe this is all out of the kindness of his heart.

"Thank you for sharing this with me. It's really nice of you . . ."

"I feel a *but* coming on." He fills in my pause, accurately reading my tone.

"But . . ." My smile is weak as I confirm his feelings. "I don't understand why you're telling me this or why my dad feels so comfortable telling you his plans. Who exactly are you, Connor Walsh, and what are you planning to do here?"

He reaches into his pocket and pulls out his wallet. Flipping it open, he pulls out a card and hands it over to me. I take the embossed business card from his hand like it's a snake about to bite. Familiarity dances on the outskirts of my mind, and when I flip it over, everything finally snaps into place.

I walk around to the back of my desk, pulling open the top drawer and shuffling papers and pens around until I find what I'm looking for. I grab the business card I found all those months ago when I was organizing Gran's files and hold it next to the one Connor just handed me. Prose and Fable's name is in bold print with their calligraphy pen logo at the top of both cards. Beneath it, Connor Walsh's name in simple script, followed by his chief operating officer title.

"I knew your name sounded familiar." I keep my eyes on the matching business cards. "Now, are you going to tell me the full truth this time? What's going on here and how did you know my gran?"

# CHAPTER 20

I DON'T KNOW HOW LONG I STAY IN GRAN'S OFFICE AFTER CONNOR leaves, but by the time I head home, the sky is dark and the store is empty. I think I remember Dani stopping by my office to let me know she was leaving, but I can't even be sure. I was frantic, tearing apart Gran's desk to try to find anything that might confirm what Connor told me.

But of course, there was nothing.

The drive home is a blur as I try to fight back the demons threatening to consume me. I haven't felt like this in months. Not since the day Gran passed. Somehow, though, it feels worse this time.

Because at least when Gran died, I was able to be mad at the world.

Right now, I'm mad at her.

I walk into my apartment, slamming the door shut behind me. The pictures on my wall rattle and I revel at the feel of my floors vibrating beneath my feet. It's small, but it's something. Getting any of my anger out, feeling the release I've spent months and months denying myself, helps ease some of the resentment starting to bubble over.

I think about calling my mom, asking for her advice, but I shut down that idea almost as soon as it comes. Every time I talk to my mom, there's a sense of hesitation in her voice. It's as if she's waiting for me to finally snap. I've worked for months to convince her I'm okay and she's safe to settle into her life in Tennessee. If I called her now, I'd have a permanent guest in my one-bedroom apartment and neither of us want that.

I drop my purse on the rug leading into my apartment, not bothering with the hooks where I usually hang it. I pass my couch, ignoring my TV, which is currently housing two unwatched episodes of *Housewives*, and march into my bedroom. I throw the shoes scattered around my closet haphazardly over my shoulder until I get to what I'm looking for.

I yank the box I shoved in the back corner months ago out of the dark. I hope I'm not opening Pandora's box, but I don't think it's possible for things to get worse.

I dump the contents across the emerald-green down comforter I splurged on a year ago. Pictures and papers fly across my bed, the rosary Gran kept hanging on her bedroom mirror scatters to the floor, but no answers come spilling out.

I toe off my Birkenstocks and climb onto my bed, desperate to make sense of something I have no control over. Hoping Gran didn't throw me to the wolves without leaving me with any clues about how to navigate it.

I keep thinking back to the sympathetic look on Connor's face as he recalled the meetings he had with Gran. How she sought him out, not the other way around. How she expressed her desire to sell the Book Nook but wanted to make sure that if she did, her family would be well taken care of. Apparently that's why he took my dad's calls at first. He didn't realize my dad wasn't the family she was talking about in those meetings.

I don't know what to believe, but a part of me that I want to ignore is screaming that Connor is telling the truth. I called the lawyer in charge of Gran's will, hoping he had something I may have overlooked in the pandemonium following the reading of her will. Of course, because my luck is what it is, he's on vacation and won't be back for another week.

So now I'm stuck riffling through old notes, old pictures of her curly white hair and bright smile, remembering the way she made me feel as if I had a place in the world. I'm stuck staring at pictures of a woman so full of life and knowing she's gone. I'm frozen, lost in the past, trying to figure out how in the hell the world hasn't fallen off its axis without her powerful presence holding it upright. Wondering how Earth is still spinning without the force of her laughter and the comfort of her patience.

I pick up the picture of her standing beside me in the back room of the Book Nook. We're facing each other, and I'm laughing, my curls all over the place as my head is thrown back and my eyes are closed. Gran is wearing a bright pink sweater, her pendant resting on her chest. Her white hair is curled and tucked behind her ears, and her cheeks are nearly as rosy as her sweater. She's watching me, her smile's huge, and I feel like if I stare hard enough, I'll be able to feel her hand on my shoulder again.

I remember this day. I was in college and had come home for spring break. She was my first stop. I remember her face when she saw me as I walked through the door, but for the life of me, I can't remember what we were laughing at in this picture. The pride she had for me is practically bursting off the matte paper and I remember that. But at the same time, I've forgotten, and as I try to recall this moment, this conversation, I realize that what I have left of her is fading. I can't remember the exact tenor of her voice or what her perfume smelled like when it mixed with the scent of her shampoo.

No matter how hard I've tried to cling to every piece of her, she's still drifting away.

A knock at my door breaks my concentration. I glance at my watch and my heart rate kicks up a notch when I see how late it is. Nobody should be knocking at my door at this time of night.

Slowly and quietly, I climb off my bed. I look around my room for something that could be used as a weapon and vow to buy a baseball bat after work tomorrow. I start to tiptoe through my apartment, cursing myself for not bringing my phone to my room with me. There are a few more knocks as I creep around my living room like I'm the burglar, when a voice I've become very familiar with calls my name.

"Drew?" Jasper calls from the hallway. "Are you in there? It's Jasper."

I take a deep breath, willing my pulse to slow before I unlock the door.

"Jesus." I swing open the door, my eyes narrowing on him for a millisecond, before stepping out of the way as an invitation to come inside. "You can't knock on a person's door at eleven o'clock at night. You scared the crap out of me."

"You said you were coming over to my place after work. I called you like ten times." He never takes his attention off me as I go to my purse and pull my phone out. "I was worried about you. Are you okay?"

When I finally find my phone buried deep beneath old receipts, the screen stays black until a battery icon flashes across the screen.

"It's dead." I show him the screen even though I'm pretty sure he already saw it. "I'm so sorry. I can't believe I forgot to come over."

"It's fine." His eyes are alert, but his tone is gentle as he walks toward me. "Are you okay? You seem upset."

"Connor Walsh stopped by the Book Nook today and filled me in on a few things I didn't know." A humorless laugh falls out of my mouth as I realize what a gross understatement that is. "So yeah, you could say I'm a little bit upset."

He comes to a sudden stop and his head jerks back.

"Connor came back?" He says Connor's name like it's acid on his tongue. "For what?"

"How much time do you have?" I fall onto my couch, suddenly feeling beyond exhausted and wanting this all to be over. "It was quite the doozy."

His lips quirk at the corners. "A doozy? I haven't heard that word in a long time."

He drops onto the couch beside me, not hesitating at all before his arm's around my shoulders and he has me tucked tight into his side. I don't fight it. I push in closer, needing all the comfort I can get if I'm going to rehash this story.

"Well, apparently, Connor knew my grandma. They spoke a few times before she died because she was considering selling the Book Nook." Jasper's body goes tight beside me, but he doesn't say anything as he listens to me recall the earlier conversation. "Connor works for Prose and Fable. I guess one of their new ventures is acquiring small bookshops that already have ties with the community, but putting them under their name. Because of the Book Nook's long-standing relationship with its customers and prime Denver real estate, it made Gran the optimal target for them."

I leave out the part where Connor told me they offered Gran a high six-figure offer if she sold everything to them outright or that she said she would get back to them . . . but passed before she could.

"Just because they spoke doesn't mean she was planning to sell." His voice is like a balm to my soul, but it's too little, too late. The hurt and anger have been marinating for so long that I don't know if anything can extract it.

"She was interested, Jasper." My voice breaks when I say his name. All the emotions I've been suppressing are coming to the surface. I close my eyes and take a deep breath, trying to push them back into submission, but they power through, the tears falling silently down my cheeks, the pressure in my chest deepening with every breath. "I gave up everything so I could run the store in a way that would make her proud. I wake up and I go to sleep wondering if I've made the right decisions by her. I don't do anything in that store if I don't think it will fit the vision she had. And now I find out that she might not have wanted it at all anymore?"

I bury my head in Jasper's chest. I don't want him to see me this way. I'm ashamed of the things he'll see written across my face.

"It's been a year since I found out I got the store. A year of stress about money. A year of fighting with my dad more than normal. A year of ignoring my career to nurture her legacy and try to keep this piece of her alive." I hiccup, my tears coming harder as Jasper turns me fully into his body and wraps me tight in his arms. "Why would she do this to me?"

And there it is.

The real reason for the tears. The real reason this pain feels like someone has plunged a knife into my chest and made me watch as they twist it.

"She's the only person I had." I feel like I'm drowning. The grief I've worked so hard to ignore, the fucking anger I've pretended didn't exist, is bursting out of the neat little box I tucked it away in. And now that it's tearing at the seams, the messiness is leaking all over my life, destroying what I was working so hard to preserve.

"It's okay, Drew." Jasper's voice cuts through the fog threatening to swallow me whole. "It's okay to feel hurt. It's okay to be angry. Let it out."

The pain trapped in my chest claws at my throat, fighting for a release. I can't breathe; the magnitude of my grief is too big. It's been a part of me for too long. I've grown around it, trapping it where I thought I could control it.

But I can't anymore. It's too heavy. If I don't let some of it go, it's going to pull me down and I don't think I'll ever be able to recover.

I grab onto Jasper's shirt, twisting the fabric around my fists so tight that my fingers ache—anchoring myself to him like he's a lifeboat. And when I feel like I have a strong enough hold, I let it out.

Even to my own ears, it's unrecognizable. It's ripped from the very bottom of my soul, etched in pain and hurt, wrapped in love and grief. It's horrifying and it's beautiful, the sound of love that has fought to live on well after a person's final days.

I've battled so hard to ignore the pain, trying to patch up the gaping hole losing my grandma left in my life, that I didn't realize I was only feeding the hurt. Even though I feel like I'm being ripped in half, something deep down inside starts to mend.

And for the first time in a year, I feel a hope that while I know the pain will never go away, I might be able to walk with it instead of struggling against it.

Jasper holds me tight, whispering words that I hear but can't understand through it all. His arms never loosen as he absorbs my sobs and feels my tremors as my body succumbs to grief a year in the making.

When the sobs finally begin to fade, my body feels as though it was just wrung dry of every tear, every emotion. I feel like I climbed a mountain. I've never felt so exhausted in my entire life.

"Let's get you to bed," Jasper whispers into my ear before settling his lips against the top of my head. I nod into his chest but make no move to get up. I don't know if I have enough energy to make it across my apartment.

But it doesn't matter.

Before I can find out, Jasper adjusts his grip, keeping one arm behind my back and dropping the other beneath my thighs.

He carries me to my room and lays me on my bed, gently draping my comforter over me. I couldn't keep my eyes open if I tried, but in the distance, I hear the faint rustling of papers and distant footsteps before the mattress dips behind me and Jasper pulls my back tight to his front.

"Thank you," I whisper into the darkness. "I'm sorry you had to see that, but thank you."

"Don't ever apologize for that, Drew." His long fingers flex into the softness of my hip. "Thank you for feeling safe enough with me to allow me to be here for you."

I didn't think it was possible for my body to produce another tear, but at least this time, the tears don't fall from sadness.

I roll from his grip, turning so we're facing each other. "Thank you for staying."

"I'm not sure you've realized this yet, but I really like you, Drew." The faint light from outside my window filters in through the small crack in my curtains, just enough so I can see the shadows and lines of Jasper's face soften. "I always want to stay with you."

"Careful." I bring my hand to the side of his face. "Those are the kinds of things a man says to make a woman think they're in a relationship."

"I know." He pushes his cheek into my palm, a slow and lazy smile tugging at the corners of his mouth. "Is it working? Because there's nothing I want more than to be able to call you mine and me yours."

Holy shit.

Okay.

Maybe I do need to read his books because wow.

My breath catches in my throat, but not for long. After falling apart in his arms, I thought he would run for the hills, but instead, he's lying in front of me, asking me to call him mine.

And I realize that's all I want too.

"That sounds good to me." I don't wait for his reaction before I pull his face to mine, pushing my lips against his and tangling my tongue with his as we explore this new dynamic between the two of us.

One where we are each other's and I'm not so alone after all.

# CHAPTER 21

WE SHOULDN'T HAVE LEFT OUR BUBBLE.

After I'd spilled my heart out to him and we became an official couple, we stayed locked in my apartment for days. I called out of work and Jasper set an autoresponder for his email. The only place we went was to my couch and the front door to get the food we ordered.

Jasper sat with me as I went through the box of papers and pictures I had from my grandma, never judging me as I tried to start processing my grief against the new information Connor had told me. It wasn't pretty a lot of the time, but it was real, and for the first time in a long time, I feel like I'm on the road to healing.

Oh . . .

And we had a lot of sex.

Like, loads of it.

"Are you sure you want to do this?" I ask Jasper before he hands his keys to the valet. "This is your last opportunity to back out."

"I'm sure." He aims a smile my way, and despite my anxiety about tonight, my insides turn to goo. "This is going to be great, stop worrying."

"Fine." I climb out of the car. "But don't say I didn't warn you."

He rounds his rental car, linking his fingers with mine the second he gets close enough. It's what he does whenever we're together. I didn't think I was a fan of touchy-feely, but whenever Jasper is within reach, some part of him is touching me. And when we're in private, lots of our parts touch.

"Drew." He pulls me in tight and brushes his lips across my forehead. It's so sweet that the lady waiting for her car to arrive sighs. "Elsie is your best friend and I've already met her. What are you worried about?"

"Oh, you sweet summer child." I tighten my hold on his hand, fully aware that he has no idea what he's walking into. "Just you wait and see. Just you wait."

While we were locked in my apartment, I finished the latest book on my Jasper Book List. There was a lot of cooking in it, so I told him about this cooking class that takes place once a month in a boutique hotel downtown with their head chef. She creates a menu based around seasonal foods and then teaches a small handful of people how to cook it.

I'd heard really amazing things about it from a few acquaintances who had gone, and it was even ranked in *5280* as one of the best date-night ideas in Denver. Of course, Jasper, being Jasper, decided this needed to be a date activity to pair with the book, and when I charged my phone and called Elsie back, I mentioned this to her. And Elsie, being Elsie, insisted that we make it a double date— something I turned down immediately.

I love Elsie to the moon and back, but the last time I went on a double date with her, she scared the guy away before dessert arrived.

I just forgot how determined she can be.

Between her tenacity and Jasper's inability to say no, she somehow talked him into adjusting our reservation from two people to four.

So really, if this night is a total disaster, it's not my fault at all because I said no. I can't help it that nobody ever listens to me.

We walk through the lobby of the hotel, following the directions of the staff as they point us in the direction of the cooking class. Each hallway is covered with a different ornate wallpaper, giant light fixtures hanging from the ceiling until we reach the class.

Where I'm always early for events, Elsie is chronically late. Something that has been made way worse with every child she's birthed. I figured we'd at least be able to have a drink alone before the Coopers joined us.

Wrong again.

"Drew! Jasper!" Elsie shouts across the industrial kitchen scattered with prepared cooking spaces. "Over here!"

Whereas I dressed in my favorite pair of jeans, a button-up blouse from Madewell, and my fancy flats with a bow on them, Elsie is wearing a dress that shows off every curve motherhood has blessed her with and heels so high, I fear for her safety as she runs across the space to greet us.

"I can't believe you beat us here." I give her a hug when she reaches us. "You're always late."

"Correction." She pulls away and narrows her perfectly lined eyes at me. "I'm always late when the kids are with me. Tonight, we're alone. We sprinted out of that house the second Brandon's mom got there."

"That makes sense to me," Jasper chimes in. "It's hard enough for me to get out of the door on time and I'm a single man. I can't imagine what it's like being in charge of kids on top of that."

"Yes, thank you!" She looks to Jasper, grateful to have someone on her side. "Just loading them in the minivan takes like ten minutes." She swings her head around and points a finger in my face. "Don't you say one word about my swagger wagon, Drew Young."

I hold up my hands in surrender. "I wasn't going to say anything."

I always give her a hard time about driving a minivan, but in reality, I love the damn thing. One day, the twins asked me to sit in the back with them and I got to watch *Moana* in a very spacious middle seat the entire ride. It was glorious.

She rolls her eyes but drops the subject.

"Brandon and I ordered drinks for the table." She points to the table where Brandon is still sitting, watching his wife with a gentle smile on his face. "They have a bar if you want to order something else, but this is the one the chef recommends with the menu, so I figured we should all at least try it."

"Thoughtful of you." I bump my hip against hers.

"I know." She bumps me back, her bright smile growing even wider as she turns to Jasper. "You'll see, Jasper, I'm a really good friend like that."

Jasper doesn't miss a beat before saying, "From the stories Drew has told me about you, I don't doubt that for a second."

Some of the mischief behind Elsie's eyes disappears and they go soft at the corners. In that moment, I have no idea why I was ever worried in the first place about going on a date night with Jasper and my best friend. Instead, my imagination takes flight as I picture a future where I join Elsie and Brandon for date nights with a man I adore at my side.

It's a fantasy I never allowed myself to have. But like everything with Jasper, he's allowed me to envision a life I never thought was a possibility before.

And now it's all I want.

I FORGOT THAT WHEN ELSIE meets new people, she turns into a master interrogator.

It's a habit I've tried to break her of since the day we met. She's somehow convinced herself that her method of rapid-firing questions at people makes them feel comfortable and not like they're under investigation.

"And where are you from?" She takes another sip of the wine she switched to after the initial cocktail she ordered.

"Originally I'm from Maine, but we moved to California when I was in middle school for my dad's job." Jasper answers this question like he's answered all the others, fast and with a smile on his face. "But I haven't lived there in a while. To be honest, I haven't really had a home base since I got my first publishing deal. I bounce around from place to place, enjoying the scenery before finding someplace new."

The happy buzz I was feeling courtesy of four courses of delicious food and three martinis that had more gin in them than anything else fizzles away hearing Jasper talk about leaving.

"Really?" Elsie rests her elbow on the table and leans her head into her fist. "Where were you before you came to Denver?"

"Seattle." He moves his hand from my leg beneath the table and drapes it across my shoulders. "I liked it, but it was too gray for me. I decided to leave it and try out the sunny state of Colorado instead."

"I went to Seattle once. I loved it there, but it was definitely a huge difference coming from Denver. I did love being right on the water though." She turns her attention to Brandon, who, like me, has been a quiet observer since we finished dessert about twenty minutes ago. "Didn't you like it there? Maybe we should go back one day, take the kids for a family vacation."

"If that's what you want to do, that's what we'll do." Brandon's soft smile as he watches his wife is everything, but it grows when he turns to Jasper. "I'm just glad she doesn't want to do Disney yet. I'm not sure I'm ready to dad that hard."

Jasper and I laugh as Brandon pretends to flinch when Elsie shoves his shoulder.

"Oh, stop it," she says. "You know you already picked what matching T-shirts you're ordering us and where you're making reservations for the entire trip."

Brandon lifts his glass of water to his lips but does not deny that she's absolutely right.

"Anyways"—she turns her line of questioning back to Jasper— "where are you planning on going after Denver?"

There's a shift in her voice that I don't think Jasper can pick up on, but as her best friend, I absolutely do. And I don't know if I want to yell at her or hug her for asking the question I've been too afraid to bring up.

I know it's something we should've talked about before—or definitely after—the whole boyfriend/girlfriend discussion, but I just started processing one thing in my life; I couldn't add another. Thankfully, one of my strong points in life is avoidance, so I've been pretending not to think about it while I deal with the Book Nook and trying to figure out what Gran really wanted when she left the store to me.

"I'm not sure." There's an unfamiliar thread of unease in Jasper's normally confident voice.

My heart stutters in my chest as fear and hurt begin to register with his words. I know this is a conversation we can't avoid forever, but I also know having it at the dinner table with my best friend and her husband is not the place I want my fragile little heart broken.

"No need to make a decision right now." My hands ball into fists beneath the table and I try to focus on the pinch of my fingernails instead of the conversation at hand. "You still have a while until your book deadline."

"I'm actually ahead of schedule for once." Jasper's fingers flex against my shoulder, and for the first time, his touch makes me nervous. "I should be finished in a couple of weeks."

"Oh. Wow!" The saccharine excitement in my voice tastes like a grape Popsicle leaving my mouth. "Congratulations, that's great."

I wait for Elsie to speak up and take over the conversation like she usually does, but she's chosen this moment to be quiet.

And now I definitely want to yell at her.

"Yeah, it is." Jasper sounds even more hesitant this time. "I was going to tell you later, but—"

"Oh, don't worry about it." I cut him off, not needing an audience for what's coming after that *but*. "I'm happy for you. Really. I'm sure you're getting restless here, ready to move again."

"Actually—" He tries to talk again, not getting the hint that I want to wait to talk about this later.

And by later, I mean never.

"I get it." I cut him off again before grabbing my drink off the table to drain the remaining gin at the bottom of the glass. "It's fine—ow!"

Pain explodes up the front of my shin. I look beneath the table and move my leg just in time to avoid getting struck by Elsie's pointy-toed stiletto for the second time.

"Did you just kick me?" I glare across the table at my best friend, who's glaring right back.

"I did and I'll do it again if you don't shut up and let the man speak." She's using the mom voice she uses with the twins when they are in trouble. I don't want it to be effective, but I cower beneath the force of it. No wonder her kids are so well-behaved. "Good." She nods before turning her attention back to Jasper. "Now you can continue."

I look at him with wide eyes and then resist the urge to continue the kicking onto Jasper when I see he looks like he wants to laugh.

I knew this was a bad idea. Double dates are the worst. I hate them and I'm never doing this again . . . Not like it matters since the only guy I'm interested in is likely moving across the country, never to be heard from again.

I try to pull away from him, but I don't get far before he tightens his grip and tucks me deeper into his side.

"Thank you, Elsie," traitor jerk number one says to traitor jerk number two. "What I was going to say is that I'm thinking about staying in Colorado this time."

I can't say for sure what angels' singing sounds like, but I'm pretty sure those words leaving Jasper's mouth is the closest I'll ever come to hearing it here on earth.

All urges to yell at and kick the wonderful people I'm here with fade into oblivion as hope, a feeling that has become so frequent around Jasper, begins to build.

"Really?" My voice can hardly be heard over the sound of conversation from the tables around us. I'm too afraid to speak up, terrified to wake up from whatever wonderful dream I'm immersed in.

"Yeah, really." He turns in his seat so he's looking me straight in the eyes. Elsie and Brandon disappear. Only Jasper and I exist in this moment. "I called a Realtor the other day and we've been setting up times to start looking at places. I'm sorry, I should've talked to you first. I hope this is—"

I know the last time I cut him off I got kicked for it, but I don't care. Every word that comes out of his mouth makes me want to kiss him—so I do.

And this time, Elsie keeps her feet to herself.

I grab his face between my hands and pull his mouth to mine. It's short and sweet—we are in public, after all—but somehow, this might be our best kiss yet. Like the promise of more time together has shifted something I didn't even realize was lingering between us.

"I'm really glad you're staying," I whisper against his lips, not wanting to let him go.

"Yeah, babe," Jasper whispers back, and I feel his smile as it widens on his beautiful face. "I'm getting that. And I can't tell you how happy it makes me."

"Wow. I fucking knew it." Elsie's voice breaks through my love fog, and even I have to say I'm impressed with how long she stayed quiet. "If there was one person on this planet who could make Drew smile like that and show some PDA, it's Jasper freaking Williams, creator of every woman's favorite book boyfriend."

She's not wrong.

But she's not right either.

Because while I'm sure that Jasper Williams, Author, creates some amazing characters, absolutely none of them could compare to Jasper Williams, Boyfriend.

I don't tell her that though. Instead, I tell her good night and take my man back home so we can celebrate spending many more nights together.

And maybe even a few more double dates.

Maybe.

# CHAPTER 22

---

THE DRIVE TO SALIDA HAS NOTHING ON THE ONE TO OURAY.

Partially because it's closer to Denver, but also because on our way to Ouray, Jasper wanted to make a full road trip out of it and stop at every opportunity we had to take pictures or try a store's "world-famous" fudge. He turned what is normally a six-hour drive into an almost nine-hour one.

But I'm not complaining, I loved every single second. It was the perfect Sunday.

"Welcome to the Switzerland of America!" I say to Jasper as we climb out of the Jeep—a rental this time, lesson learned—outside the cabin we'll call home for the next three days.

I had hoped to get here early enough to do a little exploring today, but we arrive as the sun is setting and it somehow feels like perfect timing. The pink and orange sky swirls above us as the sun settles behind the mountains completely encompassing this little town. I never feel as small as I do up here; the San Juan Mountains seem to touch the clouds as we nestle into the valley at their base.

"Wow." Jasper closes the car door but otherwise doesn't move. His eyes are focused on the cotton-candy sky and the pine-covered mountains. "I've never seen anything like this."

I knew going into this weekend that I was going to want to commit every second to memory, so I came prepared. I don't say anything as Jasper stands lost in the moment. I reach into the back seat and unzip my camera, which I tucked away carefully when we packed the car up. Once my fingertips touch the cool metal, the familiar weight of the camera filling my palms, a sense of peace settles over me.

As quiet as I can, I snap away, zooming in and out, squatting low and stepping onto the running board to get higher, encapsulating this moment at every possible angle. And when Jasper turns to me, his face lit only by the rapidly fading sunlight, he's never been more beautiful.

*I love you.*

I think this to myself as I look into the viewfinder and zoom into his face as close as I can before snapping one last picture.

"Get any good ones?" He winks before rounding the Jeep and pulling our luggage out of the trunk.

"Eh." I shrug, tucking my camera back inside its case. "Not sure, the model was a little iffy."

"Damn!" His laughter is loud against the quiet night. Outside the small but vibrant city, the only sounds around us are the chirps of crickets in the rustling grass and the steady flow of the nearby river.

Jasper punches the lock code into the door before bringing our bags inside, and I follow close behind him carrying my backpack and the small cooler stuffed to the rim with snacks.

His hands run against the wall until he finally finds the light switch. It's always a little nerve-racking to make decisions based on a few pictures on the internet. I mean, MTV did create an entire series based on the dangers of this. But lucky for us, our quaint little cabin is even more charming than in the pictures.

Wood from floor to ceiling; it's only broken up by the ornate rug blocking off the living room. A couch much bigger than I would've assumed in the small space is pushed against the wall, with a tiny hand-carved table in front of it. An electric fireplace is on the far wall to balance out the space and a ceiling fan spins overhead. The kitchen, like everything else, is tiny but modern. It's the perfect amount of space for us to unpack our cooler and tuck away the couple of bags of groceries we grabbed when we drove into town.

There's a tiny hallway behind the kitchen. I open the door and turn on the light, revealing a small bathroom with a shower I definitely won't be sharing with Jasper this time, before my hand settles on the doorknob to the final room. For obvious reasons, the bedroom is the space I'm most eager to see. Thanks to the rise in popularity of tiny homes, it was almost impossible to find a space where you didn't have to climb a ladder of some type to get into bed. I send up a quick prayer to the goddess of sexy times that we didn't somehow get stuck in a cabin with bunk beds and push open the door.

And when I do, I'm thrilled at what I see. The queen-sized bed covered in a cream duvet and lots of fluffy pillows is a sight for sore eyes. It takes up almost the entire room, one side of the bed is flush with the wood-plank wall, and it's perfect. When I turn to look at Jasper, he's watching me closely, and I know I'm not the only one imagining all the fun we're going to have in this room.

"Don't look at me like that. Not yet, at least." I roll onto my tiptoes in order to give him a quick kiss. "We have to get a fire started. We can't start a mountain getaway without s'mores."

"Seriously?" His eyes are huge and he looks like a little kid on Christmas. "I don't think I've ever had s'mores on a real fire. My dad used to let us roast them over his grill, but that was as close as we ever got."

I try not to look too appalled or call his parents out on what I might consider to be child abuse before I take his hand and pull him the few steps it takes to get back to the living room.

The curtains covering the huge window facing the river are open. Any remaining hints of pink have disappeared as the dark night sky rolls in. A view unlike anything possible in Denver looms overhead as what seems like millions of stars glitter in the sky.

I love living in Denver, but to me, this is heaven. There's a quiet stillness that's only possible when you're nestled deep in the mountains, outside the range of any cell tower. Sitting under the stars, realizing there's so much more to the world than anyone knows, it's freedom.

"I feel like I might be a broken record this weekend"—Jasper wraps his arms around my middle and pulls me into him—"but wow. I can't believe how beautiful this all is."

I angle my head up so I can see him taking in the view, but when I do, his eyes are focused on me.

"Most beautiful sight in the entire world," he whispers before taking my mouth with his. "Thank you for bringing me here."

I don't know why he's thanking me when I feel like the lucky one.

Unlike Elsie, I've never had my person. All my travels have been solo or with someone I met in a travel group. So sharing this place I love, with a man I think I'm falling in love with? I couldn't be happier.

But still, who am I to say that he's not feeling the same?

"You're welcome," I say before pulling out of his grip. "Now, hurry. The marshmallows and skewers are in my backpack. I'll get the fire started."

"You know," he says before he turns to follow directions, "I was never interested in Boy Scouts as a kid, but all of a sudden, I'm thinking I would do just about anything for you to guide me through the wilderness."

"Oh, but Mr. Williams"—I drop my voice to a whisper—"didn't you know that the first rule of camp safety is to always have a buddy with you? And I know exactly what kind of buddy I want."

I wink at him, taking more than a small amount of pleasure at hearing his quick intake of breath before heading out into the night sky, knowing the possibilities out here are only matched by the ones inside the tiny cabin with Jasper.

"I THOUGHT AS AN ADULT, I'd be able to eat one of these damn things without getting it all over me." Jasper tries to wipe another glob of chocolate off his ruined shirt.

"I didn't want to say anything, but I think this might be something you need to bring up with your parents when you see them." I pop the rest of my s'more into my mouth before I gesture to my shirt, which remains untouched by the campfire treat. "When you've experienced the glory that is s'mores over a campfire, you learn to keep clean. You just need more practice."

I lean back into one of the aged Adirondack chairs the cabin hosts set up around the fire pit and consider roasting one more marshmallow . . . even though my stomach told me to stop two s'mores ago.

"Maybe I'll be able to convince them to come out here to visit. We can drive up to the mountains and show them how it's done."

He throws the words out so casually, it takes me a moment to comprehend the importance behind them. Meeting the parents is already a huge thing, but hinting at vacationing with them? Am I hearing him right?

"You want us to go camping with your parents?" I repeat his words back to him and they sound just as wild coming out of my mouth as they did coming from his.

"One day." He drops his skewer on his plate. "I mean, I did already meet your dad."

I grab a marshmallow out of the bag and throw it at him, impressing myself with my accuracy when it strikes him directly on the nose.

"Hey!" He catches the marshmallow after it bounces off his face and tosses it in his mouth. "What was that for?"

"That was for bringing my dad into this. That was a low blow." I know he didn't mean anything by it, but my feelings smart with the reminder of that terrible meeting.

"Shit, I'm sorry." He reaches across the small space separating our chairs and links his sticky fingers with mine. "That was a stupid thing to say, but honest, Drew, the only thing I remember about that day was it was the day I finally got to kiss you."

"Solid recovery." I grin at him because even if I wanted to stay irritated with him—which I don't—I couldn't.

He's right. That was a great day. Not only did my dad get his ass handed to him by Collette; my ass got properly handled by Jasper.

"Thank you." He smiles huge and it's even more transfixing with the orange glow of fire dancing across his skin.

Whereas it's still too hot to turn off the air-conditioning in Denver, I made sure to pack a jacket before heading up here. Even with the fire popping and crackling in front of us, I pull my hand away from Jasper's so I can grab one of the blankets we brought out here with us. I fold my legs crisscross into the chair and spread the blanket across my lap.

"I always forget how many stars there are." I lean back, my gaze drifting to the endless black sky above us. "My mom is obsessed with astronomy. Whenever she had a long weekend off, we'd load up into the car and head into the mountains. I remember lying next to her as she would point out stars and constellations that I'd always pretend to see. I loved listening to her as she'd tell me all of the stories about how they came to be. And then one weekend, we went when there was a meteor shower . . ." I trail off as the memory flashes in my mind just as vibrant as the day it happened.

I can smell the pine trees around us and taste the hot dog I charred because I insisted on cooking mine over the campfire. I can even feel my mom's arm as she held me in her lap while we tried to keep count of every meteor that flew overhead.

I'm glad my mom is living her life the way she wants to. Every time we talk, she's telling me how much she loves being back home. But I know she's worried about me. I think when I get home, I'll call her and fill her in on everything that's going on with the Book Nook. I might even try to schedule a time to visit her.

Maybe even bring Jasper . . .

"Sorry." I shake my head, a sad smile pulling on my lips as I look at Jasper, who's staring back with watchful eyes. "Do you want another marshmallow?"

"No." He shakes his head and one of his overgrown curls falls across his forehead. "But I could use some of that blanket."

I start to reach out for the other blanket, still folded neatly beside me, before I think better of it. I untuck my legs and stand up, swinging the blanket behind me so that I'm wearing it like a cape. I move the two steps it takes me to reach Jasper before I straddle my legs around his hips and plant myself on his lap.

"Is that better?" My whisper feels like a shout as all my attention focuses on the growing bulge beneath me.

Jasper nods but doesn't say anything as I start to rock against him.

"Good." I lean forward and notice he's got a little s'more on the side of his mouth. "It looks like you have something right . . ." I drop my mouth to the spot and lick the chocolate and marshmallow off his skin. "There."

"Did you get it all?" His breathing is coming faster, and at the same time, he's growing harder.

"Almost." I drop my head into the crook of his neck as my hips start rocking harder against his as I unconsciously search for release. "Almost." I repeat the word, but this time I'm talking about something completely different.

And when Jasper's hand finds its way between my legs, applying pressure and rubbing hard circles through the fabric of my leggings, I know we're on the same page.

I'm almost thirty, and before this moment, I would've thought that was too old to come while I'm fully dressed, dry humping a man.

And I would've thought wrong.

I dig my hands into his thick hair, pulling him closer to me. Our erratic breathing is drowning out all the sounds we heard only moments ago.

"Fuck, Jasper." I pant into his ear before pulling his earlobe between my teeth.

"That's it." He hisses out, his hips matching my rhythm in perfect tempo. "Come for me, Drew."

It's something about the way he says my name, the roughness in his voice that somehow vibrates with such intensity through my entire body, that I have no choice but to do as he says. My body spasms, the shock waves of the orgasm forcing my limbs to cling to Jasper, not even dropping my legs as he stands up and flips us around so that my back is lying flat across the wooden slats of the chair.

I don't even register the chill of the crisp night air as it hits my skin once my pants are gone. I'm too entranced by this new view. Looking up at Jasper, the shadows of the flames dancing across his hard jaw, illuminating the hunger in his eyes, all with a backdrop of dancing diamonds in a sheet of black.

"You're so fucking beautiful." He leans down, touching his mouth to mine. He tastes like chocolate and marshmallow and Jasper.

And it's a craving I know I'll never be able to sate.

"That's what I was going to tell you." I breathe the words against his lips, holding his face to mine.

I've never told a man I loved him before, but I figure by the fire, beneath the stars, and with Jasper Williams is the perfect time to do it. I open my mouth—my confession on the tip of my tongue—but before those three little words can escape, Jasper pulls away.

His huge hands move from my ass, drifting down the backs of my thighs. The contrast of his warm skin to the cool breeze causes goose bumps to trail his movements. His fingers pause when they reach my knees and he hooks my legs with his arms.

And then he's inside me.

My back arches off the chair, my shoulder blades digging deep into the wood beneath me, and my hands fly out, holding tight to the armrests as Jasper moves in and out of me in the most delicious way possible.

I want to watch as the beads of sweat form at Jasper's hairline and he throws his head back, moaning into the quietness enveloping us. But as his pace quickens and the tendrils of the fire dancing overhead begin to blur with the stars, I can't keep my eyes open any longer.

I squeeze my eyes shut just as my inner muscles tighten around Jasper. I try to hold it off, I'm not ready for this moment to end. I want to stay underneath the stars and this amazing man forever.

"Don't hold back, Drew." Jasper's rough voice trembles as he moves faster, harder into me.

"No." I let go of the chair and latch on to his arms. "I . . . want . . . more," I manage to say between my heavy breathing.

And even though I'm not ready, every muscle in my body goes taut with anticipation as the pressure in my core builds to a level that is almost frightening.

"You can have this forever." He groans between clenched teeth, his arms trembling beneath my fingertips.

And that does it.

Those words. The idea of forever with Jasper—possibilities as vast as the night sky above us—pushes me over the edge.

I fall apart, the curve of the fire bright behind my eyelids as my screams of pleasure echo off the mountains. My voice ricochets around us like the final quakes of my orgasm as Jasper buries himself deep, coming apart along with me.

He drops his forehead to mine, the damp strands of his hair sticking to his skin as his breathing begins to even out.

"You undo me, Drew."

"Right back at you."

I know it's only the first night of our vacation, but I'm not sure anything can top this.

Not ever.

# CHAPTER 23

---

"Are you sure we want to try a waterfall again?" Jasper's hand tightens on mine as we start the trek to Box Canyon Falls.

"Don't worry." I try not to laugh because there's genuine worry in his voice. "I wouldn't do that to you again. The beauty in this one is it's a downward hike. We'll go to the base of the waterfall and leave the top for a time when you're better acquainted with the altitude."

I try to mask my excitement as I think of all the future trips we'll be able to take to Ouray. Blue Lakes Trail is one of my favorite hikes in Colorado, and I can't wait until the day I'll get to look at the bright blue lake standing next to a man whose eyes rival the beauty of the water.

"Oh thank god." He pretends to wipe away imaginary sweat off his forehead. "Once was bad enough, but I don't think my fragile male ego could handle getting owned by nature twice in front of you."

"Whatever." I roll my eyes and nudge him with my shoulder. "I wanted to make up for the first waterfall trip and you can't get much better than this one."

The hike down to Box Canyon Falls is short and sweet. Long before you see the falls, you hear it. The sound of the rushing water as it crashes into the creek below is a constant reminder of the power water holds. A chain-link fence keeps visitors on the right trail until the metal walkway appears, guiding us into Box Canyon. The already crisp air cools noticeably as the sun struggles to peek through the huge rock walls towering over us.

"You were right," Jasper says, taking in the breathtaking views of the narrow quartzite canyon. "You can't get much better than this one. I can't believe I've traveled to so many places these last few years and all I took the time to explore were restaurants."

"I'm so glad you let me show you around." I drop one strap of my backpack off my shoulder and pull out my camera, lining up shots in my viewfinder as I talk to Jasper. "Not to get all Mother Earth on you, but it's so important that we start protecting the planet we're on. But I think in order for it to happen, people have to actually connect with the world around them. It's why I love nature photography so much. I felt like I was the first step in reminding people what we have to fight for."

"I never thought about it like that." Jasper's huge hands find my hips, holding me in place as I lean over the railing and zoom in on the water rushing below us. "Can I see?"

"See what?" I twist around to face him. There is still more to look at, but this isn't a view to sneeze at. "We could try to go up to the top if you want to give it a go again, but I think—"

"Not that." It's too loud for me to hear his quiet laughter, but I can feel it. "I mean can I see the pictures you took?"

My heart stutters in my chest and I'm not sure if it's because I love that he wants to see them or because I'm absolutely terrified. I used to share my photography all the time. But ever since I tucked my camera away, the few pictures I have snapped I've kept close to my vest.

It crosses my mind to say no. He's an artist and I doubt he'd want to share a book before he's edited and polished it up a little bit; I'm sure he'd understand if I asked him to wait. But then something outweighs my fear and I remember that this is Jasper and I want to share with him.

"Okay, but remember"—I tighten my grip on my camera as I issue my warning—"it's not edited and the finished photo will look much different."

He grins down at me, unbridled delight making him even more stunning than the canyon we're exploring.

I pull up the tiny snaps on the small screen of my camera, using the arrow to move through them all.

"Hold on." His hand wraps around mine, stopping me from scrolling further. "This one."

I look at the picture he hasn't taken his eyes off. It's a shot of the opening of the canyon. Tree-covered mountains are just visible through the rocks, and the white creek below drifts out into the openness.

"This one what?" It's a pretty picture of a pretty location, but I don't quite understand his excitement over it.

"That's what I want my cover for this book to be." He doesn't take his eyes off the screen as his words knock the air out of me. "This is perfect."

I probably don't need to say this, but my photo being used for a novel cover was never something I ever even considered. Which is why I'm not prepared for the onslaught of emotions I feel at his request.

"Thank you." I pull my camera away from him, not ready to look at him and let him see how much that meant to me. "Have your people call my people," I joke.

"Will do." He brushes his lips across my cheek and then boxes me in against the railing. Other visitors walk behind us and snap pictures, but we don't move. I don't know what Jasper is thinking, but at this moment, I feel closer to him than ever before.

"You were right." He finally breaks the silence. "There's something so peaceful about being here. Maybe it's because we're forced to disconnect from our jobs and electronics for a bit, but I swear it's like my soul is at ease up here."

I close my eyes, listening to the water rushing below us, feeling Jasper's warmth at my back, and breathe it all in. "I know exactly what you mean."

There's something that grounds you when you're entrenched in nature. I don't think humans were designed to never experience fresh air and stillness. Hustle culture has somehow shifted the narrative so that we feel guilty when we rest instead of accepting the truth, which is that we need rest to thrive. Add in the constant rise in the cost of living but never increasing pay? We've forgotten about work-life balance because we're all killing ourselves to survive.

And even though I'm well aware of this, when I needed to get away and experience nature firsthand, I retreated into my tiny apartment, only leaving it to go to a tiny office. A tiny office Gran might not have even wanted—

"Should we keep going?" Jasper breaks me out of my thoughts before they're able to make an unwelcome turn.

"We should." I put my camera over my head, enjoying the familiar weight of it as it dangles around my neck. "A condensed lesson for your trip," I shout over the rising noise of the waterfall. "This sits on the Ouray fault. Millions and millions of years ago, a deep crack appeared, and thanks to erosion from alpine glaciers, it carved this glorious little slice of heaven. The end."

What can I say? I take pictures; I am not a geologist.

"Impressive," he says without a hint of sarcasm. "I think I remember the word *erosion* from middle school, but that's it. I hope there's not going to be a test later, because I'm not sure I'd pass."

"No test." I draw a cross over my heart. "All you need to do is enjoy the view and make sure you don't get altitude sickness, because after this? We're heading to the hot springs."

He pulls me close and drops his voice so low that I can barely hear him over the waterfall that's now right in front of us. "Does that mean I get to see you in a bikini?"

I put my hands in the middle of his chest, giving him a half-hearted shove because if I'm honest, the entire reason I picked the hot springs is to spend some extra time around Jasper with his shirt off.

What can I say?

There are perks to being the travel planner after all!


BEFORE THE MINERS CAME TO Ouray and the government did their typical government thing, this land belonged to the Ute people. Up until they were removed from their land, the Ute people considered the hot springs to be sacred and healing. In fact, they would refer to them as "Miracle Waters"; some tribes would travel days to visit them.

I don't know if there's any truth to it, but as we sit at dinner now—my fingers still pruney from how long we soaked in them—I feel better than I have in months. Maybe even years.

"See, this is what I call balance." I lift up the icy mug filled to the brim with a beer made in-house and tap it against Jasper's. "You can explore nature and the food. It doesn't have to be one or the other."

And thank goodness, too, because I love the outdoors, but I also really love to eat. And drink. Eating and drinking while outside is basically my euphoria.

"This might be the best beer I've ever had." His tongue darts out of his mouth and he licks the foam off his lip. "Actually, this might be the best vacation I've ever had."

"It has been pretty good so far, hasn't it?" I follow his lead, taking a deep sip of the amber liquid. I never thought of myself as a beer fan before, but maybe I'd only had the crap stuff, because this is delicious. "Hopefully tomorrow will be just as good."

Tomorrow will be a little more low-key, breakfast in our cabin and hopefully a little morning delight before we come into town. Much like Salida, Ouray has worked hard to preserve the Victorian buildings coloring this town. We're going to do some shopping, look at some art, eat—of course—and what I'm most excited about is bringing him to a local bookshop here.

I'm more shocked than anybody that Jasper's plan actually worked. I'm not sure I'm what anyone would call an avid reader yet, but I could see myself getting there. I've released the anger and disappointment I felt as a young girl and enjoyed the stories for what they are: an opportunity to relax and allow my mind to wander. When I get lost in these books, life feels a little bit lighter, as if there are endless opportunities for me. I found courage to take the lead in my relationship with Jasper and I feel like I'm in charge of my life for the first time in a long time. I feel closer to my customers and to Gran. I didn't realize how therapeutic reading is; I'm just glad I know now.

"It will be." He nabs one of the tortilla chips and loads it with the elote dip I will dream about. "You really could start your own travel company; you're that good at planning expeditions."

"Expeditions?" He is so unintentionally funny sometimes; listening to him talk is my favorite. I really do need to read one of his books. "I appreciate the way you make everything I do sound fancy."

"You are fancy." He wiggles his eyebrows and I know he's referring to the lingerie I changed into after our little rendezvous under the stars.

"Oh, you know it." The sarcasm in my voice couldn't be heavier, but my cheeks get so hot, I almost break out into a sweat. "People call me Fancy Drew all the time."

He graciously laughs at my terrible pun and it makes me fall for him even harder.

"But seriously, I was thinking about what you were saying earlier." He must see the confusion on my face, so he backtracks a bit. "You know, about how you loved taking pictures of nature to connect people to the world. I want to know more about that. Where did you want to go? What were your plans?"

I'd given him a brief overview about what I'd been doing before I took over the Book Nook, but I never told him everything. If I'm honest, I don't think I've ever told anyone everything. Not even Elsie. Before, it felt like an audacious goal that I needed to keep close to my heart, but now it feels like an impossible dream, so far removed that it doesn't matter who knows.

"Well, I had a whole multilayered plan." I lean forward, ignoring my mom's voice in the back of my head telling me to get my elbows off the table. "First was to take over Colorado. I told you about camping with my mom and I think that's really where my obsession with the outdoors stemmed from. Then, when I got my driver's license and Gran gave me my Jeep? It was game over. I was in a photography class in school and one of our assignments was shooting outdoor scenery. I just fell in love. I spent every weekend after that searching out the best places to photograph. Drove Elsie insane. She wanted to go to the movies and I'd force her to come along on these ridiculous adventures I had no right taking."

One time, I accidentally got us stranded in the Sand Dunes because I decided to drive Medano Pass Primitive Road when it was my driving skills that were primitive. My mom was furious. I was only allowed to drive to and from school for two months.

"I've been traveling all over ever since. I spent more time in my Jeep and a tent than I did anywhere else. I have so many photos from all over the state; videos too. I was beginning to be regularly published in local papers and magazines. I was even in talks with a local channel to start a travel segment on a morning show." I wanted to represent young women, especially young women of color, exploring the outdoors. It was going to start out on a monthly basis with the opportunity to grow from there. "That was going to be the start. I was going to use that tape to get me funding to expand my travels. I wanted to publish a book. I know, I know," I say when I see the way his eyes narrow. "It was going to be a photography book though. What I love about photography is that while I take the pictures, everyone who looks at them sees something different. They create their own stories. But my ultimate goal was to get a show on the Travel Channel. I wanted to go off the beaten path, showcasing the lesser-known beauties. I'd sell my car, end my lease, and travel all over the place. Maybe one day, I'd build a little cabin off the grid in Colorado or even Alaska."

"Alaska?" His eyebrows scrunch together and he looks adorably confused. "I thought you don't love the cold."

"I don't like being *in* the cold." I offer my very weak explanation. "I love looking at the snow and cold from inside someplace warm. I was going to use some of the money I got from signing my contract to go on an Alaskan cruise."

"What happened to it?"

It's an innocent question and I brought it up, so I can't shut it down the way I want to. That month of my life is a period I want to block out for all eternity.

"Gran died." I start fidgeting with edges of the fabric napkin draped across my lap. "I was supposed to go in and sign the contract on a Friday. She died that Wednesday. We pushed back the day I would go in, but then I found out about the Book Nook and you know the rest."

I've thought about getting rid of all my old pictures more times than I can count. Besides the few framed prints I have hanging inside my house, I shipped the rest to my mom. It was too hard to keep them in my apartment; the beautiful story they once promised had turned into one of loss and heartbreak.

"But now . . ." His sentence dies off and he sets his nearly empty mug back on the table. When he looks back at me, knots form in my gut at the serious expression on his face. "What's holding you back now?"

I stare at him, silently turning over his question in my mind. What's holding me back now? Has he not been paying attention?

"I still have the Book Nook." I answer with the obvious. "The numbers are really starting to grow. I feel like I'm finally hitting my groove and taking the store in a direction Gran would be really pleased with."

"Okay, I understand that." His voice is low and gentle, like he's talking to a small child and not the woman he whispered very, very dirty things to this morning. "But there's been changes now and maybe you can start thinking of ways to get back to your life from before. You should see the way you light up when your camera is back in your hands, the way your shoulders relax every time we drive out of the city limits. You can still end your lease and travel. Can you imagine the adventures we could go on together?"

I know he means well and that he's saying these things from a place of good intentions, but for some reason it really pisses me off. It's nice remembering what life was like before Gran passed, but the reason I don't do it is because I didn't think anyone would understand. Jasper saying this proves that I was right.

"I don't think you get it." And how could he? I don't think anyone who isn't in my shoes could know what I'm going through. "Of course I still love to take pictures and get out into the open, but you're wrong. There haven't been any changes. She's still gone and the Book Nook is still all I have of her. That will never change."

His back straightens with the shift in my tone. I don't mean to sound so short, but I couldn't help it even if I tried.

And I'm not trying.

"I do understand that," he says. Clearly not understanding. "But now you know that she was considering selling the store, so maybe you can consider it too. I'm sure she would—"

"You're sure she would do what, Jasper? You never even met her." I stop myself, closing my eyes and taking a deep breath when I realize I'm beginning to raise my voice. "You don't know her," I repeat, but softer this time. "You weren't there to see the years and years she invested in the Book Nook."

"You're right, I wasn't there, but from all of the stories you've told me about her, I do know one thing."

"What do you know?" I don't really care what he *thinks* he knows. I just want him to hurry up and say what's on his mind so he can drop this and I can go back to enjoying his company.

"I know that she loved you and she'd want you to be happy. She wouldn't want you giving up your dream for hers." He reaches across the table and holds my hand in his. "You know she was considering selling the store; maybe it's time you let yourself explore the idea as well."

"Sure, maybe she talked to Connor, but we don't know if she was going to sell or not. Maybe you're fine making huge decisions at the drop of a hat, but I'm not. That's not something I'm comfortable doing without all of the information, and for what?" I yank my hand out of his grasp. "For a guy who thinks it would be fun to go on an adventure?"

The thing with me is that I don't lose my temper often. I get frustrated, sure. Road rage, often. But for me to truly speak without thinking? It takes a lot.

And I usually regret it.

Vaguely, I notice a change in his posture, in the way he's looking at me. But I'm too far gone. I'm in the zone and I can't stop now.

"Your book bucket list, or whatever it was, was fun. I've had fun going out and showing you around. I can admit that I got lost in it too. But the truth is, we're two completely different people. You live your life with your head in the clouds, where a happily ever after is a viable option. Not all of us have that privilege . . . *I* don't have that privilege. I can't disappoint my grandma the second something exciting comes along."

I've been too busy enjoying myself to accept that there's no way something like this could last. We're too different. But now that I know, I can't keep pretending I don't. I just wish I realized it when we weren't six hours from home.

Jasper sits across from me, staring at me like I'm a stranger. His face is a mask and his usually expressive eyes have shutters over them. Part of me wants him to say something, to tell me he agrees and this was a silly plan that had no longevity in the first place.

Another part of me, though—a part I don't care to admit to— wants him to tell me I'm wrong. It wants him to fight for me like no other man ever has.

Which might be why when he opens his mouth, I let hope stave off my smarter, more reliable emotions.

"Alice Young would not be disappointed."

His words are so quiet that for a moment, I think I've hallucinated them.

The restaurant fades around me and my vision tunnel focuses on Jasper. "What did you just say?"

It takes him a minute and I can see his mind working as he decides what his next move should be. Every second that passes causes my unease to multiply until I feel like I'm going to climb out of my skin.

"I said your grandma would not be disappointed." The stoicism in his tone is alarming, but do I ever listen to warning bells?

"And how, exactly, would you know that?" I can barely hear myself as I ask the question I'm not sure I want the answer to. I wish I could reverse time, go back to before this conversation ever happened.

Before Jasper happened.

"Because I knew her before she passed." Even though I had a feeling this is where he was going, hearing him confirm it steals my breath away. Pain I never thought Jasper was capable of causing ricochets through me, hurt turning to anger and then back to hurt again.

I feel like a masochist, but I can't stop the word as it falls from my lips. "How?"

He nods like he's coming to terms with something I have yet to understand before he opens his mouth and tells me what I know is going to ruin what little is left of me.

"It started like all requests I get from small bookstores. But you know Alice, she didn't like email, so she ignored all my emails, leaving me voice mails until I called her back." He sounds so detached from the story that it takes me a moment to focus on what he's saying, not how he's saying it. "And when I did, she told me about the Book Nook. She explained how she had a group of devoted customers who read my books and would love it if I could do a live event, but then, as she was telling me about that, she also mentioned having a granddaughter I would just love."

My heart cracks inside my chest. I have to close my eyes as memories of Gran swirl through my mind, the ones where she was so worried about me and tried to set me up with every single man she crossed paths with.

I don't say anything, so Jasper keeps talking.

"She told me you had a bit of a tough shell, but you were a softie at heart. She told me about how talented you were at photography and that you were on your way to doing big things. And she told me that you were beautiful. 'The most beautiful girl in the entire world, inside and out, still not sure how we got so lucky.' But before I could make it into the store, she passed away. I didn't hear anything until Mona reached out to me all those months later."

The tears I didn't even feel building spill onto my cheeks. Gran said that to me every single day, until the day she died. *Most beautiful girl in the entire world, inside and out.* It was the affirmation I didn't know I desperately needed until I didn't hear it anymore.

Until I heard it again right now.

"You can stop now." I stare unseeing at my lap, swiping away the tears and hoping nobody is watching as I fall apart in this vinyl-covered booth.

"I can't," he says with steel in his voice. "Now that you know this, you need to know everything."

I don't want to know everything.

I didn't even want to know this.

"No, I can't—" I reach for my purse beside me, ready to escape, when what he says next stops me dead in my tracks.

"I know she would be okay with you selling it because I'm the one who gave her Connor's number."

"You . . ." It feels like concrete is pumping through my veins. Mind, body, and spirit, I've never felt heavier. "You did what?"

"She was looking around; she hadn't made any decisions yet. She wanted to take the temperature of the market." He tells me something he has absolutely no business knowing. "She was doing it for you. She—"

So that's why he was so nervous and cagey when he ran into Connor at the store. It all makes sense and I can't take any more.

Any wishful thinking I'd dreamt up over these last few months with Jasper turns to ash.

"No, don't say another word to me." I stop him from going any further as the implications of his admission weigh down on me. "You have sat here, listening to me tell you about my grandma, about my plans for the future, about my dad."

He opens his mouth, but I don't let him get a word out.

"Don't. I trusted you. I confided in you. And you let me, not telling me that you already knew this stuff about me." Never in my life have I felt so stupid. "God."

My voice breaks and I know I'm seconds away from losing it.

I have to get away from him.

"You have the keys to the car." I pull the strap of my purse over my shoulder and slide out of the booth. "You can go back to the cabin tonight. I need some space. I'm going to find a room in town."

"Drew," he says, but I just shake my head.

"It's too late to drive back to Denver now; I'll call you in the morning and we can leave then."

I don't wait for him to respond. There's nothing for him to say.

I force my chin up and walk out of the brewery with my head held high, keeping it that way as I grab a room in the motel around the corner.

And only once I'm in the room with ugly green carpet and stiff sheets do I let the tears fall.

Everything was going too well.

I should've known better.

Some people are meant for happy, while others are meant to merely exist.

Silly me.

I thought I had a chance for things to be good.

But I'll be okay. I'm always okay. One day I'll forget all about this. Sure, it might take a while. Months. Years. Maybe even decades. But one day in the future, I won't even remember what it was like to almost have it all.

I look at my fingers after I wipe away the last remnants of melted mascara from beneath my eyes and realize they're not pruney anymore. All signs of my time in the hot springs have long gone dry.

So much for miracle waters.

# CHAPTER 24

I looked up alternate ways to get to Denver from Ouray.

The cost of a private car was more than a quarter of my rent. The bus ride had five transfers and took twelve hours. But after spending six of the most miserable hours in a silent car with Jasper, I'm reconsidering my final decision.

Jasper dropped me off at my place and I climbed out of the car without so much as a goodbye. When I walked into my apartment, I thought about jumping into my bed and sleeping for—I don't know—an eternity or so. But then I realized that even that wouldn't be enough. So instead, I got into my car and drove to the Book Nook.

I've missed my gran more times than I can possibly count. In big moments and in little moments, she's always on my mind. But right now, I need her more than ever.

I need to hear her voice as she shouts my name by way of greeting. I need to feel her arms around me as she promises me everything will be okay.

I need answers.

But she's gone and there are none.

I ignore the way my stomach twists when I turn into the tiny staff parking lot behind the Book Nook. I try to convince myself that it's residual anxiety from my time with Jasper and once I'm inside, everything will be better.

But as I walk through the front door, the bell I hear so often, it rings in my sleep, chiming over my head as the distinct scent of books filters through the air, the feeling of home I was expecting is nowhere to be found.

The disappointment is palpable. It blooms in my chest, the dull ache sharpening with every traitorous step I take. I know it's not rational, but I feel as if this place has betrayed me, and as I walk deeper into the store, I'm counting down the seconds, waiting until I can confront it.

Dani is at the front counter, checking out a customer, when she sees me.

"Drew!" Dani can't hide the surprise—and concern—on her face when she sees me walk in. "We weren't expecting you back until Thursday. Is everything okay?"

The fake smile I perfected no longer comes second nature. It strains on my cheeks and my head starts to ache.

"Totally." I lie without missing a beat. "Just missed it here. You know I can't stay away for long."

"Well, we missed you." I can tell she doesn't buy what I'm selling, but she doesn't want to make a scene in front of the customer. "Oh! By the way—"

"Why don't you finish here and then meet me in the office and tell me." I feel terrible for cutting her off, but I don't know how much longer I can keep this facade up. "I have a few things I forgot to take care of before I left."

She still looks uncertain but nods anyway and doesn't say anything as I turn my back to her. I zoom through the bookshelves with blinders on, not acknowledging any of the customers as I go. I keep my eyes planted on the floor in front of me, too afraid they might accidentally wander to one of the books I read with Jasper.

As soon as I reach Gran's office, I slam the door shut behind me, twisting the measly lock that a four-year-old could pick. No, really. A four-year-old could pick it, or at least a pair of four-year-olds. Elsie's twins have definitely broken in a time or two—they know Auntie Drew keeps candy in her desk.

I flip on the light and cringe at what I see when I do. Though I've only been gone for a couple of days, papers have accumulated on my desk as if I've been gone for weeks on end. The light on the office phone is blinking, indicating at least one but probably multiple messages left for me, and I don't even want to imagine what the emails look like.

Fast and unwelcome, Jasper's confession flashes through my mind. I try to ignore it, but here in this space, pieces of Gran all around, I can't shut it down. I wonder what she was thinking when she called Connor. Why she made all these decisions without ever letting me in. I wonder if anything I've done since she passed matters or if I'm wasting everybody's time.

I close my eyes and take a breath.

For now, it doesn't matter. I still run the Book Nook and I have people depending on me. As much as I might feel like things have changed, they're still exactly the same, and now it's time for me to get to work.

I push off the office door acting as my backrest and barely make it a step before Dani is knocking.

"Sorry," I call, knowing I must look as frazzled as I feel. "Just give me one second."

"Drew, dear?" A soft voice calls from the other side of the door, but it's not Dani.

It's Ethel.

*Fuck.*

"Ethel, hi!" I try to infuse something other than dread into my voice. "What are you doing here?"

"We had to move book club to tonight." She tells me what feels like the worst possible news at the moment. "We heard Dani call you and thought we'd come ask you to join us. It feels like we haven't seen you in ages."

She's not wrong. Between being out on dates to purposely avoiding them once I learned of Gran's maybe plan to sell the Book Nook, I've kept my distance. And now, with the way things ended with Jasper, they're the last people I want to see.

In the nicest way possible.

"Ummm . . ." I try to think of any excuse, but thanks to my terrible sleep on an even worse mattress, my mind is struggling to function and I come up empty. "That sounds great; I have to do a couple of things really fast and then I'll be out."

Technically, this isn't a lie. I do have a lot of things to do. It's just that I won't do any of them before I drag my ass out of this postage-stamp-sized office.

"Sounds good, dear," she calls back. "I'll let the ladies know you'll be joining us shortly."

I don't say anything else as I listen to the faint sound of her footsteps fade away. When she's gone, I release a breath I wasn't aware I was holding.

Considering the way everything went down with Jasper, I should feel guilty for what I did. I mean, isn't lying by omission what he did?

But I'm not going to do this forever. If anything, I'm making sure I have the full truth before I talk to them. What would happen if I told them about Connor and it turned out it was nothing like I expected? This is me putting them first. Even if I have to bear the brunt of the stress for a little while longer.

At least now when I go out there, I can paste on my happy smile for a while before coming up with a reason to leave. And maybe, if I do a good enough job, I'll convince them they don't need to check on me every day of my life, like they've been doing since Gran's funeral.

I love them, but I can't process everything that's happening with them watching over me like I might break at any second.

My phone beeps inside my purse, and when I pull it out, Jasper's name lights up my screen. I wish the butterflies I was becoming so accustomed to would take flight again, but instead my vision fogs over as tears threaten to reemerge. I should delete his text without even looking at it. Nothing he says can change what happened, and reading it will only cause more pain.

But I'm a glutton for punishment.

I swipe to unlock my screen and his message pops up as soon as I do.

It's simple. Sweet. Heartbreaking.

> I'm so sorry. I wish I could go back and change what
> happened.

My finger hovers over the screen. It would be so easy to just delete it. One swipe of my finger and it's gone.

> Me too.

I write, hitting send before I can think better of it.

The reply bubbles pop up at the bottom of my screen, but before his message comes through, the doorknob to my office rattles for a moment and then Collette pushes it open.

"Are you coming today or are you waiting for us to send you a formal invitation, for Christ's sake." She puts more power behind her constant resting bitch face when she sees my phone in my hand. "Oh, so you're too busy to see us because you're in here playing on your phone?"

Even though every part of me hurts right now, the sting that used to come with her biting words is missing. Ever since she let her true feelings for me slip when my dad made his last appearance, her harsh tone has lost all of its power.

"Oh, Collette." I ignore the beep of my phone and shove it back inside my purse. "I'm so sorry, I didn't realize you missed me so much."

"I didn't." The exasperated roll of her eyes is magnified behind the thick lenses of her glasses. "I just don't want to sit here all night while we wait for you to deign us worthy of your presence."

Laughter I didn't think could be possible after the last twenty-four hours bubbles up inside me when her lip curls in disgust as I wrap my arms around her in a big hug.

"This is why I should've sent Mona back here." She pulls out of my arms and turns on the heel of her orthopedic tennis shoe. "I don't have the patience for this mess."

"You don't have patience for anything." I follow her, ignoring customers as I chase after her.

"Damn straight." Her hoarse voice drifts through the store like the tendrils of smoke that used to follow her around when she would have a cigarette hanging out of her mouth. "Now, hurry up."

I fall into step beside her, forcing myself to be semisocial and say hello to old and new customers alike. A woman in the romance section offers a quick, shy smile as she flips through the pages of a book she's considering.

As we approach the final bookshelf before the nook comes into view I brace myself. The nook is where I've always felt the most connected to Gran. On days I'm missing her extra, I'll come back here and sit in her rocking chair. But since I talked to Connor and had my not-so-minor meltdown right after, I've avoided this space.

We round the corner and I'm met with the same symphony of greetings that have surrounded me for the last year. I take in their bright, smiling faces, lined with proof of lives well lived, as their eyes crease with happiness to see me. I don't know if this brings me comfort or makes me more confused. Surely knowing that Gran wasn't connected to this place as much as I thought she was should change things. The paint shouldn't look as shiny, the projects we've completed should look more shabby than chic.

But they don't.

Everything is exactly as it was before.

"There she is!" Mona pushes out of her rocking chair. She looks as stylish as ever in her stilettos with her pink-painted lips as she rounds the table, her arms spread wide before she wraps me in a tight hug. "You know, when we decided to set you up with Jasper, we didn't realize it would mean we wouldn't see you anymore."

The dull pain in my chest turns sharp at the mention of Jasper's name, but it's the confirmation of what I already assumed that has me pulling away.

"I knew your devious brains were up to something more than book club when you pulled Jasper in here." I try to joke, but all I want to do is cry.

Thankfully she doesn't seem to notice.

"Well, considering you're always out with him, going on all sorts of dates, you can't complain." She looks down her nose at me. "And don't think I haven't noticed the way your skin has had an extra glow the last few times I've seen you."

Oh.

My.

God.

I've heard of a lot of ways to forget about a breakup. One way I didn't know—and still wish I didn't—is your grandma's friend telling you that she knows you've been getting some good, good loving.

Kill me now.

"Mona!" I bury my face beneath my hands. I will never be able to look Mona in the eyes ever again. "I can't believe you said that."

"I don't know why not." She sounds offended as she peels my hands from my face. "I know not everyone needs it. However, since you've taken some time away from the store and spent time with a man who clearly adores you, the Drew you were before Alice left us has returned to us. So we might have meddled a little bit, but when you're our age, you know how to decipher what someone needs. And you, my lovely girl, needed the love of a good man."

Oh no.

This is why I didn't want to come out here with them. Because now I'm going to cry . . . again. And they're going to pester me until I tell them everything that is going wrong.

My eyes start to well up with tears—from sadness at losing Jasper and gratefulness for the love I receive from these women— but before they fall, Vivian drops her copy of the book they're discussing on the table.

"Oh good." She stands and crosses the small space to stand beside us. "We're finally telling Drew that it was really Alice who was behind introducing her to Jasper? I was wondering when we'd let that cat out of the bag."

"Wait." Ice runs through my veins, turning my blood cold. "What did you say?"

Vivian tilts her head to the side and the fine lines across her forehead deepen as she registers the change in my tone.

"Your gran was the one who initially came up with the idea to introduce you to Jasper. She was part of a group of small bookstore owners who heard him speak, and after that, she was convinced that he was perfect for you." Her eyes flicker between me and Mona as she speaks. "She told us she was close to getting him to come into the store for a speaking arrangement, but after she passed and we forgot about it."

"And then one day when I was in the back doing inventory, I found a little scrap of paper with his name and phone number scribbled across." Mona grabs the baton and carries the conversation with flawless execution. "Alice very much wanted you to be happy, so we knew it was up to us to help with her matchmaking efforts. When I reached out to Jasper, he was very upset to hear about Alice; they must have been closer than we knew."

The good news is that I no longer feel like I'm on the verge of bursting into tears. The bad news is that now I'm just about to burst.

I mean, how much can I take?

"Oh yeah." A humorless laugh falls from my mouth. "They were closer than you knew. Very close since Jasper told me yesterday that Gran asked him for information in order to sell the store."

I assumed when I let that secret out of the bag, the entire Dirty Bird crew would lose their ever-loving minds the way I did, but instead, nobody has much of a reaction at all.

"Wait." I take a step away from them, a sense of betrayal I didn't know possible seeping through me. "You all knew?"

"Well, yes." Mona is watching me carefully, like I'm a wild animal primed to pounce. "But it's not what you think."

"Oh, I'm pretty sure it's exactly what I think." I stop moving and point an angry finger at all these beautiful, deceitful women. "You were all in on the joke. Everyone has had a hand in molding my life the way they wanted, watching as I dove into the store you knew she didn't even care about, going on dates with a guy, as what?" The more I think about it, the more awful it all is. "As some sad, pathetic favor for the dead woman he became friends with over the phone?"

The tips of my ears burn with embarrassment as I imagine what Jasper must have been thinking when he agreed to this whole charade. My stomach churns and I feel like I might be sick as I begin to fully grasp the entire situation.

"Drew, stop it." Collette's raspy voice scolds me like somehow I'm the one out of line here. "You know it wasn't like that. You need to listen to Mona."

I don't say anything, not because I've taken a turn for the obedient, but because there is nothing to say.

Not one single thing could make this okay.

"Alice loved this store and she loved you." Mona sounds so concerned as she tries to explain the unexplainable. "But she was getting old, she knew she wasn't going to work here forever, and you—"

"And I loved this store!" I shout, cutting her off. "I loved coming here with her, I loved being with all of you, and now that's ruined because you all, every single one of you, have been lying to me for months. Maybe even years! And now I have nothing."

My throat clogs; the tears that I thought were gone now choke me as the dark realization settles around me.

Nothing.

No more Gran. No more Book Nook.

No more Jasper.

I have nothing but tarnished memories and broken promises.

I spin on my heel, ignoring the crowd that has gathered to witness this sad scene, and run out of the building, knowing I might never return.

# CHAPTER 25

---

ONCE I TURNED OFF THE "ARE YOU STILL WATCHING?" OPTION ON Netflix, time truly ceased to exist.

Armed with nothing but a remote and more snacks than I can count, I stay camped out on my couch for the rest of the night . . . and maybe even the next day.

Even though I no longer care about the store, I still sent a text to Daisy, asking her if she had time to watch over it. Not even a minute passed before she responded saying she'd be happy to. Her internship hasn't been what she was hoping it would be and I think she is grateful to spend time at the store.

So now I'm free to mope on the couch for at least another week.

I'm on my phone, scrolling through the results of my "movies that make you cry" Google search, when it starts to vibrate in my hand. A vaguely familiar number pops onto the screen and I contemplate sending it to voice mail. But a part of me I don't want to admit exists is begging me to answer, whispering treacherous thoughts like maybe it's Jasper on the other end, calling for forgiveness.

I swipe my finger across the screen, the bright light illuminating my poor nail that has been chewed to the quick, and put it against my ear. "Hello?"

"Is this Ms. Young?" an unknown voice that definitely doesn't belong to Jasper asks from the other end.

"This is. May I ask who's calling?" I push through the disappointment and a sense of unease takes its place.

Nobody calls me Ms. Young.

"Of course, Ms. Young. This is Jacob Wilson, I was in charge of your grandmother's will. I saw that you called and I'm so sorry it has taken me so long to get back to you, but—" He takes a deep breath and I hit the mute button on my remote. "Some things have arisen and it seems as though Andrew Young is intent on giving you a hard time. I know you have some questions and I was hoping we could schedule a time for you to come in and speak with me so we can clear everything up at once."

My freaking father. Only he could take my lowest moment and bring me lower.

"Of course, when do you need me?"

"Sooner is better," he says, not easing any of my worries. "We aren't worried about Mr. Young's claims, but there are some things I want you to be aware of so you can move past this as quickly and easily as possible."

I would also like that, but considering nothing is ever quick and easy with my dad, my hopes are low.

"Okay, ummm . . ." I look around my dark, messy apartment. "I'm free today if that's not too soon."

I'll definitely need a shower, but I could still be out of here within thirty minutes.

"Well." He hesitates, sounding a little bit confused. "It's a little late for today; how about we plan for the first thing tomorrow morning. Does nine o'clock work?"

I pull my phone away from my ear and check the time. Just after five.

See what I mean about time not existing?

"Nine is perfect, Mr. Wilson," I tell him, failing to mention that I have an undetermined amount of time off due to a slight nervous breakdown. "Thank you."

"Not a problem." His deep voice is softer this time, apologetic even. I'm sure in his line of work we aren't the first, and we won't be the last, family he's seen who are not at their best. "I'll see you soon."

I toss my phone on the table, forgetting about my quest for the next great tearjerker, and unmute my TV so I can hear David and Alexis arguing again.

The good news about hearing back from the lawyer now is that things can't get any worse. I've hit many a false rock bottom before in my life, but I'm pretty sure this time it's the real thing.

Or at least I really, really hope so.

"Ms. Young." Jacob Wilson outstretches his hand as he greets me in the waiting room of his office. "How are you doing?"

"Please, call me Drew. And I'm fine, thank you." I lie without missing a beat. "Ready to move on from this mess and put it all behind me."

I'm just not sure what putting this behind me looks like anymore.

"I'm sure you are." His deep voice is oddly soothing as he guides me into his office. It's the perfect mix of authoritative and sympathetic. It's clear he chose the perfect career for himself. "To be honest, it was quite a surprise to hear from you and your father. We don't often hear from families this far after a will is distributed."

"I really am sorry about this." I take a seat across from his desk and try not to wring my hands. "I was hoping maybe you could give me a little more insight into what my grandmother was planning. I thought I knew what she wanted for the Book Nook, but I've recently come across some information about her store and I'm not sure what to do with it."

He tilts his head to the side and his already warm smile softens around the corners. "Drew, it's not her store; it's yours."

I smile back even though I know it doesn't reach my eyes.

"Yes, my store," I repeat after him. "But I found out she was planning on selling it before she passed. I thought she wanted me to push the store forward, but now I'm not so sure anymore. I know it might be a stretch, but I was hoping maybe she gave you some information that I may have missed during the craziness of taking over the Book Nook."

He leans into his brown leather wingback chair.

"That is a perfect question to address what you're needing and also what your dad is trying to accomplish."

"Okay." This might be the first time in history that what I need and what my dad wants complement each other, but I don't question it. "So what is it that my dad wants?"

I don't know why I ask. I know what he wants. He's always been a greedy SOB, and it's only gotten worse with Gran's death.

"He wants to dispute the will," he says, which I'm already aware of. "He's claiming that you manipulated Alice Young to leave the store to you even though he is her rightful next of kin."

Even though this is not even a little bit of a surprise to me, I still didn't anticipate the way it causes my blood to boil. Maybe it's because after feeling like I'm the only person who's been manipulated lately, it strikes a pretty raw nerve.

"He's the worst kind of human." I don't mean to say it out loud, but I don't regret it when I do.

"If it makes you feel any better, this isn't anything we haven't dealt with in the past." He mistakes my rage for sadness and pushes a box of Kleenex across his massive desk. "This might have been something he could've argued when the will was first read, but it's pretty late in the game to bring up these concerns. It also doesn't look great that he already accepted the part of the will where he was left a very valuable property."

A property he didn't even let me walk through before I was forced to attend the estate sale like the rest of Denver to buy Gran's old jewelry box and the silver tray I helped her polish every Christmas.

Again, have I mentioned how big of an asshole my dad is?

"Yes, he acted very fast on that." I hesitate before what I tell him next. I don't want to drag Daisy into this mess, but I also can't let him bully me out of the Book Nook, no matter what I feel about the store right now. "From what my sister told me, he pocketed a cool million from the sale."

I'm pretty sure he called a real estate agent before the funeral took place. The house sold before her grave had a headstone. I don't have much faith in him as an overall human, but I still can't get over the fact that he moved on so quickly from his childhood home.

"Good for him," Mr. Wilson says, and I can't tell if he's being sarcastic or not.

I sit up straighter, wondering if I read him all wrong. *Wouldn't be the first time* . . . "I'm sorry?"

"Good for your dad," he repeats his earlier sentiment. "That's what Alice wanted."

My argument dies on my tongue, those four little words knocking the wind out of me.

"I first met your grandmother two years ago. She worked with my predecessor to get her first will written, so when she came to me, it was just updating a few things." He opens a file on his desk that I didn't even notice was there and hands me a stack of papers. His voice is very soft and his eyes are attentive. He's tracking my every movement and it's clear he can read that I'm ready to bolt. "You can see there, the first things were easy. She wanted to leave Daisy Young her wedding ring and ten thousand dollars. She also had one of her brokerage accounts transferred to Daisy."

I vaguely remember hearing all of this at the reading of the will, which feels like ages ago, but I was in such a fog that this feels like the first time I'm learning all of this.

"Then we know she gave her house, car, and possessions to Andrew Young. She did this with the firm understanding that he would sell these things and make money from the sale. I can tell you that she was not under the illusion that he would sit on that property and hold vigil. She knew what the outcome would be."

He leans forward and flips the page for me again, and on this one, my name is listed in bold print. I can't look at it. I'm not sure why seeing this makes me feel so emotional, but I promised myself that I was done crying and I'm not ready to renege on that.

"I need you to know that I have a lot of clients. I don't remember the details of these meetings off the top of my head for many of them because there's simply too many." He pauses, holding my eye contact in a way that causes me to brace. "But I remember talking to Alice Young about a Drew Young with a clarity that still surprises me."

I suck in a sharp breath, my pulse speeding up as my sinuses start to go all wonky.

He waits to see if I say anything, only continuing on when he's met with silence.

"Alice Young was very worried about leaving the Book Nook to her granddaughter. I didn't understand why, but she told me that her granddaughter was a very talented photographer with an adventurer's soul and a heart that would bleed for the ones she loved."

Okay.

Now he's just playing dirty. I swipe away at the tears I can no longer hold back, still staying silent.

"She told me that you didn't like books much but would still spend the little free time you had indulging her and her friends at book club or helping around the store. She knew the store was worth a small fortune for the property alone, and whether you decided to sell or rent out the space, you'd be set for life. But she was concerned that you wouldn't sell."

"What?" I feel a little dizzy, and even though I've never had blood sugar issues, I feel like I should ask for a glass of orange juice or something. "She was worried I *wouldn't* sell?"

I spent this entire time thinking she would've been worried about me selling like Dad did. Tossing everything she worked for away in order to make a quick buck.

"I know, that's what I thought." His wry grin tugs at the corners of his mouth. "I couldn't believe that she was worried about a twentysomething-year-old who loved to travel and didn't read not selling the moment the opportunity arose. But she insisted. And actually, I owe you this." He pushes away from his desk, opens the top drawer, and hands me a crisp twenty-dollar bill that he pulls out.

I look at the money. My head is beginning to ache from how tight my eyebrows are furrowed. "I . . . I don't understand."

"Your grandmother bet me twenty dollars that this would be an issue. Told me if you called about the Book Nook, I was to give you a twenty. I'm a man of my word." He drops the money in front of me when I still don't take it. "Plus, she said she would haunt me if I didn't honor my end of the deal."

That finally makes me crack a smile, because Gran making jokes about haunting someone while planning her will is so something she would've done.

"Not that." I leave the money on the desk. "I don't understand what she wanted me to do. I know how much the Book Nook meant to her—it meant a lot to me. It was her legacy. How could she expect me to sell that?"

"She said you'd say that too." He chuckles and pulls out a hundred-dollar bill this time, along with another folder. "She gave me this with strict orders to only give this to you if you came back with questions. She wanted you to come to your own decision with the Book Nook. In her heart, she knew you wouldn't sell it and she didn't want to pressure you to do something you weren't comfortable with. But she also knew that you wouldn't be happy there."

He places this folder on top of the unexpected payout, his hand lingering above it. The good-natured humor on his face only seconds ago is gone, replaced by a look one could only describe as concern.

"There's information in here she wanted you to have. There's property values from before she passed that would've gone up by now, same with rent prices. She also had contacted someone at Prose and Fable to ask about selling them the Book Nook with the understanding that it would stay the Book Nook, but they would pay you for the rights to take over."

My heart flips and my stomach turns.

That must've been what she was talking to Connor about, and to Jasper as well. She wasn't trying to get rid of it; she was doing what she always did, taking care of me.

Even when I didn't know I needed it.

"But before you go and look these options over, I need you to know what Alice told me when I asked her why she wanted to wait to give you all of this."

My cheeks are wet and my mouth is dry as I nod for him to continue.

"She said that you'd been through a lot and she knew you would need the Book Nook if anything happened to her. I don't know all of the details, but she made it clear that there was a community there that would support you and help you move on. She didn't want you to have the Book Nook to continue her legacy—you were her legacy. She wanted you to have the store in order to take care of yourself so you could live out your dreams like she lived out hers. Alice Young adored you in a way that I will never forget and I really hope you never do either."

Well, if I wasn't already crying, I would be now.

Because this man, this stranger, reminded me of what I'd somehow forgotten. I buried my pain in the work. I tried to hold on to the memory of my grandma through a place, when that building was never what made my time there special. It was her.

And it still is.

"Thank you." It's not enough for all he's given me, but it's all I have.

Well, that and one hundred and twenty dollars, because long after she was gone, Gran is still making sure I'm winning.

Now it's my turn to take care of myself.

# CHAPTER 26

"I DON'T UNDERSTAND WHY YOU'RE STILL HERE." ELSIE IS DIGGING through my desk drawer, tossing out piece of candy after piece of candy until she finds the watermelon Blow Pop she was searching for.

"Where else would I be?" I don't want anything sweet, but since she dumped so much on my desk, I feel like it's my duty to help her clean up by nabbing a piece. I peel open the Laffy Taffy, toss the wrapper, and pop the bite-sized candy in my mouth.

"Ummm . . ." She aims her glare at me, but it hits differently with her cheek puffed out from the sucker. She pulls it out of her mouth with a loud pop and points it much too close to my face. "I don't know. Literally anywhere else. Your grandma basically laid out every option possible so you could fund your worldly travels. But if you don't want to start there, you could always drive your ass to a little bungalow in Wash Park to smooth things over with Jasper."

I check the time on my phone.

It's been seven minutes since she last brought up Jasper . . . which is about two minutes longer than the time she brought him up before this.

I've been trying to be gentle with her the last couple of weeks because she was one thousand percent as invested in my relationship as I was. When I went over to her house the other night, Brandon told me she ate an entire pint of ice cream after I told her things were over between me and Jasper.

But it's getting ridiculous.

"Elsie, I love you, but you gotta let it go."

"I'll never let it go." She flops into the chair across from the desk and accidentally bumps into the double stroller currently housing a sleeping Milo and Finn. We both freeze, not so much as breathing as Milo readjusts, and only exhaling when he settles back into his sleep. "I'll never let it go," she repeats. "This was a misunderstanding and there's no way Jasper won't get over whatever it is you think he's holding on to."

The problem is, I know she's not wrong.

Even though I know he was helping Gran set up some things I doubt he even knew the details to, it was still beyond fucked-up that he didn't tell me he knew her. Maybe I didn't handle it the best—you know, forcing him to spend a night alone in a secluded cabin and subjecting him to the silent treatment over the course of a six-hour car ride—but I wasn't wrong to react the way I did. No matter how you spin it, he lied to me and that's fucked-up.

However, I'm over it now. And I miss him.

A lot.

Beyond the thoughtful dates, good kissing, and better sex, I loved talking to him. He laughed at all my jokes and seemed really, authentically interested in what I had to say. So many times over the course of my life, I've felt like the people around me didn't see me.

It was the opposite with Jasper.

It felt like he saw parts of me that I didn't even see in myself. It was so easy to be myself around him because he wouldn't let me be anyone else.

But the due date for his book was two weeks ago and I doubt he stayed in Denver any longer than he had to. He mentioned his next book taking place in Texas; he's probably already scouting the area—hanging out with some blond woman in cowboy boots and a crop top.

"He only rented the house he was in until the beginning of October." I tell her of the fact that now haunts me in my sleep. "So even if he did decide to stay in Colorado for a bit, I don't know where he'd be living."

This is the totally valid, totally plausible lie I've been telling myself as a perfectly good excuse to never reach out to Jasper again. Yes, it's flimsy, but it works for me.

And apparently only me.

"That's dumb." Elsie stares at me dead in the eyes, destroying my reasoning in two words. "Does he change his phone number with every move too? Or could you still type out a text like, 'Hey, it was fucked-up that you lied to me, but maybe we could talk it out,' or, I don't know . . . literally fucking anything."

Elsie's been more high-strung than normal since Jasper and I crumbled to the ground. Part of me feels terrible, but the other— more prominent—part is wildly amused by the things she now says to me.

"I see what you're saying, but I also feel like he could reach out as well. I might have called things off, but he's the one who messed up. It was more than a misunderstanding. He completely left out knowing Gran. Maybe I could forgive him now that I've cooled off, but he has to apologize first."

And herein lies the major problem.

I am stubborn to a fault and Jasper is kind to a fault.

He knows he messed up, and beyond the few apologies he issued right after we returned, I haven't heard from him since. I actually really respect that. As much as we normalize fighting for someone, it's nice to see a man simply taking no for an answer and not pressuring me to change my mind.

Except for the very small detail that I want him to fight for me to change my mind.

"Drew!" Elsie whisper-shouts, aware of her sleeping babies in the room. "You're ruining this for me! Please let me love you loving Jasper. I need this!"

I'm about to explain to her, once again, that he has to be the one to make the first move, when my email chimes with a notification from an address I've never seen before. The subject line reads "Photography Inquiry for Drew Young" and successfully piques my interest.

"Shoot, hold on." I hold one finger up—something she hates, which is obviously why I do it—and click open the email. And as I start reading, the world that has slowly been rebuilding itself around me since my meeting with Mr. Wilson bursts into a kaleidoscope of color. Possibility and hope spiral back to life, and my feelings for Jasper break through any lingering hurt I had.

"What is it?" Elsie leans out of her seat, trying to sneak a look at my computer screen. "Why does your face look like you just won a million-dollar sweepstakes?"

"Because"—I turn the laptop to face her so she can read the email—"I pretty much did."

"Oh my god." She breathes out as her eyes travel down the screen. "Jasper's publisher wants to pay to use your photographs for the cover of his book."

She tells me what I already know, since I read the email before her, but my excitement only grows when I hear her confirming that I didn't make up this entire thing.

"I can't believe it. He mentioned wanting my picture for his cover, but that was the day I called things off with him. I didn't think he would still want it." I gather my mass of curls and twist it into a bun on the crown of my head. "I don't know what to do. What should I do?"

"Duh, Drew!" she shouts, forgetting about the small humans for a second. "Did you read those books with Jasper?"

I scrunch my eyebrows together, not following at all. "Uh, yeah . . ."

"Oh my god, I have to tell her everything." She closes her eyes and tilts her head to the ceiling, taking a deep breath and maybe muttering a prayer before looking back at me. "What happens in the final act when the hero has to win back their love? They make a grand gesture! Jasper did his, linking himself to you forever through your photography, even if he can't have you." I swear, she swoons talking about it. "Now you have to come up with something so that we can make up with Jasper and live happily ever after with him forever."

"We?" I ask.

"Fine, you. Whatever." She rolls her eyes like I'm the one being ridiculous. "But you know I'm going to be right there with you. So what do you say, do we forgive him or not?"

She clasps her hands together and looks at me with her giant puppy-dog eyes. I'm half-convinced she's going to drop to her knees soon and start begging.

And how can I say no to that?

I can't.

"Fine." I try to sound a little put out by all of this when really I want to bust out into cartwheels and squeal like a little girl at whatever boy-band concert is hot at the moment. "I guess we forgive him."

"Finally!" She punches the air above her and I'm concerned that her face may crack in half with how giant her smile is. "Time to come up with the perfect grand gesture."

"ARE YOU SURE THIS IS going to work?" I ask Elsie and Daisy for what feels like the millionth time.

"Yes!" they both shout back at me.

Maybe I have asked it a million times.

"Seriously." Elsie finger-twists the curls on the back of my head. "You need to relax. This is going to be amazing."

"But is it grand enough? I'm not sure it's grand enough."

I mean really, who do I think I am? How can I do a grand gesture to a man who literally makes a living dreaming them up?

"The fact that it's you makes it grand." Daisy uses the lipstick applicator to apply one final layer of lipstick before she takes a step back to admire her work. "It doesn't matter what you do. It's not the scale that makes the gesture grand; it's the motive and the meaning behind it that make it special."

"Okay, but are—"

"Yes," Elsie cuts me off. "We're sure."

"You know you're very rude for someone who has pretty much forced me into this situation." I glare at her and she smirks at me in the mirror as she finishes up with my hair.

"I admit to being fully invested in this relationship." Elsie squirts a final pump of olive oil spray onto my hair before stepping in front of me and taking my hands in hers. "But you know the only reason I am is because I saw how happy you were when you were with him. You're my best friend in the entire world and I will do anything I can to make sure you're happy. That includes helping plan a grand gesture to mend fences with Jasper, but also finding a secluded spot off the grid to bury him if he ever hurts you again."

"I second that." Daisy walks back into the room holding my Dr. Martens, which we compromised on me wearing tonight. "And one of my friends' dad owns a ton of land up in Montana that we could totally use."

Awwww.

The life of rich people; it will never not be wild to me.

"Okay, but what happens if he's not happy to see me? What then?" As much as I want to do this, part of me is screaming to back out. This could go wrong in so many ways, and according to my history as a human on this Earth for the last twenty-eight years, the odds are stacked against me.

"Good vibes only." Daisy repeats her life mantra but thankfully doesn't cite *The Secret* this time.

"Daisy's right," Elsie says before I can groan at their non-advice/ advice. "If you think this isn't going to go well, you're going to talk yourself out of it before we can even get there. You have to think this is going to be the best night ever and everything is going to be perfect."

"Or should I maybe grab a mini bottle of tequila from the minibar?" Because my armpits are starting to sweat and maybe liquid courage is exactly what I need to get this final boost.

"Absolutely not." Elsie shuts down my idea immediately. "I didn't pump all week and ask my mom to babysit overnight for you to miss out on your moment because you decided to be Tequila Tina instead."

You do tequila shots and end up singing Tina Turner songs on the bar one time and you're judged forever. But still, I guess she's not totally wrong.

"Now, come on." Daisy shoves my shoes into my hand. "We have five minutes before you need to be down there."

Thanks to the internet and having a sister and best friend who are determined to get Jasper and me back together, Daisy and Elsie found out that Jasper was speaking on a panel for a small book conference in Colorado Springs. At the Broadmoor, to be exact, the same hotel where our first outing, to Seven Falls, was. I guess it's only fair that I'm the one feeling queasy this time.

Elsie drapes the lanyard with my name and conference pass over my head before giving me one final look-over . . . scowling when she lands on my feet.

"Are you sure you don't want to wear the heels? I brought a pair with a block—"

"Nope," I cut her off, because I don't care what shape the torture device is, it still hurts. "I'm sticking with my boots, thank you very much."

"Fine, if you insist." Elsie gives in. "You still look great."

Daisy nods in agreement. "You really do. And are you sure you don't want us to go with you?"

I think about it for a moment before sticking to my guns. "I'm sure."

This is going to be hard enough for me to do in a room full of strangers. I'm not sure I could do it with Daisy and Elsie watching . . . especially knowing that Elsie's hopes and dreams for double dates and early looks at his books hang on my shoulders.

"All right." Daisy pulls open the door for me, slapping my butt as I walk into the hallway. "Go get 'em, slugger."

I don't look back, because I know if I do, I'll run back into the room with my tail between my legs. Instead, I keep my head held high and go to get my man back.

The walk to the conference room on the far side of the hotel is a blur of faces and overthinking as I go over and over what I want to say to him. But as soon as I walk into the room and see him sitting behind a long row of tables, immersed in a seemingly intense conversation with the man beside him, I forget it all.

Just being this close to him again soothes the aching in my heart I haven't been able to get rid of since I saw him last.

He cut his hair; the long locks I loved so much are nowhere to be found. It's cut low on the sides, but the waves on top are still kind of there. Even from across the room, I swear I can see the turquoise eyes I've dreamt about every night since we first met. But something about him seems different.

Maybe I'm making it up, but his smile seems smaller. Dimmer. Like maybe he's been every bit as miserable as I've been since he left.

I sit in the last row, strategically planting myself behind a man who is much taller and much wider than I am. If I'm going to do this, I need to make sure it's of my own accord, not because Jasper saw me in the crowd.

Plus, where's the drama in that?

The rest of the attendees filter into the room, finding open seats and settling in when the moderator introduces herself along with all the members of the panel.

She starts asking questions, directing each one at a different author, sitting back as the conversation begins to flow naturally between the panelists. I thought I'd be bored to tears, but I'm shocked to find myself immersed in the conversation and hanging on to every word they exchange.

"And now"—the moderator stands from her stool on the side of the stage—"time for audience questions. If you have anything to ask or say to one of our amazing authors up here, please raise your hand and Lachlan here will bring the mic to you."

This is my moment.

All I need to do is raise my hand and I got this.

But I don't.

I sit quietly in my seat, safely tucked away from knowing eyes, listening to one audience member after another as they speak into the mic, asking mind-numbing question after mind-numbing question. Until finally, I've had enough.

I lift my hand in the air, pretending that it's not shaking like a leaf as soon as Lachlan places the mic in my palm.

"Um, yeah, thank you. I have a question for Jasper Williams." I take a moment before standing up, and when I do, I can feel Jasper's eyes burning a hole into me despite the neutral look on his face.

"Jasper, in your last book, *The Fall*, Liam shows up for Isabella just as she needs him most. You do a great job of exploring their dynamic and showing Isabella growing with the help of Liam's love and support, but I have a question about the ending."

My mouth feels dry and I'm really regretting not at least sticking the shooter into my purse for this moment.

"Yes." Jasper doesn't take his eyes off me as he speaks into the microphone. "And what's your question?"

The sound of my heavy breathing echoes through the room on the speakers set up in every corner, and I'm sure if I were to hold the mic against my chest, my thundering heartbeat would be heard as well.

"My question is, even though Liam messed up, because he definitely did, what does it say about Isabella that she still loves him?"

There.

I did it.

I told Jasper I loved him in front of a room full of people . . . well, kind of.

And while the people sitting around me might seem confused, the only person I care about isn't. The bottom of his chair scrapes across the floor as he pushes away from the table. Whispers around us begin to rise to a crescendo as he moves to me down the long aisle, his pace picking up until he's in a full-out jog and pushing past the other people in my row.

"You're here," he says when he's finally close enough for me to touch.

I hand the microphone to the woman beside me, who's watching us like we're her favorite soap opera. "I'm here."

"I should've told you that I knew Alice. That was my plan when I first walked into the Book Nook. I was going to tell you I knew her and give you my condolences." He stops, not aware of anyone around us, and he reaches for my hands—a question in his cautious movement that I answer when I touch my palms to his. A small smile pulls at his lips, but I hardly notice it when I see his eyes shimmer with tears, relief so stark across his face that everyone around us lets out a collective sigh. "But then I saw you," he continues, and now I'm the one who wants to cry. "And I forgot everything other than I wanted to get to know you. Other than . . . I wanted to be your hero."

"Jasper, I didn't need you to save me." I shake my head, because that was part of the problem. "I can take care of myself. I just needed you to stand by my side, supporting me as I figure things out."

"I know." He says those two small words like they have been pulled from the deepest part of his soul. "You're the most amazing person I've ever known. You're smart, talented, adventurous, and heartbreakingly beautiful. You push me to do things I never thought I could do, and nobody makes me laugh harder. And"—he tightens his grip on my hands—"I love you."

My vision fogs over and not just because Jasper loves me.

But because I know he sees me. All of me. I've shown him the messy, ugly bits that I spent my entire life trying to hide from people, yet here we are.

And he loves me.

"I love you too," I tell him again, just a little more direct this time. "I know I'm new to this grand gesture thing, but at the end of your book, Liam and Isabella kiss, so I think that's next."

"You read my book?"

*I read five.*

"I did. And while I can see the appeal of Jasper Williams, Author"—I roll onto my toes, needing to get closer to his mouth—"I have to tell you, Jasper Williams, Boyfriend, is way, way better."

He grins down at me, but I only see it for a second before his mouth is on mine and whoops and applause surround us.

Who would've thought that I, of all people, would end up with a love that's even better than fiction?

Talk about a plot twist.

# EPILOGUE

---

"You sure you'll be okay without me for a couple of weeks?"
I ask Daisy.

Turns out, owning a store is easier when you have someone to share it with. Daisy ditched her internship and, in a move that has Dad seeing red, decided to join me at the Book Nook.

"Of course! Dani and I are hosting a book club on Thursday and Elsie is coming for story time. We'll be fine without you." Daisy pushes a steaming mug across the counter of our new coffee bar. She's been working on perfecting her latte-making skills for the last week and I've been vibrating from the amount of caffeine I've had as her test subject. "Try that one. It's snickerdoodle."

I take a small sip—she's inconsistent at best and I've had more than one spit shot over the week. Lucky for me, though, this one is delicious.

"Oh my god." I take another sip. "This might be your best one yet!"

She rounds the counter and pulls the mug out of my hands, taking a sip for herself as the bell over the front door chimes.

"Welcome to the Book Nook," I shout out before I turn and see Jasper walking toward me.

I thought it would wear off. I didn't think it was sustainable for me to still feel giddy beyond belief every time he walks into a room. But it hasn't and I hope it never does.

"Hey." He only has eyes for me as his long legs stride through the store, only slowing once he's reached me. Just like he does every day when he greets me, he slips his arms around my waist and pulls me into him, touching his lips to mine so gently that even Daisy sighs. "You ready?"

"Yeah." I kiss him once more, wanting his mouth on mine as often as possible. "My bags are in the office."

"You two make me sick," Daisy says, sounding anything but sick. "You don't need to rub your happiness in our faces all the time. The poor people of Alaska don't even know what's about to hit them."

"Hater." I stick my tongue out at her and wink. She loves us.

Ever since learning about all the possible exit plans Gran mapped out for me and the Book Nook, the pressure I felt running the place has disappeared. Getting to choose to keep it open instead of feeling it as a burden I'd placed on myself has changed how I feel about everything.

I don't know if it's what I'll want to do forever, but for now, I'm happy running it with Daisy and getting to know my sister better.

Plus, I've incorporated more of a work-life balance where I'm making time for photography again. Jasper keeps his weekends free and we hop into *his* Jeep—I still haven't parted with mine—and go exploring. We never have a plan; we go where the wind takes us, enjoying each other's company and the beauty that is Colorado.

Then, for my birthday, Jasper surprised me with a trip for two to Alaska.

Apparently when I told him about my Alaskan dream, it spurred a story idea for him. But this time, instead of moving there while he writes, we're going to experience a ten-day guided tour. It's the best present anyone has ever gotten me and I couldn't be more excited.

"You have all of your camera stuff, right?" he asks. He's so protective of my creative time and it makes me love him even more. He knows it's more than a hobby and he goes above and beyond to be sure that I have what I need to pursue my passion.

"Yup. It's all tucked into my backpack so I don't have to check it." I follow him as we move to my and Daisy's shared office, which we're in the middle of renovating. "I can't believe we're going to Alaska!"

I've basically been squealing since I opened my present a week ago.

He stops before we reach the office, turning around, wrapping me tight in his arms, and kissing me senseless.

"What was that for?" I ask when I catch my bearings again. "Not that I'm complaining."

Because wow.

Yes, please. More, please. Thank you.

"I can't wait to spend this time with you." His lips graze across my forehead. I'm so focused on him and the way his eyes darken as his voice drops with his confession that I don't even notice the way he mindlessly pats the pocket of his coat as if he's making sure something very important is still tucked safe and sound inside. "I've never been happier and I feel very lucky that I get to be the person by your side. Hopefully forever."

"Definitely forever."

# ACKNOWLEDGMENTS

This book was written not only in the middle of a global pandemic, but also in the aftermath of losing my mom. This was the hardest and most satisfying book I've written. In months that felt so dark and hopeless, I was able to get lost in Jasper and Drew's love story. I explored with them, laughed with them, and processed my grief alongside Drew. So while I have a lot of people to thank for this, thank you, the reader, for allowing me the opportunity to go on this journey and trusting me enough to come along with me. I am forever grateful to you.

Kristine Swartz and Jessica Watterson, thank you for not only putting up with me, but encouraging me. These books literally would not be possible without you both. Thank you for believing in me and helping me grow as an author.

To everyone at Berkley, I am endlessly thankful for all that you do. Thank you for making this book happen and for being absolute magic.

To booksellers everywhere. As an author and a reader, I thank you for all that you do to spread joy and create community within your walls. More than ever, you are a haven for us. The world would be a much darker place without you.

Since being in lockdown, I've had the wonderful opportunity to get to know so many members of the book world. Melissa Gill, Amber Burns, Crystal Perkins, Emily Santana, Shay Tibbs, Allie Boedeker, and so many more, thank you for being such bright lights. I feel so lucky to know you and call you friends.

Maxym and Lindsay, I honestly don't know what I would do without you two brilliant women by my side. Your friendship means the world to me! Suzanne, Sarah, and Falon, I thought Pitch Wars couldn't give me any more until I met you! Love you ladies to the moon! Harper, Clubhouse might've been a dumpster fire, but I'm so glad I found you!

Lin. I mean, what can I say that I haven't already? Joining that Facebook group was the best thing that's ever happened to me. You keep me sane. I honestly don't know if I could've made it through these last years without you. You are a saint. I am so freaking thrilled to watch you shine. It's long overdue, but I can't wait to scream my head off and cheer for you as you take the world by storm. They aren't ready!

Abby, Taylor, Brittany, and Natalie. It's an embarrassment of riches, honestly, to have friends like you. You inspire me every single day. I love you so much.

Jean, I hope you're reading this. I missed you, my life wasn't as bright without you in it. Thank you for being there for me.

To my children, DJ, Harlow, Dash, and Ellis, you blow me away every day. You're kind, funny, smart, and more than I ever wished for. I don't know what I did to deserve to be your mom, but I'm eternally grateful. I love you beyond measure.

Derrick, look at us still going. Fifteen-year-old Alexa could've never dreamt of this future; thank you for standing by my side.

Mom, Grandma, and Grandpa, I'm still a little angry that you all left me so soon. I know people like to say that grief gets easier as time goes by, but I'm beginning to think that's a lie. I love you too much; I don't think it will ever lessen. I hope you're all together and happy. I really hope I'm making you proud.

# Better than Fiction

## ALEXA MARTIN

# QUESTIONS FOR DISCUSSION

1. *Better than Fiction* opens with the Dirty Birds inserting themselves into Drew's life. Who are the well-intentioned people involved in your life?

2. Drew is a bookstore owner who dislikes books. What is something ironic in your life that might give others pause?

3. If you turned a book into date inspiration, what book would you choose and where would you go?

4. The Book Nook plays a huge part in this story. What is your favorite bookstore? Why do you love it?

5. Drew says she feels completely seen in her relationship with Jasper. What do you think that means? What are things someone can do to ensure their partner feels this way?

6. Drew hates books; Jasper writes them. Do you believe that opposites attract? Why or why not?

7. Although Drew is falling in love, she is still grieving the loss of her grandmother. How does this dichotomy affect her as she attempts to move forward with her life?

8. When Drew is fighting for Jasper, Daisy tells her, "It doesn't matter what you do. It's not the scale that makes the gesture grand; it's the motive and the meaning behind it that make it special." Do you agree with Daisy? Why or why not?

9. Near the end of the story, Drew feels betrayed by those around her. Have you ever unintentionally hurt someone by trying to protect them?

10. You can invite one author (dead or alive) for coffee. Who are you inviting?

Keep reading for a special look
at another exciting novel from Alexa Martin

# Mom Jeans
# and Other Mistakes

*Available now from Berkley*

# PROLOGUE

---

# *Lauren*

"And just one more," our landlord, Miss Morielli, says as she hands Jude and me the final paper to sign before our town house is legally ours.

The irony doesn't escape me that I've had to sign more paperwork to live in a town house with brass hardware and popcorn ceilings than I did to take my daughter home from the hospital. I'm pretty sure being granted a tiny human should at least require a background check.

"Thank god. My hand is starting to cramp," Jude moans beside me. "I thought people signed this stuff over the computer now? Did you know they aren't even teaching kids cursive anymore? I wonder what Addy's signature is going to—ouch!" She finally stops talking and glares at me for kicking her beneath the table. If she's expecting me to feel bad, she's going to be waiting awhile because I don't. Not even a little bit.

HGTV has really tricked people into believing that house hunting is this joyful experience where the only downside is the previous owner's terrible taste in wallpaper. And maybe it is when you have unlimited funds and don't have to worry about all the ways your five-year-old could possibly conduct a vault flip off the loft railing or mistake the terrible green paint for a chalkboard she can deface.

So after weeks of looking and lowering our standards until I'm not sure they could get much lower, the last thing I need is for Jude's complaining to throw a wrench into everything when we're one signature away from finally crossing the finish line.

"We'll sign as many papers as you want. We're just so grateful to live in your beautiful property." I sign my name on the final line and push the paper over to Jude—who is still glaring at me. I'm definitely the suck-up between the two of us. And I'm good with that. "Adelaide hasn't stopped talking about how she wants to decorate her room or asking if the cookies she had when we toured the house will be there too."

"Oh, the pleasure is all mine." She takes the document from Jude, a wide smile spreading across her face. Probably from knowing how much money she'll be making off a condo she no doubt paid off ten years ago. "It can be so hard finding the right people to rent to in this city. But the last lesbian couple I rented to was so nice and respectful, I was thrilled when your family walked through the door."

My eyes nearly pop out of my head as I register her words, but Jude, my very reactive and not at all measured best friend, almost comes out of her seat. "Oh my god, what? No!" There's no masking the shock in Jude's voice. I'm not sure if I should laugh along or be offended she's so horrified at the idea of kissing me. "I mean, not that I haven't swum in the lady pond once or twice, but never with Lauren. She's my best friend, we're practically sisters. Gross."

Okay.

Not offended. Just wildly embarrassed.

Thank god this happened after we finished signing the paperwork and the condo can't be revoked.

Poor Miss Morielli's cheeks look like we set them on fire, and I've never related to a person so much. Jude really knows how to work a person up. "Well, I guess it's a moot point, with as much paperwork as you both just signed together, you may as well be married. At least for the next twelve months."

"I'm not sure I believe in marriage." Jude stands up and rounds the table. I swear, the woman is incapable of keeping any of her thoughts to herself. She's lucky she's too far away to kick this time. "But I am a fan of sister wives . . . without the husband, of course. It's all of the support with none of the dude drama. I guess you could say that's what we're doing."

"Sister wives, huh? I think you might be onto something." Miss Morielli holds out two keys. "I hope you'll enjoy your new home."

"Are you kidding me?" Jude grabs the keys out of her hand and crosses the room, placing them next to the only photographable plant in the room. I have no doubt in about two minutes the photo will be on her Instagram feed with about a million filters. "We've only been planning this for our entire life. This is going to be the best year ever."

I think about asking Miss Morielli for her notary and making Jude sign that statement. Because as much as I've warned her and she's said I'm crazy, I have a feeling having a rule-following mom and a five-year-old for roommates is not going to be everything she thinks it will be.

But like it or not, she's stuck with us now.

# CHAPTER 1

---

## *Jude*

CHILDREN AND HANGOVERS DO NOT MIX.

I'm sure it's common sense to most people, but this is not a problem I ever thought I'd have.

For one, my uterus is under heavy protection. And two, by the time I have kids—if I ever do—I'll be a real adult who makes grown-up decisions. You know, like one glass of heart-healthy red wine with a well-balanced meal and not the parade of low-carb vodka shots I had after eating a side salad, no dressing, last night.

But as the sticky, tiny fingers literally peel open my eyes, and my tongue is uselessly stuck to the roof of my mouth, I have the very unkind realization that this is my new life . . . at least for the next year. And for the millionth time, I hope that if a giant sinkhole were to open up, it does so underneath Asher Thompson's feet.

"Auntie Jude, Mommy made pancakes. She said to ask you if you want some before you go to your special meeting." Adelaide holds my eyelids hostage and stares into my eyes, which are no doubt bloodshot, with the most innocent expression that it almost makes me smile. *Almost.*

"Addy." I push her hands off my face and resist the urge to hit her with my pillow. But, seeing as she's only five, I feel like society and her mother might frown upon that kind of thing. "We have to find a new wake-up technique. You're going to give me crow's-feet."

Her mouth purses and her little nose scrunches, giving her these wrinkles on the top of her nose that are adorable now but might make her consider Botox in about thirty years. I don't tell her that. "You'll get a birdie's feet?" Her voice is a screech, and she honestly sounds appalled. "What happens to the rest of the bird? How will it land with no feet?"

"Oh my god." I wrap my arms around her and pull her down to me, covering her chubby cheeks with kisses until she squeals. "This is why I'm obsessed with you," I shout over her peals of laughter before sitting up with her and ignoring the slight pounding against my skull. "Crow's-feet aren't birds. They're the little lines around eyes that make your grandma Keane always look so sleepy and old."

"Ooooh." She nods, but I'm pretty sure she still has no idea what I'm talking about.

"Yup." I crawl out from under the duvet I spent way too much money on, but photographs like a dream, and climb over the boxes I have yet to unpack. "And you don't want Auntie Jude to look like Old Grandma Keane, do you?"

Instead of answering and then apologizing profusely for endangering my skin, she shrugs, and I'm pretty she couldn't actually give a fuck. Rude. "Are you going to eat pancakes with me?"

"No pancakes for me." I grab her hand and walk with her down the stairs of our new townhome. "Repeat after me: carbs are evil."

"Carbs are evil," she mimics. For a five-year-old, she follows direction beautifully.

"Carbs are not evil," Lauren says from somewhere. And even though I can't see her, I know she's glaring at me.

But whatever, sue me. Someone needs to teach kids the importance of diet. That high metabolism and glowing skin they are unfairly blessed with aren't going to last forever.

"Mommy!" Adelaide drops my hand like a bad habit and takes off running to the table, where a plate of cut-up pancakes is waiting for her, complete with eggs and a healthy serving of fruit. "Wanna know what Jude taught me?"

Lauren walks around the corner, a coffee mug to her lips, looking way too hot in her mom pajamas and headscarf. The glare I knew she had is directed at me before she drops it and aims a bright smile at Addy. "Sure, baby."

"She said that Grandma Keane looks so old because of all the birdie feet on her face." She pops a grape in her mouth, completely unaware of the rising tension in the kitchen. "And what's a carb anyway?"

We're going to have to work on keeping secrets.

"Carbs give you energy to make you big and strong. And Grandma Keane doesn't look old, she looks wise." Lauren goes to put down her mug before grabbing the organic maple syrup and drizzling the saddest little sprinkling that I've ever seen on her pancakes before making direct eye contact with me. "Can we talk for a second?"

Crap.

I know that tone. It's the same one she used in sixth grade when we were locker partners and I took one of her glitter gel pens out of our locker without asking . . . and every time I've pissed her off since.

"Actually." I make a move to the coffee machine, in desperate need of both caffeine and an excuse. "I'm really thirsty."

Lauren grabs my arm and pulls me out of the kitchen with a smile that both terrifies and intrigues me frozen on her face. "Eat your food, Adelaide, we'll be right back."

I look to Addy for help since she's the one who ratted me out, but instead her eyes are closed and her shoulders are bouncing as she chews her pancakes.

Maybe I do want carbs and sugar. I'm not sure I've ever looked as happy as Addy does. And if pancakes and organic syrup are the answer, who am I to argue?

"What the hell, Jude?" Lauren snaps me out of my syrup-coated fantasy. "You can't talk to Adelaide like that. Do you understand the hell Ben will give me if she goes to visit him and she tells him we're over here talking about how old his mom looks?"

"Fuck Ben and his mom. She's a bitch and he's trash. He should really just be happy I'm not saying more." I have to fight back the rage that always tries to claw its way to the surface whenever I think of Lauren's piece-of-shit ex. I really try to be Zen- and peace-like, but that dirtbag always fucks up my chi.

Lucky for me, I guess, my anger seems to defuse Lauren's.

"What're you fucking smiling at?"

"You're just so cute when you're mad." She pinches my cheek, something she knows I hate. "Plus, my mom still defends Ben whenever he comes up, so it's nice that someone has my back."

"Well, your mom's a bitch too. But she's still goals AF when it comes to aging well, so I couldn't use her for an example with Addy." I'm sure you're not supposed to talk about your friend's family like that, but Lauren and I don't lie to each other, and Mrs. Turner really is a bitch. She never liked me and I'm a fucking delight. But I never liked her, either, so it was completely mutual. Even eleven-year-old me knew I never wanted her approval. The same could not be said for my people-pleasing best friend . . . which only made me hate Mrs. Turner more. I wouldn't mind if she shared her beauty routine, though, but I'm thinking my lack of melanin might prevent me from ever being on her level.

"I can't say you're wrong about any of this, but you still can't say it to Adelaide." Lauren fidgets with an imaginary string on the sleeve of her flannel pajamas. "You know how hard it's been for us. I just don't want her to go see him and say something that gives him an excuse to walk away from her and blame me for being the crazy baby mama."

Lauren is a spitfire. She's confident and strong and the smartest person I've ever known. Whenever I have a problem, she's the first person I tell. She gives me the best advice, and when she's done talking to me, I feel like fucking Wonder Woman. She knows what she wants in a way that both intimidates and inspires me. But whenever she talks about her douchebag ex, it's like I can see her visibly fold into herself. She shrinks right in front of my eyes and becomes this meek person I don't even know. And if he wasn't my favorite five-year-old's dad, I'd have already paid a hit man.

Well . . . I would've when I wasn't broke as a joke.

"I'll try to be better," I reassure her, but when she glares at me, I know I've failed. "Fuck. Fine." I uncross my fingers from behind my back and hold them in front of me. "I promise not to say anything about Ben or his stupid family in front of Addy."

"Thank you." She smiles and her perfect white teeth gleam against her brown skin. "And when she's not around, you can talk all the crap you please."

"I guess that's fair." I pout like Addy did the other night when Lauren told her she had to take a bath. "You know, it's still so weird to me that you're a mom. Like, you grew a fucking human! A really cute one at that. But, now when you give me the mom eye, it actually scares the shit out of me."

Even before Lauren had Addy, she would look at me like I was crazy. I do have a knack for putting myself in not the greatest of situations. I used to laugh her off and try to get her to join me (which never happened), but I guess losing countless hours of sleep and wiping butts for years just gives that look more authority, because now I cower.

"I know, and as a mom, I have to ask if you remember that you have a photo shoot in an hour?"

"Duh." I totally didn't remember. Because where Lauren is an actual adult, I just play one on Instagram.

"Mom . . ." Addy's hesitant voice calls from the kitchen. "I think I might've put too much syrup on my pancake."

"Crap," Lauren whispers underneath her breath before calling into the other room, "it's okay, accidents happen, here I come."

And on that note . . .

"You have fun with that!" I run to the stairs, not missing Lauren flipping me off before I go.

I might be living with a small child, but at least I'm not responsible for keeping her alive. Because for real? I'm not doing the best job of it for myself.

But at least I look fucking fantastic doing it.

**Alexa Martin** is a writer and stay-at-home mom. A Nashville transplant, she's intent on instilling a deep love and respect for the great Dolly Parton in her four children and husband. The Playbook series was inspired by the eight years she spent as an NFL wife and her love of all things pop culture, sparkles, leggings, and wine. When she's not repeating herself to her kids, you can find her catching up on whatever Real Housewives franchise is currently airing or filling up her Etsy cart with items she doesn't need.

## CONNECT ONLINE

AlexaMartin.com
🐦 AlexaMBooks
❶ AlexaMartinBooks
📷 AlexaMBooks

Ready to find
your next great read?

Let us help.

**Visit prh.com/nextread**

Penguin
Random
House